Lindsay was standing between the two men. With one rapid motion she reached and grabbed the flashlight and swung it hard, hitting the man on the temple. The other one turned and started for her. She ran through an opening deeper into the cave. Suddenly, after a few slippery feet she was sliding down a slick surface.

She slid for an eternity, the walls of the cave a mere kaleidoscopic flicker as the light of the flashlight illuminated her passage like a strobe. Then she was in the air, but only for a second. She hit something, slid farther for several moments, then rolled off onto the ground, rolled again and stopped. She lay there, numb, afraid to move. There was no sound but her heart beating furiously in her ears. The flashlight was still on, and she moved the light around the chamber. She saw a beautiful cascade of stalactites with stalagmites growing up to meet them. The long water slide was like a lava flow. She couldn't see the top, even with the light. She heard a mild explosion and a vibration. After several moments, debris came sliding down the flow.

They had sealed the entrance to the cave.

★

"...an intriguing mix of mystery and history..."

...oklist

"...a

...imes

"...an intriguing mix of mystery and history."

—Booklist

"...a real treat."

—Northwest Arkansas Times

Questionable Remains

Beverly Connor

WORLDWIDE®

TORONTO • NEW YORK • LONDON
AMSTERDAM • PARIS • SYDNEY • HAMBURG
STOCKHOLM • ATHENS • TOKYO • MILAN
MADRID • WARSAW • BUDAPEST • AUCKLAND

To my mother, Edna Phillips Heth

QUESTIONABLE REMAINS

A Worldwide Mystery/May 2001

First published by Cumberland House Publishing Inc.

ISBN 0-373-26385-6

Printed in U.S.A.

Acknowledgments

I would like to thank Diane Trap, Jean Stiles and all the members of the Harriette Austin Writer's Group for their critiques and support. Thanks to my husband and my mother for their support. My gratitude to David Hally, who taught me to love archaeology.

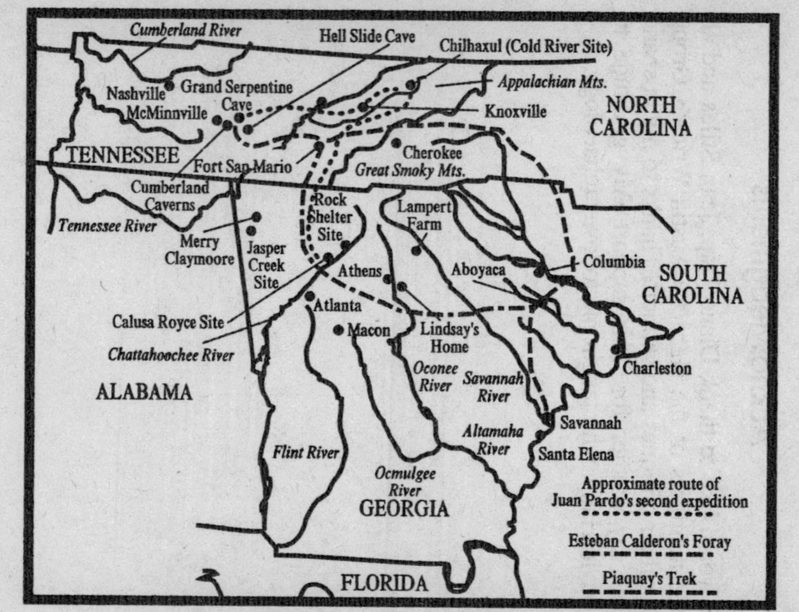
Cumberland River
Hell Slide Cave
Chilhaxul (Cold River Site)
Appalachian Mts.
Nashville
Grand Serpentine Cave
McMinnville
Knoxville
NORTH CAROLINA
TENNESSEE
Cherokee
Fort San Mario
Great Smoky Mts.
Cumberland Caverns
Rock Shelter Site
Lampert Farm
Tennessee River
Merry Claymoore
Jasper Creek Site
Athens
Aboyaca
Columbia
SOUTH CAROLINA
Atlanta
Calusa Royce Site
Macon
Lindsay's Home
Chattahoochee River
Charleston
Oconee River
Savannah River
ALABAMA
Savannah
Altamaha River
Santa Elena
Flint River
Ocmulgee River
GEORGIA
Approximate route of Juan Pardo's second expedition
Esteban Calderon's Foray
Piaquay's Trek
FLORIDA

Questionable Remains

ONE

"DR. CHAMBERLAIN." Gerald Dalton, Denny Ferguson's defense attorney, lay a hand on the mahogany witness box. "Dr. Chamberlain." He made a sweeping gesture with his arm, taking in the entire jury, who sat fanning themselves with their notebooks and gazing at Lindsay through skeptical eyes. "You ask these twelve men and women to believe that you can positively identify my client as being the man who shot Ahyoung Kim, even though the perpetrator wore a ski mask...and you only got a glimpse in his mouth as he was yelling at you to hand over your purse?" Dalton removed his glasses and pretended to clean them with his handkerchief, shaking his head as he focused his gaze on his task. "My client could go to the electric chair," he said, replacing his glasses on his nose. "Are you willing to have that on your conscience? Weren't you scared? This fellow, whoever he was, had just shot Mr. Kim and now he fixed his attention on you. You must've been terrified."

"Your Honor." The prosecutor, Max Gilbert, rose to his feet. "Is Mr. Dalton going to cross-examine Dr. Chamberlain, or is he going to testify himself?"

"Get on with it, Mr. Dalton," said the judge.

"Dr. Chamberlain, don't most bone experts like yourself use dental records to identify people, or are you able to Zen your identifications?" Dalton gave Lindsay a broad, sarcastic, toothy grin.

"Your client has very distinctive overlapping teeth," Lindsay replied, "as I have described in detail. I saw them clearly and noticed them in spite of my fear, because observation is automatic for me. It's my job."

"It's your job," Dalton repeated. "Haven't you told your

students on many occasions that you need much more evidence to make a positive identification than to rule out a person?''

''Yes,'' she answered. The heating system in the old, small-town courthouse was on high, and Lindsay could feel the prickly sensation of perspiration forming on her forehead. *I must look guilty,* she thought ruefully. She saw Mrs. Kim and her son Albert out in the spectator seats. Mrs. Kim understood little English, but she could read faces; her own was filled with worry. Albert, who had dropped out of the university to help his mother, looked angry. The defendant, Denny Ferguson, sat staring down at his hands; occasionally he would look up at Lindsay with a half smile on his face.

Dalton's cocounsel sat tapping a pencil silently on her pad of paper. She watched the jury for a moment, then shifted her attention back to Lindsay.

''Well, then,'' Dalton continued with exaggerated sarcasm, ''forgive me if I don't quite understand. It seems to me that all you can say about my client—after your brief look in the perpetrator's mouth—is that you can't rule him out. This is a far cry from saying that Denny Ferguson is positively the man you saw.''

''The man who shot Mr. Kim was your client.'' Lindsay realized she sounded more stubborn than professional.

''Dr. Chamberlain, you require more supporting evidence when you identify skeletal remains. Why are you requiring so little for a man's life?''

''I have described your client's dentition in great detail. I am sure of my identification.''

The jury wasn't convinced. Lindsay could see that. Too much rested on her testimony, and they didn't believe she could identify Ferguson by having seen only his teeth. They would not have noticed his teeth in that detail, and they didn't really believe she would either. Denny Ferguson would go free, even though Lindsay knew he was the one who shot and killed Mr. Kim, the neighborhood grocer—simply because

Mr. Kim did not have enough money in the cash drawer to satisfy him.

"You like the Kim family, don't you?" The defense attorney's voice was quiet, almost gentle.

"Yes."

"You want to see the murderer caught. We understand your sadness and sympathy for the Kim family." Again he gestured with a sweep of his arm, including the jury as if they were on his side. He shook his head and raised his voice, drawing out his words. "But, just how can you convince me, and these twelve very sensible people that you can say for sure it was my client who shot Mr. Kim and not someone else with bad teeth?"

"Mr. Dalton," said Lindsay, raising her hands to grip the top of the witness box and leaning forward slightly. "You had orthodontic work as an adult. You had four teeth pulled. Two upper second premolars and two lower first premolars. You wore your braces quite a long time, and the constant soreness caused you to develop the bad habit of grinding and clinching your teeth at night."

Gerald Dalton gawked at Lindsay, surprise evident on his face; his mouth dropped open, speechless for a moment. It was that moment of surprised hesitation that swayed the jury. Lindsay could see them shift their gazes to one another the way people do when they simultaneously see and understand a truth. In that moment she saw Albert nod his head and turn to whisper something to his mother; she saw the prosecutor smile and the defendant look around as if someone told a joke he did not understand.

"OKAY, HOW'D YOU DO IT?" Gilbert asked Lindsay, handing her a cup of coffee from the cappuccino machine in the corner of his office. He grinned broadly. "Your timing was perfect."

"My timing was from desperation."

Gilbert sat down and propped his feet on his dark oak desk. "But tell me how you did it."

"It wasn't that hard. His theatrics made it possible. The

way he tried to intimidate me, leaning over me, drawing out his words with that big voice of his, gave me a good look into his mouth. I saw that he had premolars missing. When he looked down to clean his glasses, I caught a glimpse of a permanent retainer behind his lower incisors. A retainer is used to prevent shifting of teeth.''

''And grinding his teeth?''

''His lower incisors were beveled where they ground against his upper incisors.''

Gilbert gave a satisfied laugh. ''I'll bet there's going to be a great gnashing of teeth in his office when the verdict comes in. With circumstantial evidence and a witness who only saw in the perp's mouth, ol' Dalton thought this was going to be an easy one.''

''You think they will find Ferguson guilty, then?'' asked Lindsay. She couldn't quite share in Gilbert's confidence.

''I think so. Of course, I've been surprised and even shocked by juries before, but I feel good about this. You're a good witness.''

Lindsay took a sip of her coffee. ''I can't stay for the verdict. I have to give an exam. Call me when you know something.'' She set down her cup and rose, offering Gilbert her hand.

He stood up quickly and shook her hand with a firm grip. ''Sure. Glad to work with you, Lindsay. We don't usually have this kind of thing going on in our little town. I hate to see this kind of crime come in.''

''Me, too,'' said Lindsay. ''I'm going to miss Mr. Kim.''

Sally, Lindsay's graduate assistant, was setting up the classroom for the honors course final exam when Lindsay returned to Baldwin Hall, home of the Department of Anthropology and Archaeology. Sally's dark blond hair was pulled back into a ponytail, one wayward strand falling into her face. She had on a pair of well-worn jeans and a black T-shirt showing a white skeleton of a rat on the front along with the words: *Rattus Rattus.*

''I like your shirt,'' said Lindsay.

Sally looked down at the picture on her chest. "Yeah, I do, too. We're selling them to raise money for the anthropology club." She paused a moment before she asked, "Is it over?"

"It's with the jury."

"I'm sorry about Mr. Kim, Lindsay."

"So am I." Lindsay tried to fight off the depressing mood in which the trial had left her. "Did you get students from the advanced osteology class to help you with the exam?"

"They'll be here in a few minutes."

The graduate students came in, followed by six honors students from Lindsay's class. There were the usual moans, groans, and the predictable question, "Is it hard?"

"I don't think so," said Lindsay, smiling. She gave each of them a long strip of black fabric.

"What's this?" asked one of the students.

"A blindfold," she answered.

"I knew it," said another. "A firing squad. She's going to shoot us if we fail."

"We have to get our bones somewhere," offered Sally.

Lindsay smiled at the group of four male and two female undergraduate students as they dropped their backpacks on the floor and sat down. "Okay, everyone listen up. As you have probably guessed, your test will be to identify some selected bones by touch alone. After you've named each bone, the graduate student assigned to you will write your answer down for you. You can get extra credit if you can identify the correct side—left or right. Don't try to listen to what the other students are saying because I've put different bones in each of the boxes on the tables. Now, pick a box and begin."

Each student picked a spot next to one of the covered boxes on the laboratory tables and tied their blindfold across their eyes. Lindsay watched as they removed the lids from their boxes, reached in, took a bone, and felt for identifying characteristics. She smiled when their faces lit up as they felt a trochanter or a condyle or when they frowned as they searched with the tips of their fingers for a fossa or muscle attachment. Sometimes they would roll the shaft of a bone in their hands to determine the shape of the cross section. After a while she left the exam in Sally's supervision and went to her office.

Lindsay's office had no windows. The walls beside and behind her desk were lined with bookshelves filled with books and journals. Her walnut desk had belonged to her grandfather, the only other archaeologist in the family. The brown, straight-grained wood surface was marred, and the left front leg still had her father's initials carved into it where he had tried out a new pocketknife on his ninth birthday. Her mother had wanted to have the desk refinished before they gave it to her, but her father had said no. Lindsay was glad because the marks left on artifacts reveal their history in a kind of code that she took pleasure in deciphering. The coffee cup rings told of her grandfather's long nights sipping coffee and working on articles. The cuts and scratches were evidence of the stone tools he laid out on the surface to examine and catalog.

The desk faced the door to the archaeology lab. An oak filing cabinet inherited from the previous occupant stood behind the door. On the other side sat a single stuffed leather chair next to a brass floor lamp. Her grandfather's trowel rested on a bookshelf, and an old photograph hung on the wall behind the chair, showing her grandfather as a young man dressed in a tie and rolled up shirtsleeves, holding a shovel and standing in front of an Indian mound in Macon, Georgia.

There were no artifacts or bones displayed in Lindsay's office. The only artifact she possessed was in an old cigar box inside her desk. It was a treasured possession: the first Indian artifact she had ever found. When Lindsay was five, her grandfather had taken her on the first of their many trips to do surface collecting. She had earnestly examined the freshly plowed ground as she walked beside her grandfather getting hot, tired, and restless. Then, there it was: the tip of a point partially covered by the moist earth. She had dug it out with her fingers and wiped off the dirt that clung to it. The point was beautiful, and it was huge, longer than her hand and almost as wide, made from black flint.

"It's a Clovis point," her grandfather had told her. "The

oldest point there is. It could have killed a woolly mammoth.'' Lindsay had held on to her find so tightly the edges had cut her hand, but that didn't matter because she had found something wonderful. Since that day she had found many things, but no discovery had ever made her feel as she did that time she found the Clovis with her grandfather. From that day on Lindsay knew she would be an archaeologist.

Lindsay was reaching for a term paper to grade when a figure appeared in her doorway. She thought it was a student before she recognized Gerald Dalton's cocounsel. Lindsay hadn't gotten a good look at her in court. Now she saw that she was a small, fine-boned woman, not over five feet four inches tall. Lindsay guessed she wore a size two. She looked as if she had the hollow bones of a bird, she was so thin and delicate looking. Her short, glossy-black hair was cut in a pageboy, and her skin looked as though it would be translucent if her makeup were washed off. She stood stiffly in the doorway, still in the snug-fitting dark blue suit she wore to the trial.

''Can I help you?'' asked Lindsay.

''Have you heard the verdict?'' Her voice belied her small frame. It was low and husky.

''No, I had to give an exam...''

''Yes. I saw your blindfolded students. I suppose that fits...teaching them that they can make a positive identification without looking.'' The woman walked into Lindsay's office and stood, put her palms on the desk and leaned forward.

''Is there a point to your visit?'' asked Lindsay.

''I wanted to be the one to tell you that the jury found Dennis Ferguson guilty. I hope that pleases you.''

Lindsay frowned. ''Nothing about this event pleases me.''

''What really gets to me is that you don't have any misgivings about convicting a man on the flimsiest of evidence.''

''I was sure.''

''How can you possibly not have doubts? Are you that arrogant?'' She stopped and looked at Lindsay for a moment, her green eyes clearly showing her anger. ''God, you are, aren't you? You've set yourself up here as some great… bone…guru, haven't you? And that performance today really topped it.''

''Performance?'' asked Lindsay.

''The way you pulled the rabbit out of the hat on the stand. It was the drama that convinced the jury, not the facts…it was the damn show you put on. You are the most arrogant, manipulative woman I have ever met.''

Lindsay started to speak when the woman turned on her heel and left.

Sally, who had been standing just outside the doorway, watched after the retreating figure before she came into Lindsay's office. ''Well, who peed in her Wheaties?''

''I suppose I did,'' replied Lindsay.

Lindsay finished grading the papers and tests, turned in the final grade sheets to the department, and locked her office. Before going home she put on her running clothes and drove to Memorial Park where she jogged on the wooded trail that wound around the duck pond. It was a cold February day, and there weren't many people on the trail. She was glad for the solitude and content to empty her mind of everything but running. After twenty minutes of jogging she slowed to a walk and went back to her car.

Driving through the town of Trowbridge, she passed Mr. Kim's grocery. It had been closed following Mr. Kim's murder. She saw Albert Kim walking down the sidewalk toward the store. She pulled her Land Rover into a parking place and got out.

''Albert,'' she said. He turned from unlocking the door of the grocery store to greet her. ''How's your mother?''

Albert smiled and nodded. ''She's better. Thanks to you and the jury, she's better.''

''Are you going to stay here and run the store or go back to school in Chicago?''

Albert shook his head. ''I don't know. I will have to stay here for a while anyway, you know…'' He paused, not knowing what to say, and seemed filled with despair.

"You could transfer to the university here. If you need a letter of recommendation, I would be glad to write you one," Lindsay offered.

"Thank you. You're very kind. I may ask you..."

They turned to look as a woman with a shopping bag in hand crossed the street, waving at Albert. "It looks like you have a customer," Lindsay said. She took her leave and drove home.

Home was in the middle of thirty-six acres of oak, hickory, walnut, and pine trees. Lindsay had moved a nineteenth-century square-logged cabin onto her property and was in the process of restoring it. She had added the modern conveniences of electricity, plumbing, bathroom, and kitchen. The dark, oak-log cabin sat on the edge of a small pond where Lindsay often fished.

Mandrake, Lindsay's horse, stood behind the white board fence, tossing his head as she drove up. The black Arabian stallion was a birthday gift from her mother. Lindsay loved the horse, but it was not the horse that to her was the best part of the gift. It was the fact that Ellen Chamberlain bred, raised, and trained the horse for her. It took seven years to bring Mandrake to the level of training that Ellen wanted for her daughter's horse. During that time Lindsay, of course, had seen Mandrake, but had had no idea he was to be hers. Seven years of patient training—that was what Lindsay found so remarkable about her mother's gift. She got out of her car and, hugging herself against the cold wind, walked over to Mandrake with an apple she had not eaten for lunch. He took it from her hand, and she stroked his soft nose as he ate. She made a mental note to call Susan Gitten to house-sit for her when she went on her summer vacation. Susan, a trainer herself, was one of the few people with whom Lindsay trusted her horse. She was a reliable woman a year younger than Lindsay's twenty-seven years, honest, pleasant, and totally lacking in sense of humor. Seeing a friend or watching a horse do what she trained him to do would bring a smile to her face, but jokes were lost on her. Lindsay thought Susan must be completely bewildered by sitcoms and comedians.

Lindsay was a minimalist when it came to furnishing her house, a trait she got from her mother. The living room had a couch and two rocking chairs facing the fireplace. The mission-style oak pieces had tan, leather-covered cushions and were draped with lap comforters. A painting of Mandrake, the only original painting she owned, commissioned from a local artist, hung over the fireplace. Her other paintings were copies. Lindsay could not hope to afford or acquire original Vermeers. The woman quietly pouring milk hung on a walk over the kitchen table; the woman reading a letter was over a desk in her bedroom; the woman looking over her shoulder hung opposite the front door, greeting guests as they entered her house. It was the quiet gentleness of the everyday lives of the women in the pictures that appealed to her, just as what she saw in many of the archaeological sites she excavated: people going about the commonplace tasks of living.

LINDSAY SAT PROPPED up in her four-poster bed, comfortable in her green cotton nightshirt, reading the latest osteology journal. The television on a table against the wall beyond the foot of her bed went mainly unnoticed as it flashed the news of the day, but as she turned a page in the journal a scene on TV caught her eye. She aimed the remote at the television and turned up the volume. Denny Ferguson's cocounsel, the angry young woman in the dark blue suit, was talking to a reporter. The lettering at the bottom of the picture said her name was Sarah Kelley Banks.

"I am absolutely outraged," she was saying, "that a man's life depended on the testimony of that woman." Lindsay cocked an eyebrow as Sarah Banks went on to attack her professionalism and competence. She hit the off button when the reporter announced that Lindsay could not be reached for comment.

The shrill ring of the telephone startled Lindsay. She glared at the device on the nightstand as if it were a traitor, letting the machine answer it. At the sound of Derrick's voice on the speaker, she picked up the receiver.

"Derrick, I'm here," she said.

"Good. I called late, hoping you'd be home. How'd it go today?"

"The jury convicted him."

"I'm glad."

"Derrick, do you think I'm arrogant, manipulative, and unprofessional?"

Derrick gave a surprised laugh. "Self-assured, yes. Manipulative? Definitely not. And you're the most professional person I know. What's this about?"

Lindsay told him about the angry confrontation.

"Well, I can see why they might be choking on sour grapes. Forget them. I have some good news."

"I could use some good news. What is it?" She settled into her pillows and looked at the smiling face of Derrick in the picture at her bedside.

I'm going to be the principal investigator of the Cold River Site this summer."

"Derrick, that's great." Cold River was potentially a huge site, probably covering more than fifty acres. It had seven mounds. The largest covered four acres and rose to a level of fifteen feet. The site had been known to archaeologists for more than a hundred years, but the landowners had never given permission to dig. The land was in different hands now and permission had been granted to the University of Tennessee, where Derrick was working on his doctorate. It was a gem of a site. Lindsay let the sound of Derrick's easy voice soothe the tension of the day from her.

"I won't be able to come see you for a while," he said with regret. "We're starting excavation in the spring."

"I know you must have a lot to do to prepare," she said. "I'll put Cold River on my summer itinerary."

"Bring your dancing shoes."

"Always, when I see you."

"I miss you, Lindsay."

"I miss you, too. I wish you were here," she said. He was silent. Lindsay imagined the look of surprise on his face.

"I'll come if you need me," he said.

"I need you, but don't come. I'll be fine. It's just the trial and Mr. Kim. It's so sad."

"I know," he said.

"I'm pleased about Cold River," Lindsay told him.

"So am I," he said.

THE MARCH WINDS lingered into April, and it was unseasonably cold as Lindsay showed the students at Barrow Elementary School how much you can learn about people by examining their tombstones. Lindsay and the class of sixteen young students were in the old cemetery beside Baldwin Hall. Campus lore said it was where the university buried deceased students in centuries gone by when it was inconvenient to ship the bodies back home. The story may have been true, but the graveyard was actually the remnants of the old City of Athens Cemetery, encroached on over the years by the expanding university. Most of the residents had been exhumed long ago and moved elsewhere so that only a fraction of an acre of the cemetery remained on the campus. Lindsay had just finished talking about identifying the different kinds of rock the tombstones were carved from and asked if there were any questions.

"Can we dig one up and look at the bones?" asked a nine-year-old dressed in a red and black UGA sweatshirt.

Lindsay was saved from answering by Sally, who had come to tell her she had a phone call from Max Gilbert, the prosecutor of Denny Ferguson. She left the students and their teacher with Sally and hurried to see what he wanted.

"I have some bad news," he told Lindsay when she picked up her office phone. "Denny Ferguson is on the loose."

"How?" asked Lindsay, clutching the telephone.

"Sometime after midnight last night he complained of severe stomach pains and had a fever. The county jailer on duty called for a doctor, who thought it was his appendix and had him sent to the hospital. He found himself in a momentarily unguarded hospital room and walked out. Simple as that."

"What do you think he will do?"

"Try to get as far away from here as possible. He does have a lot of relatives who could hide him, and that's bad, but I don't want you to worry, just be cautious. Normally, these guys are caught within forty-eight hours."

Lindsay hung up the phone. She decided not to tell Derrick. He would probably interrupt his work to come down, and she didn't want to be the cause of that. Besides, the prosecutor was right. Ferguson would be caught soon if he stayed in the area. The life of a fugitive is hard, particularly when his face has been seen on TV by nearly everyone.

Ferguson's escape caused a flurry of news items about the role of Lindsay's testimony in his conviction. His lawyers talked about the tyranny of expert witnesses and how their credentials and reputation can unduly interfere with some jury members' exercise of their own good judgment. Sarah K. Banks gave a teary interview, saying that Denny was afraid he was going to be put to death for something he didn't do. No wonder he bolted, she told the interviewer. He felt as though he had no hope for justice.

DENNY FERGUSON was not caught within forty-eight hours. Two months passed before Max Gilbert, the county prosecutor, called to tell her, "A car stolen from the hospital parking lot about the time of Ferguson's escape turned up in South Carolina. It's a safe bet it was him. He'll turn up. He's not smart enough to stay hidden for too long. Maybe we'll get lucky and *Unsolved Mysteries* or one of those programs will pick up the story."

Lindsay thought that sounded as if they didn't have a clue where to look for Ferguson, but she had stopped worrying about it. If he had a grudge against her, he would have tried something before now. She directed her attention to her plans for the summer: a leisurely trip through North Georgia and Tennessee, visiting archaeological sites. The three she was most interested in were directed by friends she had gone to graduate school with who were in the process of finishing up their doctoral programs: Brian Parker's Royce Site, Jane Burroughs' Rock Shelter Site, and, of course, Derrick Bellamy's Cold River Site. She had spent the larger part of spring quarter planning her trip. If Denny Ferguson came after her, at least she would be a moving target.

"THERE'S A CALL for you." Susan Gitten leaned from the door of Lindsay's cabin, yelling to her. "Do you want me to tell them you've gone?"

Lindsay turned from stroking her horse's neck and glanced at her Land Rover, packed and ready to go. "Yes...no. I'll take it." She rested her cheek on Mandrake's velvet-soft nose, gave his neck another pat, and walked to the cabin.

"Lindsay Chamberlain," she said.

"Dr. Chamberlain, this is Sheriff Howard, over in Cordwain. We met last year at that cemetery flooding thing."

"I remember. What can I do for you?"

"A farmer up here's found a skeleton in a field he's plowing. I wonder if you'd come take a look. I got a deputy guarding it right now." Lindsay looked at her watch. She had planned to be on the road by now, but then, she had also vowed to have a leisurely trip and a flexible schedule. "We don't have anybody here who can tell us what to do with it," he added, as he gave her directions to the farm.

"I'll leave right now. It should take about forty minutes."

"Thanks. I sure do appreciate this. It's probably an Indian burial ground he's stumbled on, then again..."

TWO

LINDSAY SAW THEM standing in the field: two men in uniform, slim with military bearing, and another man dressed in work clothes. A large green tractor was sitting idle a few feet away. A woman in a print housedress stood at the edge of the field. Next to her a young boy about twelve sat cross-legged, petting a dog lying beside him. A girl of about five pulled at the woman's hand, straining to see what had gotten the grown-ups' attention. All faces turned toward Lindsay as she parked her vehicle and walked across the plowed field.

The sheriff held out his hand to Lindsay. "This is Miles Lambert. He owns the land. This is my deputy, Mike Murray. Glad you could come."

Lindsay smiled and shook each hand in turn. "No problem," she said as she looked down to where two ribs lay on the surface of the ground.

"Lambert thinks it may be a dog he buried a few years ago," said the sheriff, as Lindsay kneeled to look at the yellowed bones. She picked them up and stood to examine them.

"No, I'm afraid they're human," she said.

The sheriff shook his head. "Well, damn."

"How can you tell?" asked the deputy. "I've seen some pretty big dogs."

"If you look over at that dog, you'll see his rib cage is a different shape from ours. It's a consequence of walking on four legs rather than two."

Lindsay watched as they squinted at the dog, who sat up and wagged his tail as if expecting to be called. They looked at the ribs again, not seeing what Lindsay saw. Lindsay asked the young boy to bring his dog over, which he did eagerly.

The dog was a large black and tan hound that wagged its tail and sniffed with mild interest in the direction of the bones.

"What's his name?" Lindsay asked the boy.

"Casey," he told her.

Lindsay petted the dog and said his name. He licked her hand and gave her his paw. She shook it, then held the rib bones next to his chest. It was obvious from the comparison that the ribs could not be those of a dog.

"I see what you mean now," said the sheriff. The others nodded in agreement.

"These are the left sixth and seventh ribs of a human," Lindsay said. "They've been in the ground a good while, well over a hundred years from the looks of it. But ground that is routinely fertilized," she motioned toward the field, "has an effect on bones that can make them look older than they are. I need to see all of the skeleton to be sure of its age."

"I've got some shovels," Lambert offered.

"I have excavation equipment in the Rover," said Lindsay. "It probably will take the rest of today and most of tomorrow, maybe longer."

"Deputy Murray here will help," said the sheriff, and Lindsay was somewhat surprised when the deputy readily agreed.

"I got a camera in the car," he said.

Mr. Lambert was able to supply her with a makeshift screen to sift the surrounding dirt for items that might belong with the bones.

Lindsay drew a tentative outline in the soil indicating where she believed the grave's edges would be, then sat down in the plowed ground and began gently moving away dirt with her trowel. She started where the ribs had protruded through the surface, and she quickly found more bone. After an hour or so the sheriff realized that this was going to be a slow and meticulous task. He left the deputy in Lindsay's charge and drove back to his office. The Lamberts had left earlier. Lindsay heard Mrs. Lambert admonish her children not to bother them while they worked.

Mike proved adept at excavating and at sifting the fill taken out of the burial. The ground was soft and the task went more quickly than she had expected. By noon the upper half of the skeleton was partially uncovered. She was brushing dirt away from the forehead of the skull when, to the side of the excavation, she spied a pair of small tan feet with pink toenails in tiny brown sandals. She looked up into the wide-eyed cherubic face of the little girl she had seen earlier. The girl was staring down at the protruding skull.

"Hi," said Lindsay.

The girl grinned and waved a hand at Lindsay.

"Marilee, does your mama know you're here?" asked the deputy.

Marilee nodded emphatically twice. "She said for you to come in for tea and sandwiches."

"That sounds mighty good," said Mike. "How 'bout it, Dr. Chamberlain?"

Lindsay dusted her hands. "Maybe you and Marilee could bring me a sandwich and something to drink. I think I'd like to continue working."

"I found one just like that." Marilee pointed to the ground.

"What?" asked Mike.

Lindsay's gaze followed the direction of Marilee's finger. Lindsay saw it immediately. She took a tongue depressor and gently shaved the dirt away from the object, then dusted it with a soft paintbrush. After more shaving she was able to lift it from its place in the ground.

"What is it?" asked Mike.

"A copper earspool," said Lindsay.

"An earspool?" Marilee sounded incredulous. "What's that?"

"It's like a pierced earring, but the hole in the ear is stretched over this part. See how it kind of looks like a spool of thread?"

"Well, what kind of person wears something like that?" asked Mike.

"Indians of a certain time period wore them," answered

Lindsay. "Where did you find the other one like it?" she asked Marilee.

The little girl looked around the field as if gathering her bearings. She pointed toward the middle.

"Do you come out and collect stuff after it rains?" asked Lindsay.

Marilee nodded that she did.

"I'll bet you find a lot of good stuff. Could I see it?" she asked.

A worried look came over the little girl's face, and Lindsay remembered how tightly she had protected the Clovis point she found when she was Marilee's age, how she hung on to it still, keeping it safe in her desk.

"I won't take it," said Lindsay. "I just want to look at it."

Marilee smiled and said, "Okay."

"Well, I guess that tells us who the bones belong to," said Mike, rising and mopping his brow with a large blue bandanna.

"Looks like it."

Lindsay took the brush and dusted the skull. It had been partially flattened from years of decay, heavy topsoil, and, Lindsay supposed, farm equipment running over it, but certain features caught her eye. First, the very narrow nasal passage, then the slightly rectangular eye sockets: telltale signs of a Caucasion skull. She looked closely at the teeth, which she believed had overbite instead of the usual even-edged occlusion of people of Asian ancestry. Lindsay touched the zygomatic arch with her finger. She would have to wait until the skull was out of the ground, but she was relatively sure that these were not the forward-projecting cheekbones of an Indian skull, but the more recessed ones of a European.

"This is interesting," she said aloud.

"Found something else?" asked Mike.

Marilee squatted by the grave and looked at the bones.

"His facial characteristics are not those of an Indian, but of a European," she said.

"What does that mean, exactly?" asked Mike. "We got us

some guy from Europe wearing spools in his ears getting hisself buried here in this field? Maybe it's some hippie, you know, from the '60s, and the bones are not as old as they look. You said fertilizer and stuff make a difference."

"These are authentic Mississippian earspools, and the bones are definitely over a hundred."

"He from Mississippi?" asked Marilee. "My kindergarten teacher's from there."

Lindsay grinned at the little girl. "How old are you?" she asked.

Marilee held up five fingers.

"You sure are smart for five."

Marilee grinned.

"But no, Mississippian is the name of," Lindsay hesitated, searching for an explanation that Marilee would understand, "a big tribe of Indians that lived about five hundred years ago."

"Wow," Marilee whispered.

MARILEE'S MOTHER, Grace Lambert, made tuna sandwiches, chocolate cake, and tea for Lindsay and Mike. They were sitting cross-legged in the grass at the edge of the plowed field eating when they heard the screen door of the house slam and turned to see Marilee running across the grass holding a cigar box.

"These are the things I found out here," she said, handing the box to Lindsay.

Lindsay set her plate down and opened the box. Marilee scooted close, guarding her treasure, Lindsay thought. The green copper earspool lay on a wadding of cotton. The design cut into the copper, as far as Lindsay could determine, was similar to the one with the skeleton. In the box with the earspool were two arrowheads, a bottle cap, half a horseshoe, and a rusty bolt.

"Nice collection," Lindsay told her. "It looks like this earspool is the mate to the one we found today." Marilee looked troubled again, and Lindsay handed the box to her and she set it on her lap.

"Mama and Daddy told me I have to give it to you," Marilee said quietly.

"No, you can keep it. But maybe sometime I can borrow it and give you a paper that says that it is yours and I must give it back. Would that be all right?" Marilee nodded her head. "I don't need to borrow it now," Lindsay continued, "so you keep it safe."

Marilee smiled. "Will you tell Mama and Daddy that?"

"Sure," said Lindsay. "Are these all the things you found?"

"Yes. I look all the time."

"Let's look in the field now, while Mike finishes his lunch."

"I can go back to work now if you need...," he said, with a mouth full of chocolate cake.

"I want to do a little surface collecting. Take your time."

Lindsay and Marilee walked in the fine, dark brown dirt of the field. Lindsay's practiced gaze swept the ground with each step, but she found nothing.

"If you come back after a rain," suggested Marilee.

"Sometimes, if you don't find anything, it's still like finding something," said Lindsay, and Marilee gave her a sideways glance filled with such skepticism that Lindsay repressed a laugh. "You see, when you find a burial that looks like an Indian burial, it's usually near a village. If it's near a village, you'll find a whole lot of pieces of broken pottery and arrowheads. But there's nothing here."

"Maybe Mr. Moore got it all," offered Marilee.

"Who is he?" asked Lindsay.

"He lived here 'fore we did."

"No, probably not. Most people don't recognize pieces of clay pottery. It looks just like dirt sometimes. I think this means that there is no village here and this is a lone burial. Which is interesting." Lindsay was mostly talking to herself; she doubted Marilee understood what she was talking about.

"They got no trash here," said Marilee, and Lindsay glanced at her.

"That's right. That is very smart of you."

Marilee grinned.

THEY DID NOT FINISH unearthing the Lamberts' unexpected tenant that day, so Lindsay covered the bones with a sheet of plastic and went home after asking the Lamberts to not allow the dog to run free until the bones had been removed. When she arrived back at her house, she told Susan to ignore her, that she was not really there, and she slept in her own guest room.

Lindsay returned to the Lambert farm at sunrise and had been working two hours when Mike arrived. They finished about four o'clock that afternoon. Lindsay swept the bones clean, and Mike took photographs. He was slow but thorough, taking shots of the full skeleton and close-ups of the skull, hands, feet, and torso.

The skeleton was extended, arms lying out to the side. It looked embossed into the ground. The Lamberts had come out to look at the finished work.

"I called our pastor," said Grace Lambert, a gracious woman who fit her name and who, Lindsay noticed, had the bone structure of a Native American. "If you rebury him, he said we could do it in the church cemetery. Poor fellow can't stay out in the field."

"There's other Indians buried in the cemetery," offered Joshua. "A lot of people around here are part Indian."

"Mike said that the fellow was wearing earrings," said Miles Lambert. "Are you sure it's a guy?"

"Yes," said Lindsay, and she pointed out some of the features: the coarse brow ridge, square jaw, the shape of the pelvis. "What is interesting," she said, "is his race. I think he is European. I'll know more when I measure the bones."

Something on the edge of Lindsay's mind had been nagging her about the skeleton. She stared at it as she talked to the Lamberts. It was the right hand. The middle and distal phalanxes were under the proximal ones, and they were reversed so that their distal ends were now facing the proximal direction. The hand had been curled into a fist when the man was buried.

Lindsay took a tongue depressor, knelt down beside the skeleton, and began digging around the bones of the hand.

"Hand me that dental pick," she said to Mike.

"Found something else?" asked Mike.

"I don't know." Lindsay worked as the others peered over her shoulder. "Would someone give me a tissue?"

A white tissue appeared over her shoulder and Lindsay spread it on the ground. After some meticulous work with the burial tools she lifted an encrusted object from the ground and laid it on the tissue.

"What is it?" they asked.

"It's green," said Mike. "More copper?"

"Yes," Lindsay answered, staring hard at the piece, teasing it with the pick. "And it has something attached to it that has been preserved by the oxidized metal."

The object was mainly a mass of green oxidized copper with four thin extensions at ninety degrees to one another. It was attached to what looked like wood carved into small spheres or beads.

"A rosary," Lindsay said with surprise. "I think it's a rosary."

"My goodness," said Grace Lambert. "The fellow was a Christian."

"What do you reckon he was doing in them earrings?" asked twelve-year-old Joshua Lambert.

ROBERTO RAPHAEL LACAYO squinted as he looked out over the ocean at the speck he had been observing for the last two days, wondering if he was hallucinating or if it could be a ship. Oddly, he felt the taste of red wine in his mouth; odd because he had not tasted wine for how long? Twenty years? Twenty-five years? Who knew anymore? He unconsciously fingered the copper ornaments in his earlobes and looked down at his deerhide clothing and tattooed arms. Only his hirsute appearance gave a clue that his origin was not here in this alien wilderness, but across the ocean. Roberto remembered the day he had left Spain: Cristina crying and laughing at the same time. His mouth twitched into a slight smile. She was an adventurer, too, and she would have come with him if she had been allowed. His mouth turned down again. She had probably married. Her children would be grown now. Cristina would have grandchildren. Roberto couldn't imagine it; she was still so young in his mind—young, but faceless. He couldn't remember what she looked like. He had expected to go home rich, marry Cristina, and be a powerful man. But instead... He sighed and dug in his doeskin pouch. He pulled out his prayer beads and began to whisper as the salt water lapped at his feet. "Ave marie, gratia plena, Dominus tecum..."

The ship—Roberto now could see that it was a ship—was heading along the coast, northward. Estúpido, estúpido, *he thought.* No hay oro aquí. *He could tell them, "There is no gold here," but they would not believe him. They could take him home. He felt his ears again; the lobes were permanently stretched. So much about him was different. But he still wanted to go home. He began walking northward. There were only a few safe harbors where a ship could anchor.*

LINDSAY PACKED the bones and gave them to Mike with directions as to where at the University of Georgia to deliver them for further analysis. Now she would drive home, get a good night's sleep, and make another start tomorrow on her vacation. She was getting into her Land Rover when the Lamberts approached.

"Please stay for dinner," Grace asked.

"Thank you," said Lindsay, "but I need to shower and change..." She looked down at her clothes.

"We have a guest room," interrupted Grace. "You have your luggage. You could stay the night and leave from here."

"I couldn't impose—"

"You wouldn't be imposing," said her husband, putting an arm around his wife's shoulders. "We would be honored if you would stay."

The trip to the Lambert farm had been an interesting diversion, and Lindsay was looking forward to resuming her vacation plans, but there was an urgency in their request that caused her to consent. Besides, she was tired. Excavation was hard work.

Marilee jumped up and down when she heard that Lindsay was staying. After Lindsay took a shower and changed, the irrepressible five-year-old took her on a tour of her bedroom, which shouldn't have taken long in a ten-by-ten room. But Marilee was a collector: rocks, leaves, various kinds of teeth, bird nests, dolls, and just things she found, all nicely categorized and neatly placed on shelves in her room.

Lindsay named the teeth for her. She had a tooth from a cow, a horse, a dog, a raccoon. As Lindsay identified each one, Marilee asked, "How do you know that?" and Lindsay showed her the identifying characteristics of each. Marilee listened, wide-eyed, soaking up the information.

"Is this your brother's?" asked Lindsay, holding a small square box containing a deciduous human molar on a piece of cotton.

Marilee nodded. "He traded it to me for this rusty thing I found."

Lindsay smiled and set the box down. Interesting, she thought. Joshua's molar had a rare extra cusp.

"What is this?" Lindsay picked up a deep red-brown piece of weathered wood leaning against the wall next to Marilee's shelves.

"It's a piece of wood from a ship," Marilee said proudly. "I found it on the beach. See the holes? Daddy said they had wooden pegs instead of nails to hold the ship together. It's real real old."

"I'm impressed," said Lindsay. Marilee beamed.

"I'm glad you're staying tonight," she said.

Lindsay took hold of Marilee's hand and walked with her

to the dining room. Dinner was pot roast with potatoes and carrots, green beans, squash, and cheesecake for dessert. The setting was elegant white china and silver on an off-white lace tablecloth. The buffet, hutch, and chairs were of polished cherry. On the wall hung a Norman Rockwell print of Thanksgiving dinner, which Lindsay imagined matched this dining room on holidays. The Lamberts were going out of their way to make Lindsay's stay enjoyable, but it was always a little uncomfortable for her to be in the home of strangers, even ones as nice as the Lamberts.

They passed each dish of food around the table, and Lindsay helped herself to some of everything. Grace filled Marilee's plate, but Lindsay could see she wanted to do it herself. "That's not the calf, is it?" she asked as her mother cut up her meat. "Joshua said we were having it for supper."

"Joshua, why do you tell her such things?" said Grace, frowning at him. "No, it's not the calf. That's buried and gone."

"Calf?" asked Lindsay.

"When we were on vacation," young Joshua volunteered energetically, "one of Mr. Stevens' calves got loose and got its head hung up in a hold in our shed and died. Boy, what a stink when we got back."

Lindsay was sorry she had asked.

"No talk about the calf at the dinner table," said Miles.

Joshua laughed. Marilee clearly did not think the episode funny at all.

Marilee and Joshua chattered throughout the meal, and Lindsay commented to their parents on how smart they were.

"Both our children are smart," said Miles with pride. "Joshua is a straight-A student, and the teachers are already planning an accelerated program for Marilee. They sure didn't get their brains from me." He smiled at his wife. "I hardly made above Cs. It must have come from Grace."

"We got lucky with the kids," added Grace. "Maybe they got it from my brother. He was the smart one in the family. He was good at figuring things out."

Everyone was quiet for a moment.

"It's time for you kids to go to bed," said Miles.

"It's early," Joshua protested.

"Then you can play in your room," said his father. "Marilee, it's your bedtime."

Marilee shook her head and pointed to Lindsay. "I want to show her my books."

"Now, Marilee. Dr. Chamberlain is our guest," said Grace.

"I don't mind, really," Lindsay said.

"Show her just a few. I'll make a fresh pot of coffee," Grace told Lindsay. Marilee went happily off to get ready for bed.

Marilee had quite a collection of books. Lindsay picked up one about collecting seashells and rocks; the one beside it was about Native Americans. Another one was about what different people, like teachers, policemen, nurses, and doctors, do at their place of work. "These are good books," Lindsay told her.

"Kelley gave me a lot of them. She always brings me a book when she comes to visit."

"Kelley?"

"She's my cousin."

"Would you like me to read you a story?" asked Lindsay.

"I'll read," Marilee said confidently.

Marilee took the book about Native Americans and crawled up on her bed. Lindsay sat beside her. Marilee read, pointing to each word and pronouncing it clearly and deliberately. Lindsay was surprised and pleased that the book was as accurate as it was simple.

"You read very well," she told Marilee.

"I like to read," she said, smiling up at Lindsay.

"I'd better let you get to bed."

Marilee shook her head. "More."

"I think your mother made coffee."

"Just one more page, please?"

Lindsay relented and listened to just one more page, which

turned into two pages, after which Lindsay tucked her in and turned out the light.

Miles and Grace Lambert waited for Lindsay in the sitting room. Miles sat uncomfortably on the white and gold brocade sofa, his hands gripping the seat as though he were not in that room by choice. Grace poured coffee from a silver coffeepot that was part of a silver service sitting on the cherry coffee table. A large manila envelope lay next to the tray. Grace handed a white bone china cup and saucer to Lindsay.

Lindsay took a sip of coffee as she sat in a wingback chair that matched the sofa.

"We're glad you stayed," Grace said. "It's been a treat for Marilee. She's always bubbling with questions, and we can't always answer them."

"She has quite a collection of things."

"She's a little pack rat all right," said her father. "Did she show you the piece of wood from the shipwreck?" He seemed as proud as Marilee.

"Yes. She said she found it on the beach," said Lindsay.

He nodded his head. "We took our vacation back in April. Went to Florida—bad timing, too many young people." He shook his head. "But we had fun, didn't we, Grace?"

"It's the first trip we'd been on since our honeymoon. We took the kids to the beach and Disney World. Then we came back..." She didn't finish her sentence, but took a sip of coffee.

As they made light conversation, Grace eyed her husband the way one does when they want someone to bring up an agreed upon subject. Miles set down his cup and took a breath. Lindsay quietly sipped her coffee.

"Dr. Lindsay," he began. "We—my wife and I—have a question. We understand that you can tell an awful lot about what happened to a dead person from just looking at their bones."

"Sometimes," Lindsay said cautiously.

"Grace's brother, Ken, died and—"

"No, he was killed, murdered," interrupted Grace, leaning forward. "I believe I know who did it, but I can't get anybody to listen to me."

THREE

LINDSAY DIDN'T KNOW what she had expected to hear from the Lamberts, but it wasn't this. She stared at Grace a moment, but before she had a chance to speak, Grace began telling her about her brother. She handed Lindsay a photograph in a silver frame of a thin, lanky young man with handsome features leaning casually against a restored Mustang convertible. He had brown, almost blond, hair falling onto his forehead. As Lindsay looked at the picture, Grace told her how much she adored him, how good he was to her, how much he loved life.

Lindsay had observed that people seem to feel that if they could only make her understand how much a person was loved—that they were a real persona and not a statistic—she would understand how important it was to do her best and make no mistakes when she examined their bones. Above all, she would treat them with dignity. Grace wanted Lindsay to know her brother as she knew him.

Miles, however, did not seem to share Grace's opinion of Ken's good nature. When Lindsay cast glances at him during Grace's narration, he had his head down or stared out the window lest he be called on to verify his brother-in-law's virtues—or so Lindsay suspected.

"The last time I saw him," Grace continued, "was the first week in January a couple of years ago. He and his wife, Jennifer, went to Colorado to visit her folks at Christmas. We drove up to Tennessee to see them right after they got home. He'd had a bad skiing accident out there. He broke his ankle and a couple of ribs, bruised up his face real bad. He looked terrible." Grace bit her lower lip.

"He was doing that—I can't remember what you call it—some kind of daredevil skiing, where you go straight down a mountainside. Had a fall. It's a wonder he didn't kill himself then,'' said Miles. Lindsay could see he was having a hard time keeping quiet about his brother-in-law. She also saw that Miles believed Grace's brother's death was his own fault, and it was only for his wife's sake that he was going along with asking for Lindsay's help.

''How did he die?'' Lindsay asked, still being cautious.

''Ken was a caver,'' answered Miles. ''He had a caving accident.''

''Ken was a good caver. He was safety conscious. He took care of the people who went caving with him,'' Grace said.

''Caving is dangerous,'' insisted Miles. ''Even the best cavers have accidents. Caves are unpredictable.''

Grace looked at her husband with no malice. ''Miles thinks I'm wrong,'' she said. ''That I'm too grieved. But I know my brother.''

''We need to just tell her what we know,'' said Miles. His wife nodded and looked to him to tell the story.

Miles went on. ''Grace is right: Ken knew caves, around here and all over in Tennessee and Kentucky, too. But he would sometimes go off caving with friends and not tell anybody where they'd gone. They might've taken off to Atlantic City of California as far as anybody knew.''

''Ken was always a little wild,'' said Grace, ''full of life. He liked to see and do things.''

''Two years ago, Ken and a couple of friends went off like that, not telling anybody, and just didn't come back. Nobody knew where they were. The sheriff thought they'd left town. His buddies were just as likely to up and take off as Ken was.''

''He had a business,'' said Grace. ''He wouldn't have left his business. Ken was serious about that.''

''That's true,'' said Miles. ''He sold sporting equipment, expensive stuff. Did pretty good. He was in it with his wife. It was her money that started it.''

''It was her that killed him,'' said Grace. ''She got a ton of insurance money. Extra for accidental death.''

"How was he finally found?" asked Lindsay.

"Some other cavers in Tennessee found him," Miles said. "Just this past May. We'd not been back a month from our vacation. The cavers just happened on his remains, his and his friends'. I understand it was a pretty hard cave to explore, one of the most dangerous. That's why it took so long to find them. The cave is on private property, and hardly anybody goes there. Apparently a cave-in of some sort trapped them." Miles took Grace's hand. "They died there."

"Jennifer arranged it. I know she did."

"Is his wife a caver?" asked Lindsay.

Grace stared at her a moment, puzzled at the question. "No, I—"

"It would be hard to arrange a cave-in so that you wouldn't get caught in it, too, and so that the authorities wouldn't find evidence," said Lindsay.

"There was some talk of Jennifer having an affair with some guy," offered Miles. "Grace thinks that the two of them killed Ken and his buddies in the cave, then somehow removed the evidence."

His wife nodded. "When they were found, they were nothing but bones. We were thinking that maybe you might be able to see something from the bones that the authorities missed."

"Surely they are already buried," said Lindsay gently.

"That's true," said Miles. "But the sheriff took pictures when they were found, and I had them blown up." Miles picked up the manila envelope from the table and opened it. Grace averted her eyes.

Lindsay looked at the black-and-white photographs he handed her. The first one showed a pile of rocks with blue jeans and boots sticking out from under the rubble. The next photograph showed three individuals who had been crushed under the rubble, looking all the more flattened because they had been skeletonized. The other photographs were close-up shots of bony hands that were still articulated. The skull of one of the skeletons had rolled away and come to rest about two feet from the body. Miles identified that skeleton as Ken Darnell, Grace's brother. The other skulls were apparently still attached by remaining ligaments. The photographs were good, but the skeletons were clothed.

"Do you have any photographs of the bones by themselves?"

"No, that's all we have. We know it's not much," said Miles.

"Who identified the bones?"

"The authorities in Tennessee," answered Miles.

"Do you know what person? Was it the medical examiner? Did they show the bones to a forensic anthropologist?" asked Lindsay.

"We don't know that," said Miles. "We were lucky to get these photographs."

"Were you asked to identify any of his belongings?"

Miles nodded. "Yes. We went up to Tennessee, and they showed the effects to us and Jennifer, his wife. They were Ken's, without a doubt."

"You said they were found last month. When did they disappear?"

"February 26 two years ago was the last day anybody remembered seeing any of them," Miles said.

"It's been two very hard years," said Grace.

"What exactly do you want me to do?" asked Lindsay.

"Dean Howard, our sheriff, is a friend of Sheriff Duggan over at Merry Claymoore. Sheriff Duggan told him that you are really good with bones."

Lindsay wanted to tell them that yes, she was pretty good with bones, but she needed some bones to work with. Here she had only pictures of bones, and they didn't show much. Instead, she asked, "Why do you think someone murdered your brother, Grace?"

"The insurance. He and his wife were partners in the sporting goods store, and she had insurance on him for the business, and she also had personal insurance on his life. Since he died by accident, she got over a million dollars."

Lindsay raised her eyebrows. ''That is a lot of money, but—''

''Like Miles said, she was seeing somebody else while they were married. I think he might have helped her,'' said Grace.

''Do you know who she was seeing?'' asked Lindsay.

Grace shook her head. ''A friend saw them together. He had dark hair, that's all I know.''

''She is a businesswoman,'' said Lindsay. ''The person she was seen with may have been a client or a business associate.''

''You don't kiss clients or business associates,'' Grace Lambert said emphatically.

''All right,'' said Lindsay. ''However, none of what you have told me is evidence of murder.''

''She got the money to open their sporting goods store from insurance money when her first husband died,'' Grace said.

''How did he die?'' Lindsay asked.

''A heart attack,'' Grace answered.

''Was the death investigated?'' Lindsay asked.

''Not that I know of,'' Grace replied.

''It could have been a heart attack,'' Lindsay told her gently.

''Look,'' said Miles. ''I know we haven't got much to go on. We don't even have his bones. But we thought maybe they'd give information to you where they wouldn't to us.''

''You just want me to have a look at the medical examiner's report?'' Lindsay was still not sure what they wanted her to do.

''Yes, and anything else you can find out.'' Grace looked down at her hands and back up at Lindsay. ''Maybe there's something in the pictures. Maybe they took other pictures they didn't show us. Maybe there's something you can find. He was my brother, and I have to do all that I can.''

Lindsay understood that. She had a brother, estranged from their family, but he was her brother, and even if she wasn't his favorite person, she loved him and was glad to know that he was somewhere in the world.

"Tell me what county he died in, and I'll see what I can discover."

Both Grace and Miles looked relieved.

It was almost ten when Lindsay went to the guest room to get ready for bed. She was about to turn down the covers when she heard a gentle *tap-tap* at the door and opened it. Marilee was standing there in her nightgown.

"Hello, Marilee. Do you need something?"

Marilee came into the room. "Why is Mommy crying? Is it for her brother?"

"Were you listening?" asked Lindsay. *Of course she was,* Lindsay thought. When you're a kid, you make it a point to listen to adult conversations. And a child as smart as Marilee could understand a lot of what they talked about, but she still had a five-year-old's fears and anxieties, and it worried her when her mother cried.

Marilee nodded. "Are you going to look for him? Will that make Mommy feel better?"

"I'll try to find out what happened to him," Lindsay said as she carried Marilee back to her room.

"I hope you find something," said Marilee.

Lindsay tucked her in. "I can't promise anything. Sometimes a person just can't find the answer. But I'll try."

Lindsay awoke early to the confusing sound of a rooster crowing and the aroma of bacon frying. She smiled as she realized where she was and that today she would be starting, for sure, her long-needed vacation. She showered and dressed, stripped the sheets from her bed, and folded them to be put in the hamper before she carried her things to the Rover. On the way back to the house she met Grace at the door.

"I've made breakfast. We can't send you on your way on an empty stomach."

The Lamberts' kitchen was a sunny farm kitchen: large, bright, and shiny clean. Lindsay sat down to a meal of bacon, eggs, fried apples, and biscuits. Miles and Marilee were already at the table. Grace called for Joshua. He came carrying something wrapped in a handkerchief and handed it to Lindsay.

"Joshua, what is that?" asked Grace.

"That's what I want to find out."

Lindsay unwrapped the object. It was a rusty piece of metal.

"Joshua, don't bring that dirty thing to the table," Grace said.

"Where'd you get it?" Miles asked.

"I traded Marilee my tooth for it."

"Joshua!" Grace cried.

Marilee laughed.

"Well, you guys would only give me a dollar. Marilee had a better deal."

Miles shook his head with a bemused smile.

During the conversation Lindsay had been examining the object. "Joshua, I'm not sure, but I believe you have a five-hundred-year-old Spanish knife."

"What?" Marilee slapped her hand to her head.

Grace, who had been passing the food around the table, stopped and looked over at the object again.

"Wow, really?" said Joshua.

"You're kidding," said Miles. "A five-hundred-year-old Spanish knife? You can tell that from that chunk of rusty metal?"

"I'm not sure, but I believe it may be. We know that expeditions of the Spanish conquistadores passed through this general area, and I have seen similar objects recovered from archaeological sites in Georgia. If you like, I'll have it cleaned for you."

"You can make it like new?" asked Joshua.

"No, not like new, but it may clean up so that we can tell more about it."

"Yeah, I'd like that."

"Find a box for it, and I'll mail it to someone at the university."

"Well, I like the tooth," said Marilee.

Lindsay grinned at her. "It's a fine tooth."

"Do you think the knife belonged to the gentleman in our field?" asked Grace.

"It might very well have," said Lindsay. "There is no real way to know for sure."

"Well, we just have all kinds of interesting things on the property," said Miles.

"Dr. Terry said it's a rare tooth," said Marilee.

"It is," said Lindsay, trying not to laugh.

"Yeah, that's what he said about my back teeth," said Joshua. "What did he mean?"

Lindsay wrapped the knife back up in the handkerchief. "Your tooth has an extra cusp," she said as she went to the kitchen sink to wash her hands. "Those are the lumps on the tooth that help you chew food."

"Does that mean I chew better?" asked Joshua.

"Could be," said Lindsay, taking her seat again and helping herself to fried apples that Miles passed to her. "This is good."

"Grace is an excellent cook," said Miles, smiling at his wife.

"My niece is coming over sometime this morning," said Grace. "I hope you're here to meet her. You'll like her. She's the first one in our family to get a college degree. We're real proud of her."

"She's a lawyer," said Joshua.

"She's dating the children's pediatrician," said Grace. "A really nice young doctor in that new medical building with Dr. Terry."

"He's Dr. Tim," said Marilee.

"Did someone mention my name?"

Lindsay looked over to see a handsome man in his mid-thirties, dark blond hair, athletic build, coming into the kitchen carrying a bouquet of daisies and daffodils. "Kelley will be here soon. She called and said she was leaving the same time I did," he said, giving the flowers to Grace.

"How pretty," she said.

"Aren't they?" replied Dr. Tim. "I don't think Mrs. Stevens will miss them from her garden, do you?"

"Oh, you..." began Grace, cuffing him on the shoulder as she rose and took the flowers to put them in a vase. "This is Dr. Lindsay Chamberlain," said Grace. "Lindsay, this is Dr. Timothy Scott. Lindsay is a bone specialist."

He reached across the table and shook Lindsay's hand, then sat down between Miles and Joshua. "Bone specialist?" he asked.

"Lindsay identifies bones," said Miles.

"Yeah, you won't believe what we found buried in the field," said Joshua.

"What did you find?" he asked as he reached for a biscuit.

"An old skeleton of a Christian with spools in his ears," said Marilee.

Tim stopped in the middle of buttering his biscuit.

Joshua and Marilee giggled at the look on his face. No one noticed the kitchen door opening until they heard the voice.

"What are you doing here?" The statement was not loud, but it was severe enough that everyone stopped and looked.

Lindsay was surprised to see Denny Ferguson's cocounsel standing in the Lamberts' kitchen glaring at her.

"Kelley," said Grace. "What's wrong, dear? This is Dr. Lindsay Chamberlain. She's our guest."

"We've met," said Lindsay. "Miss Banks and I were on opposite sides of a recent court case."

"Oh." Grace smiled. "I guess that would happen in your lines of work. Lindsay came here to identify some bones for us."

Kelley looked sharply at her aunt. "Excuse me?"

"Yeah," said Joshua. "Dad was plowing and found some bones in the field. The sheriff called Dr. Chamberlain."

"What was it?" Kelley asked.

Dr. Tim nodded to her. "Marilee just explained to me it was a Christian with spools in his ears. I'm waiting to find out what that means. Sit down and pull up a biscuit and let them tell us." Tim looked at Lindsay. "Well, bone doctor?"

Miles moved his chair and Kelly sat down beside Tim and gave Lindsay her attention. Her eyes sparked with antagonism as Lindsay explained about the skeleton and the Mississippian earspools.

"I found the other one," said Marilee.

"And the poor fellow was holding a rosary," added Grace.

"A rosary?" said Tim.

"That's how it appears," said Lindsay. "The bones and artifacts have to be examined in the laboratory to be sure."

"I'm surprised you couldn't tell at a glance," said Kelley.

"She pretty nearly did," said Miles, oblivious to Kelley's sarcasm.

Lindsay could see that there was a good chance things were about to go downhill from here. She folded her napkin and rose. "I had better be on my way. I want to thank you for the hospitality you've shown me.

"We enjoyed it," said Grace.

"Yes," agreed Miles. "It has been a bit of excitement for us."

"Let me get a box for the knife," said Joshua, jumping up from the table.

Lindsay shook hands with Grace and Miles and said good-bye to Marilee, who wanted to shake her hand, too.

"Come back and see us. Won't you?" said Marilee.

"I'll tell you what," said Lindsay. "I'll return the knife personally when it is cleaned and analyzed."

Lindsay went out to the Rover to wait for the package. She was followed shortly by Kelley Banks.

"What's this Uncle Miles is telling me about your investigating my uncle Ken's death?" she said.

"Grace and Miles asked me to look into it for them," Lindsay told her.

"Aunt Grace is having a difficult time with Uncle Ken's death. I don't want you dragging it out for her."

"What are you talking about?" asked Lindsay.

"Aunt Grace just can't accept his death. She has some notion that Aunt Jennifer had something to do with it. It's part of her grief. She needs to get over it, not have you feeding it. Aunt Grace has been through a lot. She doesn't need this."

"I take it you don't think Ken's wife had anything to do with his death?"

"No, I don't. Jennifer isn't the nicest of people, but she's not a murderer."

"Why are you so hostile? Are you like this with every expert witness every time you lose a case?"

Kelley narrowed her eyes. "I've never had an expert witness refuse to admit that there was room for doubt, when there so clearly was. You went beyond stubborn, to criminal, and I'm taking steps to have you sanctioned by the courts."

"I couldn't express doubts I didn't have."

"No doubts? You had—what—a ten-second glimpse of his mouth? Denny's a troubled kid, an easy target when someone is throwing blame around. You didn't know for sure it was him, but because you're labeled a so-called expert, they believed you. You know that you need more corroborating evidence to make a positive ID."

"I said this at the trial, but I'll say it again. Denny Ferguson's lower incisors overlap in front, his lower left second premolar has a pronounced lingual lean. He was missing his right second mandibular molar and his upper incisors both had a mesial chip that made a V-shape in front. Even if he had a twin with the same occlusal pattern, his twin wouldn't have broken his teeth in the same way. Denny Ferguson has a distinctive tooth pattern that is unique to him that I recognized and could reproduce in a drawing. It was that drawing that both Albert Kim and the policeman recognized. I think you have a deep misunderstanding about identification. Take all the steps you want. You'll only look like a fool."

They stared at each other silently for a moment. Finally Kelley spoke.

"I didn't come out here to retry the case. I came for my aunt. She is a very nice, sensitive woman who loved her brother dearly. We all did. He was a bit of a rogue, but a fun guy and a good uncle. Grace is in denial about his death, a natural process of grieving, but she needs to get on with her life. I don't want her hurt."

"I understand that. Your aunt and uncle asked me to do something for them, and I agreed. There is very little evidence, no bones to examine, only pictures of clothed skeletons. I will do my best for them, but I told them that there is little that I can do."

"Aunt Grace has pictures? That must be horrible for her." Kelley looked at the house and wrinkled her brow. "I'll talk to Uncle Miles."

"I don't think she's looked at them," said Lindsay. "She averted her eyes when Miles showed them to me."

Kelley looked back at Lindsay. This time she had a softer expression and her eyes weren't like glittering daggers. "Can't you see what this is doing to her?"

"I think she needs a closure she can deal with. Perhaps if I see what the authorities in Tennessee have and I can tell her it was only an accident, she can go on."

"Perhaps you're right." Kelley rubbed her eyes with the tips of her fingers. "What's the story on the guy in the field; how did he get there?"

Lindsay smiled. "I don't know. It's a mystery at the moment. I told your uncle I'd like to send some archaeology students to look around to see if they can find anything else. It won't take long. They'll try not to interrupt his planting."

Kelley shook her head. "It's so late for planting, I suppose he was just plowing under the field. It's been so dry lately, I think he lost the last planting."

Kelley seemed almost friendly. Lindsay hoped she had lost some of her hostility.

Joshua came out of the house holding his package. Grace and Marilee followed with Miles and Dr. Tim. Lindsay gave Joshua a receipt for the object, and she promised to keep them informed about the progress with the remains and with Joshua's knife.

As Lindsay drove off, she saw Kelley holding Marilee's

hand. She felt a pang of envy. She shook her head and reached for her map to the first stop on her trip: Brian Parker's sixteenth-century Indian village.

FOUR

PIAQUAY ORDERED HIS men to set down the heavy ransom. He stood, grim faced, and waited for the devils. Concealed beneath deerskins on litters were the most treasured objects in his chiefdom. He heard the sounds, like birds: the calls of his scouts warning of the arrival. They were coming; marching the stolen women and children, they were coming.

ESTEBAN CALDERÓN licked his lips when he saw the litters laden with treasure. He wanted to savor the moment he removed the hides, revealing the silver, gold, and diamonds. He was moments away from being wealthy, a few short weeks away from returning to Spain a prosperous man. He pictured himself riding down the streets of Madrid lined with cheering throngs of people, the iron shoes of his horse announcing his presence with every step, banners flying. Already he was thinking how he was going to keep it to himself. He watched his men, tired, gaunt, and as hungry for gold as they were hungry for food, hot in their armor, bitten unrelentingly by the insects of this sweltering world with its dark shadowy forests. And there was that stupid Pardo to outmaneuver. Calderón would have to exercise care if he was to keep his treasure.

Calderón sat astride his horse, looking down at Piaquay, who was naked except for the doeskin wrap that hung like a skirt from his waist to his thighs. He stood with arms folded over a smooth, hairless chest, his dark skin tattooed with intricate dark blue and red designs, snakelike down his arms, around his neck, and on his chest like a sunburst. There were bands, like flowers, around his legs and pointed designs along his abdomen. His black hair, streaked with gray, flowed down his back, except for one lock, which was tied in a topknot like a horse's tail atop his head. The chief's only jewelry was copper spools in his ears. Calderón dreaded dismounting and facing the chief; he would have to look up to him because the Indian was a good head taller than Calderón. He simply would not. He would stay on his horse and make the Indian reveal the ransom to him, treasure by treasure, as if he were Calderón the King.

Piaquay saw his family and the families of his villagers tied together and led like beasts by the devils. His sister was holding on to her son's hand. His wife, beside her, holding their young daughter in her arms. Both stood still, like trees in the eye of a storm. Soon he would be rid of these foreign devils, if they kept their word.

Calderón called for the interpreters. Three of them. It was a nuisance, but there was no alternative. The savages had too many languages. He told the first to tell the chief to bring the treasure before him and show him the bounty. The first interpreter told the second, who told the third, who relayed the message to the chief.

Piaquay stepped forward and motioned for his men to bring the litters. When the litters were sitting on the ground before the devil, Piaquay removed the hides, revealing the ransom: twenty sheets of mica, thirty sheets of copper, five clay pots filled with freshwater pearls, five baskets of flint, ten baskets of conch shells, fifty beaver hides, twenty bear hides. To Piaquay it was an enormous wealth, but worth the return of his family. His chiefdom once had a thousand times the wealth, represented on these litters, but in a mere ten seasons the sickness, the precursor to the appearance of the devils, had decimated his chiefdom to only one village. What manner of power had they that they could send out invisible warriors to weaken his people so before they arrived? While his braves revealed the treasure, Piaquay looked for the first time into the face of the devil sitting on his beast before him.

Esteban Calderón stared at the treasure in front of him, eyes wide, his brain trying to make the copper turn into gold, the mica into sheets of silver, the flint into silver ore. There was nothing of value here. Damn them, damn this place. Calderón raised his sword in a rage to cut down Piaquay. The chief evaded the attack and suffered a glancing blow to his back.

Everything erupted into a raging storm. The conquistadores, enraged by the paltry treasure and their dashed dreams, began to cut down the hostages where they stood. Piaquay and his braves tried to save them, but they were no match for the mounted enemy. When it was over, Piaquay had lost half his braves and three-fourths of the hostages. Calderón lost but five men and was driven off only when he himself received an arrow through his face, piercing him cheek to cheek.

Piaquay found his family among the dead. His wife and his daughter, his sister, his nephew. He cradled them each in turn, trying to wipe the blood from their faces with his bare hands.

His brother lifted his own new wife in his arms. "What displeased them?" he asked, to no one in particular. There was no answer.

A man, one of the devils, moaned. He was the first interpreter, lying wounded. Piaquay raised a spear to kill him.

"Please, no. Please don't kill me, please. I just want to go home." Piaquay did not understand him, but he stayed his hand. He was one of the devils, but he had the adornments of one from this world. Perhaps he could use him; perhaps he knew what kind of men they were that everything his tribe had was not enough for them.

Piaquay and the remainder of the tribe took their dead to the village on the bend of the river and buried them. He also dug a pit and buried the treasure.

LINDSAY DROVE through the hills of the upper Piedmont, winding through dark green forests of oak and pine. The rock revealed by the roadcuts changed from granite to metamorphic as the terrain became more mountainous. The number of pine trees decreased, replaced by hickory with a generous scattering of dogwood. Lindsay arrived at Brian's dig, which was in a cleared area of hardwood forest in the bend of Bigtree Creek, a small branch flowing into the Chattahoochee River. Sally met her in a small dirt area adjacent to the site used for parking. Lindsay guessed that the parking area would become considerably muddy after a rain. She waited until the dust settled before she climbed out of her vehicle.

"I'm glad you're here," Sally said. "Brian has some skeletons he wants you to look at. He thinks they may have European battle wounds on them."

"Interesting," said Lindsay, as they carried her things from the Land Rover to the tent she would share with Sally. "I hope you have plenty of work for me to do."

"Are you kidding?" said Sally. "Since this is a relatively small site, we have a small crew—a little too small. How long can you stay? By the way, did you have a good trip?"

"A few days. I'm kind of playing it by ear. And, yes, the ride up here was restful."

Lindsay looked at the view of the site from Sally's tent. She saw that about an eighth of an acre had been uncovered. Two test trenches intersected each other: one north-south and the other running east-west. The part of the site that was uncovered revealed a smooth brown surface with stakes and string creating a five-by-five grid. Several burials, two structures, and several pits were in the process of being excavated.

"It used to have a mound," said Sally, pointing to the left of the clearing, "but that was bulldozed by a landowner years ago. He thought it was a good source of dirt. It's a nice little site, though."

"I'm looking forward to seeing the bones you've found," said Lindsay.

Lindsay stowed her gear on the cot opposite Sally's. Sally followed her into the tent and sat down on her own cot.

"You're going to have to kind of tiptoe around Gerrie Chapman."

Lindsay raised her eyebrows. "Who's he?"

"She. She'd a Ph.D. student from Arizona and she thinks

she's the last word on human skeletal remains and has kind of a bad attitude.''

''Really?'' Lindsay smiled. ''I've had a lot of practice lately with hostility.''

''I'll bet. Seen any more of the lawyer person?''

''As a matter of fact, yes. And in the strangest place. I'll tell you about it over lunch.''

Sally took Lindsay across to where digging was underway. They didn't have a laboratory at the site, so everything found was bagged and stored. At the end of each week Brian or another student took the week's findings to the lab at the University of Georgia.

Brian was squatting by a pit. Lindsay had been on several digs with Brian—Sally, too—but she hadn't seen him in several months. He looked good, deeply tanned, his blond hair already bleached by the sun. He looked up when they approached.

''Lindsay.'' He jumped up and gave her a hug. ''Glad you're finally here. We've got some interesting things.''

''Looks like it.'' In the pit that was being excavated she saw the shiny surfaces of large mica sheets glistening in the sun. From all the greenish substance in the dirt, there appeared to be a sizable cache of copper. To the side, a clay pot was being uncovered, revealing a fill of small round nodules that appeared to be freshwater pearls.

''Is this a burial?'' she asked Brian.

''If it is, then this has to be the chief of the whole continent. I've never seen so many grave goods. Funny, it didn't look like a burial outline; it was a little too large and round. I guess we'll just have to see if there's bone under all this stuff.'' He turned to the diggers. ''Be careful with the copper. There might be fragile wood or something adhered to it.''

''Quite a find,'' said Lindsay.

''I'll say,'' said Brian. ''There's lots of history in this site. The test trenches show several layers of habitation. Early on, it looks like this was a pretty wealthy place. That structure,'' he pointed to a gridded section of the site, ''is one of the earliest, judging from the style of pot sherds in it. It's full of artifacts. We've found a few early burials, too, with a wealth of grave goods. The later burials have fewer goods in them. Gerri says the later burials look like a younger population, too. The very latest burials have a disproportionate number of women and children."

"Sounds like disease followed by conquest," said Lindsay.

Brian nodded. "Then we find this pit. From the design of the pot, it looks contemporaneous with the last habitations."

"Have you been able to connect this site with any historical descriptions?" Lindsay asked him.

Brian shook his head. "No. But I'm still looking. To date we haven't found any European artifacts, but we did find a cluster of burials that appear to have battle wounds. Like I said, a lot of them are women and children. This is the first sign of hostility we've seen here. I'd like you to have a look at the bones."

"Sure."

Brian turned and led Lindsay a few feet to a cluster of burials. "It's not all excavated yet," he said. "But it looks like these individuals may all have been buried around the same time."

The first group of burials had been photographed, mapped, sketched, and notated. The diggers were removing the bones, wrapping them in sheets of cotton and laying them in numbered boxes, one skeleton per box. Some small odd bones they were putting in separate numbered cartons. Brian introduced Lindsay to Gerri Chapman, who stood, wiped her hands on her jeans, and took Lindsay's hand. She was a short woman, about five feet four inches, with curly red hair and freckles.

"I believe we met at the Southwestern Archaeology Conference," Gerri said, and Lindsay remembered. She had missed the paper Gerri gave but had met her at lunch.

"Yes. We did. Glad to see you again. You're a long way from the southwest."

"Sure am. It's good to get variety. What do you think of this site? Interesting, huh?"

"Indeed it is. Brian said you had some medieval battle wounds."

"I believe so. Have a look."

Lindsay squatted down and examined a semiflexed skeleton on its side. Beside it was the skeleton of a child. Lindsay wasn't sure at a glance, but the child looked to be about six or seven. She leaned over and examined the adult skeleton more closely. It was a woman, relatively small, with a graceful head. The excavator was taking up the bones of a hand and dropping the small pieces onto cotton wadding in a carton. He cautiously lifted out the long bones of the arm and handed them to Gerri who pointed out the cut marks on the ulna where something had sliced into the bone at an angle.

Next Gerri showed Lindsay the scapula. It had a dorsal cut that went deep into the spine of the scapula and became more shallow as it extended diagonally across to the medical border.

"I'm guessing that the sixth and seventh thoracic vertebrae will show cuts as well," Lindsay said.

Gerri gave the scapula to the student wrapping the bones. "It looks like first she held her arms up like this." She demonstrated by holding her arms bent at the elbow and crossed in front of her face in the classic pose of someone warding off a blow. "Then it looks like she fell to her knees and received the final blow to her back. She must have just frozen and couldn't run."

Lindsay shook her head. "She was protecting her child. She defended herself against the first blow, which was a surprise to her. Then she bent over her child in an effort to save it."

"How do you know?" Gerri had a slightly defensive tone to her voice, but still sounded friendly.

"Her child was there with her, and that's what mothers do. That would be her final act."

"But you can't tell that from the bones," Gerri said. "The child may have already been dead."

"That's possible, too," said Lindsay.

"Grim," said Sally.

"I thought battle wounds were most often on the legs," said Brian as they sat under a giant live oak tree, eating lunch.

"They are," said Lindsay, shooing a fly from her sandwich. "European armor was made to protect the torso, so Spanish soldiers were trained to attack the legs and the head of their enemy. When they fought with Indians, they used the tactics they had learned to use against Europeans. I suspect, when these bones are analyzed, you'll find plenty of leg wounds."

"We have found several remains already with classic femur cuts," said Gerri.

"This is going to be an intriguing site to piece together," Lindsay said.

Lindsay called Derrick from her car phone that evening and was pleasantly surprised that she reached him.

"Hey, Lindsay. Where are you? At Brian's dig, I hope."

"Yep, I'm rooming with Sally," she said, leaning against her Rover. The coming darkness and emerging stars gave Lindsay a sense of privacy and intimacy as she spoke to Derrick. "It's a nice dig. Brian is doing a good job of it. I also came across something else rather fascinating before I got here. It was why I was late." Lindsay gave Derrick a detailed account of the find in the Lamberts' field.

"Well, what do you reckon?" he asked. "A lost conquistador?"

"There are historical accounts of Spaniards captured by Indians and living with them for years. Perhaps the Lamberts' burial is one of them. At any rate, it's curious."

Lindsay then called Susan to check on Mandrake and her home.

"Everything is just fine here," she said, then hesitated.

"Is there something else?" asked Lindsay.

"There have been some phone calls. Some—uh—not so much threatening as insulting. I made a list of their names and numbers. I guess the idiots don't know about caller ID."

"What are they about?" asked Lindsay.

"That trial thing," Susan said.

"You mean Denny Ferguson's? What now? Have they found him?"

"No, but his family's come on the local television station saying they're tired of being harassed by the police and that they don't know where he's got to. I think they're the ones who're calling."

"I expect it will settle down after a while. It has before. If you want, just let the machine pick up most of the calls."

"You've had some calls from reporters. I told them you're on vacation."

"That's fine. I'm surprised this case keeps recycling to the front burner of the news. I guess not much else is going on."

"I think what started it up again was a news story that the police were holding Denny Ferguson in North Carolina, but it turned out to be a false lead."

LINDSAY WALKED the short distance from her Land Rover to Sally's tent. Sally sat cross-legged on her cot, reading. Her blond hair hung forward, shading her face. "How are things with Derrick?" she asked.

"Great," said Lindsay. "His site is going well. He's fine. Some strange stuff going on at home, though. Susan has been getting several unpleasant phone calls about Denny Ferguson's trial."

Sally looked up from her book and wrinkled her brow. "Still? I'll bet it's that Kelley person. She's sure a poor loser. Did she and Ferguson have something going?"

"I don't think so." Lindsay shivered at the thought. "She has a boyfriend—a doctor, pediatrician, to be exact—that she seems fond of. Besides, Ferguson is hardly her type."

Sally went back to her book. "It'll be all blown over by the time you get home at the end of summer."

"Probably." Lindsay dug in her book bag and pulled out a mystery.

Sensing that Gerri was indeed sensitive about the burials, Lindsay stayed away from them and confined her work to helping Sally excavate a refuse pit filled with animal bones.

The excavation was done in six-inch vertical layers. She drew the bones in situ, then called Brian to photograph them, after which they removed them and placed them in carefully labeled boxes. Sally had been working on the pit for two days and had gone two layers—twelve inches—into the pit. By the end of Lindsay's first day, she and Sally had excavated another two levels and had reached the bottom of the pit.

Lindsay made a cursory inventory of the bones as she excavated and quickly identified deer, rabbit, fish, and turkey mingled in the dark soil with what looked to be many more species.

"They had a pretty good diet," commented Sally.

"Seems so. How does this oldest layer compare with the most recent?" asked Lindsay.

"I haven't noticed much difference, maybe more fish in the first level, but I'm not sure..." Sally stopped talking. Lindsay watched her gaze follow a green pickup truck pulling into the parking lot of the site. Then Brian, followed by Gerri, headed toward the lot.

"Uh-oh," whispered Sally. "Brian may need your help. Gerri's not the most diplomatic person in the world."

"What—?" Lindsay began, but she saw the Native Americans get out of the truck, and she guessed. "I'll see what I can do." She rose and walked across the site, her eyes on the parking lot. There were three of them, an elder, a woman about Lindsay's age, and a man who looked to be in his thirties. All of them had long hair, black, except for the elder, whose hair had turned gray. They wore jeans; the woman had on a white blouse, the men, short-sleeved, plaid shirts.

As Lindsay grew closer she heard Brian interrupting Gerri, no doubt trying to be a buffer for what Sally referred to as Gerri's lack of diplomacy. Lindsay introduced herself and shook hands with their visitors. Brian looked relieved that she was there. The elder introduced himself as George West. The younger man was his son, John West. The woman was his daughter, Emily West.

The elder looked Lindsay in the eye. "We object to what you are doing here," he said quietly.

"I told them that there is simply no proof that the inhabitants of this site were the ancestors of these people...," began Gerri, then stopped suddenly. Out of the corner of her eye Lindsay saw Brian grip Gerri's upper arm and step back with her.

Lindsay looked back at the elder. "I know. And we are sorry. We mean no disrespect. We take great care in the way we handle all the remains."

"You mean no disrespect," said John West, "but you give it by digging up our ancestors' bones."

The woman as yet said nothing, but merely scrutinized Lindsay. "You look familiar," she said finally.

Lindsay raised her eyebrows. "Do I?"

"Your picture has been on the TV," said John. "Something about giving bogus evidence."

"Oh. The Denny Ferguson trial. I didn't," she said simply.

"We object to this," said George West again. "We would like you to listen to our views."

"This is getting us nowhere," Lindsay heard Gerri say.

"We will listen, of course," said Lindsay. "We would like you to listen to us, too."

"We know what you will say," said John, and his father raised a hand.

"He is right, but we will listen anyway," said the elder.

"She's just a visitor here," cried Gerri.

They looked at Lindsay with suspicion. Emily West started to speak, but her father interrupted. "A visitor with influence, I would imagine."

"Yes," said Brian. "The only seat we have to offer is the ground beneath the tree."

"That will be fine," said George.

FIVE

PIAQUAY SAT UNDER the grove of live oaks. The man Roberto Lacayo was teaching him the language of the devils who had invaded his world and brought most of it, at least for him, to an end. His gaze rested on the gentle mounds of dirt that covered the people he loved, and he clenched his teeth in anger. As he listened to Roberto droning the names of the things around them, he scooped up a handful of acorns and poured them from hand to hand. He looked down at the nuts in his palm, and it reminded him of the irritating way Roberto kept fingering his beads and whispering in a language that was not even the one he spoke. Piaquay threw the acorns in disgust. Roberto looked over at the chief and fell silent, wondering what had angered him. Piaquay motioned for him to continue. This time Piaquay listened closely and repeated what he heard.

A woman from the tribe approached them and motioned for Roberto to leave. As the Spaniard rose and walked away, they watched him until he was under the vigilant eye of Piaquay's brother, Tesca.

"What is this I hear?" she asked.

Piaquay looked into her black eyes and softly lined face. "It's not your concern."

"I should say it is," she responded, sitting down in front of him.

"It is not your concern until I say it there." He pointed to the lodge on top of the large mound.

"Tell me what's in your mind," she insisted. "Why are you handing the title of chief to me?"

"It's right."

"How is it right? What are you going to do? Why do you learn the language of the enemy?"

"I'm going to kill the man who did this. The man who takes young children and women from their homes, the man who takes everything we have and when it is not enough, kills anyway. What kind of heart kills women, kills children? I'm going to rid this land of him and run out the other devils."

Cacheci shook her head. "You cannot. They are too strong."

"They're not strong. They're cowards. They don't even know how to keep the insects from biting them, they can't get food for themselves, they lose heart in battle when they have to stand on the ground and face us. It is the beasts that carry them that are strong and brave. The beasts can do all those things for themselves that the devils cannot do. Without the beasts, the devils are weak." Piaquay looked around as though the Spaniards might be listening. "Take the beasts, and they can be defeated."

"We all grieve. We all want the devils to be gone. But we must live; we must take care of our children."

"You know that. It's why it is right for you to be chief. I am too filled with hatred and revenge."

"You can't do this by yourself, and you can't take all the men."

"I will take only my brother and two more."

"I cannot dissuade you from this?"

Piaquay looked at the gathering clouds in the blue sky. A storm was coming. "No. I am changed. This is what I am now."

LINDSAY AND THE OTHERS sat facing each other under the oak tree. A breeze gently lifted their hair around their faces. Lindsay smoothed hers down with both hands as she spoke first. "We have a policy of quickly repatriating aboriginal remains after we examine them," she said.

"It would be easier if you didn't dig them up in the first place," said George West.

"Then we would learn nothing from them. They tell us so much."

John West stood up. "Why are we here? This is the same old talk. You're just using us for your pet theories. You care nothing about our people." His father motioned for him to sit down. He did, but grudgingly.

"What have you learned?" asked Emily.

"We have hardly had time to examine..." began Gerri, but Lindsay's voice rose over hers and she stopped.

"We have learned that something terrible happened to these people. Conquistadores came on horses, looking for gold and silver. They came to this village and understood immediately that it was important because at one end was a large flat-topped mound with a long series of steps leading up to a large house of clay-covered timber. The conquistadores had heard that the towns with mounds had wealth. This was a peaceful village, for it lacked a palisade around the clusters of thatched houses that circled the great plaza. No palisade meant they were friendly, and the conquistadores knew that.

"They rode in, looking for wealth similar to that of the Incas, whom they had robbed and utterly destroyed. When they did not find the riches they sought, they became angry and lashed out at the villagers. There was a woman. Perhaps she simply stood watching them, perhaps she was a hostage. She saw the sword that was coming down on her and instinctively held her arms over her face to shield it. The sword cut into her all the way to the bone. The woman had a child with her. She leaned over, protecting the child with her body, and the conquistador struck her so hard with his sword it cut into her shoulder and backbone, knocking her to the ground. She and her child were killed. Other women tried to flee and had their legs cut out from under them as they ran, holding their children. The men tried to protect them, but they were no match for the conquistadores on their battle-trained horses. This slaughter may have taken place somewhere else and the victims brought back for burial. The bones will tell.

"Conquistadores usually burned the villages they massacred, but so far there have been no signs that this village was burned. Once, this was a prosperous village. It was struck by disease, then this. The people who once lived here didn't stay long after this happened."

"That's an impressive story," said George West after a moment. "But we know what the conquistadores did."

"Not in detail," said Lindsay. "And you don't know the individual stories. You didn't know about this particular woman. We can tell you how old she was, how healthy she was, if she had other children. Sometimes we can tell if she was related to anyone else buried here. Your son was wrong when he said that I don't care about these people. I do. So does Brian. And Gerri," she added, rather reluctantly. "The people who lived here talk to me. I know what they looked like when they were alive. I would recognize them if they walked up to me."

No one said anything for a moment. They all looked at the open pits where the excavators were working. Finally, Emily spoke. "These people expected to stay buried, or at least their loved ones expected them to stay in their final resting places. But if you allow one of us to observe how you treat the burials, I could...," she trailed off as they heard another truck drive up.

Lindsay watched as a man jumped out and charged over to them. The newcomer was a young man in his early thirties, brown hair becoming bleached by the sun. He had a slender build and possibly a pleasant face, when it wasn't twisted in anger.

"What are they doing here? I want them off my property."

"Mr. Royce!" Brian said, jumping up.

"Now," he said, "or you're all gone." He looked at the three Native Americans in turn. "You took my father's property. By God, you'll not set foot on mine." He turned and stomped toward his truck.

"Damn," said Brian, running after him.

Lindsay watched as Brian caught up with him, but couldn't hear what was being said. George West looked genuinely sad;

John looked angry. Emily stared at the ground, then rose and started over toward Royce and Brian. Her brother grabbed her arm, but she threw it off. When she reached them, she sent Brian away and talked to the landowner alone. At first his manner was belligerent. Lindsay saw Emily gesturing at him with her hands; it was obviously an emotional conversation. In the end Royce got in his truck and drove off. Emily came back to the tree.

"I can stay and observe. The two of you have to leave."

"Damn him," said John. "He can't—"

"He can," said George. "It's his land, and there's been enough hard feelings. This is a compromise. We will take it."

"What about our ancestors?" said John.

"This is a compromise," the elder repeated. "We'll work with the law. It's slow, but it's starting to work for us."

"Tell me this," asked Gerri. "Why the heck did you wait until now, when we had half the burials up, to make an appearance and protest?"

"We've been busy with other pressing matters," said George, gazing down the road at Walter Royce's retreating truck. "Come," he said to John, then turned to Brian. "See that Emily gets home safely."

"Sure," said Brian. "I will. And thanks."

While Brian showed Emily West around the site, Lindsay turned to Gerri. Dropping any pretense at respecting turf, she spoke plainly.

"Look, Gerri, I know you disagree with these people, but these are their ancestors."

"You don't really know that," said Gerri.

"They are more closely related to them than we are. They feel very strongly about this. You know their worldview is very different about archaeological research from ours, and we have to respect that, even if we disagree with it."

"Exactly why are you telling me all this?" Gerri asked defiantly.

"Because I can see you are angry about their protest over the excavation of the burials. But if you let your anger manifest itself in some way that insults them, you'll hurt yourself as well as Brian and the others."

"I do know how to act."

"Good."

"Tell me this," said Gerri. "Who the heck are you to be laying all this on me? You are, after all, only a visitor here." Despite her words, there was really no malice in Gerri's voice. Only curiosity.

"According to some, I'm simply arrogant and manipulative."

"Well, if you can be arrogant and manipulative, I can be sugar and spice," said Gerri. "You'll see. Emily will be my best friend by the end of the week."

EMILY WAS AT THE SITE the next morning at the same time the crew was removing the protective black plastic from the ongoing excavations, getting ready for the day's work.

"That was a good story you told," Emily told Lindsay.

Lindsay looked up from her work, excavating another refuse pit. Emily squatted down to her level.

"It fits so far with what we've found," replied Lindsay.

"I wasn't insulting you."

"I know. But I wanted you to understand that I was being as truthful as the data allow."

"You're very straightforward. My father likes you," said Emily.

"He's a good man. Not many people see the value in compromise," Lindsay said.

"There are many people in the world with divergent viewpoints, he always says. We must get along. My brother, however, doesn't like you. I think perhaps for the same reasons. My brother and my father are very different." She hesitated a moment, then asked, "Why do you do this?"

Lindsay stopped what she was doing and looked into Emily's dark eyes. "I want to know about these people. The history of this land is my history, too. My ancestry is Welsh, Irish, French, English and, I've been told, some northern Italian. If you ask me to go back where I came from, it would be to the foothills of the Appalachians. That's where I was born and raised. There's no place else for me to go. By my thinking, I am as much native to this land as you are. That doesn't mean, however, that I believe that the government shouldn't honor past treaties or that we should completely disregard your feelings about your ancestors. It simply means that all that happened here is part of my history, too."

"I understand that. I even respect it. But what if we were digging up your ancestors?"

"I am absolutely the wrong person to ask that. If I knew nothing about them, I'd be the first in with a shovel and trowel."

Emily smiled. "We see things very differently."

"On most things, I suppose," said Lindsay. "Your differences with Royce. Was that about tribal land?"

"Yes. We've had a suit in for years. We finally settled with the government last week, and Royce's father lost his land to us in the settlement. He was paid, of course, but..."

"His family had a history with that land, too," finished Lindsay.

"Yes. Back several generations. We weren't happy to take land away from him, but it was our land before it was his. And, oddly enough, as Walter's father likes to say, a contract is a contract."

"You knew Walter Royce before this?" asked Lindsay.

Emily gazed off for a moment before she answered. "We used to go out."

"I see. For you, then, the price of the settlement was very high," said Lindsay.

"Yes. It was. But the good of the tribe is more important than my happiness."

"Your and Walter's history together—is that why he relented about you being on his land?"

"Yes."

"It looks like he might be willing to forgive one day," commented Lindsay as she went back to work on the bones of a squirrel commingled with those of a rabbit. Emily watched her work. Lindsay gently dug around the bones with a wooden Popsicle stick, brushing the loose dirt away with the kind of paintbrush used for edge work and windows. With each stroke of the brush, the bones stood out in greater relief.

"He might," said Emily after a moment, "but his father would forbid it, and he would honor his father."

"The good of his family is more important than his happiness. Perhaps our worldview is not so different from yours after all."

"In some things, I suppose not."

Emily rose from her haunches. "It was good talking with you, Lindsay Chamberlain. Perhaps we can talk more at lunch. Now I have to go observe Gerri, who seems to want to be my best friend."

Lindsay grinned to herself as Emily walked across the site.

Lunch came too soon for Lindsay. She was not finished with her animal pit. Nevertheless, she rose and went to eat the sandwich she had prepared that morning from the camp supplies. Emily and Sally sat beside her. Brian and Gerri were still on the site talking about something, and Sally kept looking over at them.

"The people on the news say that you are hiding out," said Emily.

Lindsay stopped mid-bite. "What?"

"They can't find you. They said your credentials are being looked into, that they are suspect—something about flunking a course and never making it up." Both Sally and Lindsay looked at Emily with gaping mouths. "You didn't know this?" Emily asked.

Lindsay shook her head. "I'm on vacation. Damn, this is getting ridiculous. I've never flunked a course in my life."

"I'll say," said Sally. "Lindsay's credentials are the best."

"This has gone beyond just being a sore loser, this is—this is something I'm going to take care of right now." Lindsay rose and went to her vehicle.

She first called home and caught Susan at the cabin eating

lunch. "Lindsay, I'm glad you called," she said. "The reporters' questions are getting more serious. They are asking something about where you went to school and something about not really graduating and failing a course."

Lindsay was shocked. She realized that she was tapping her foot on the brake pedal and stopped. "What are you telling them?" she asked Susan.

"Not what I'd like. I simply told them that they have wrong information and you'll straighten it out when you get back from your vacation. Of course, with their small minds, they translate that to mean you're hiding out from reporters. I hate that kind of people."

"I don't understand. My academic history is an open book. Look, I'm sorry you have to go through all this. Thanks for fielding the calls for me."

"No problem. Listen, if they start coming out here to your home, I may move Mandrake to my place. I don't want to risk them letting him out or upsetting him."

That was Susan, thought Lindsay, far more concerned about the horse than herself. "Do whatever you think best. I trust your judgment," Lindsay told her, and rang off.

Next she called her department, trying to remember if the acting head, Kenneth Kerwin, was on campus this summer. Frank Carter, the head of the archaeology department, was on sabbatical in Europe. Kenneth had been a poor choice to replace Frank, even temporarily, but the choice had been the dean's and not Frank's. She dialed the number of the main office and asked the secretary to connect her to Kenneth.

"Lindsay," said the secretary, "you can't imagine the ruckus you've caused around here. Dr. Kerwin is in a tizzy."

"May I speak with him?" Lindsay bit her tongue. Edwina would have to be working today. She wondered where Kate, the senior secretary, was.

Lindsay was put through to Kerwin. "Dr. Chamberlain," he said too loudly in her ear. "Where are you? Why aren't you here?"

"I gave you my detailed vacation plans, Dr. Kerwin. What has been going on there?"

"All these reporters. Very unseemly. They have been asking about your credentials, saying that they were tipped off that you did not finish your degree and that you have little experience or course work in forensic anthropology."

"And what did you tell them?"

"That I would look into it, of course. I told them that the Archaeology Department wouldn't tolerate fraudulent credentials."

"You told them what!" Lindsay said through her teeth. She got out of the car, stretching the telephone cord as far as it would go as she paced the parking lot.

"What did you expect me to say?"

"I expected you to defend me. You know my credentials. You know they are completely in order. You know some of the people I graduated with, for heaven's sake." Lindsay stopped short of calling him an idiot.

"Dr. Chamberlain. We need to keep calm."

Lindsay stopped pacing and drummed her fingers on the hood of the Land Rover. "I assure you, Dr. Kerwin, that under the circumstances, I am very calm."

"They asked about your identification of the teeth of Lenny Fergus."

"Denny Ferguson."

"Yes, well, I had to say that is not the way we usually do things."

Lindsay was livid. "We who? You don't know your olecranon from your coccygeal vertebrae." She looked up to see that Sally and Emily had come over to the car; both looked wide-eyed.

"Dr. Chamberlain, I don't think—"

"That's your problem. You don't think, Dr. Kerwin. Think about this. How you answer the reporters' questions will influence whether or not I bring suit against you, the department, and the university."

"Dr. Chamberlain, I—"

"If that is not clear, I'll have my lawyer write you a letter clarifying it for you."

"It's not necessary to carry on like this—"

"It is necessary. Good-bye." Lindsay hung up the phone.

"Lindsay," said Sally. "I've never, ever, seen you angry like this before. You weren't this mad at that Patrick guy for stealing your underwear." Emily raised her eyebrows. "You sure told Dr. Kerwin off," Sally added. "I wanted to tell him off when he was getting so anal about my program of study."

"Well, I don't think it got me anywhere, except letting off a little steam. I just don't understand what Kelley Banks has to gain by smearing my name. She can't take innuendos and lies to the appeals court. And if she smears everyone she loses a case to..." She left the sentence unfinished, deep in thought.

"Maybe it's not her," said Sally. "Maybe it is Ferguson's people."

Lindsay shrugged and threw up her hands. "Could be, I suppose."

Sally gave Emily a brief description of the past events as Lindsay remained lost in thought. She reached for the phone again and dialed the district attorney's office.

"Hey, Lindsay. What's up?" said Max Gilbert.

"That's why I'm calling. I'm on vacation and I keep hearing the strangest things about myself."

"You mean the news stories? Don't give it a thought. We know what your credentials are. I would never have put you on the stand if I hadn't investigated them thoroughly."

"Thanks."

"No thanks to it. This is monumental sour grapes. I can't imagine what Ferguson's relatives or Dalton expect to come of it."

"Gerald Dalton is spreading these rumors?" Lindsay was surprised.

"I don't know. Doesn't sound like him. Wish it did. I'd like to get something on him. However, I can't imagine the press paying that much attention to Denny."

"Could it be his cocounsel, Sarah Kelley Banks?" asked Lindsay.

"Could be. Do you have a reason to suspect her?"

Lindsay told him about the encounters with Kelley and how angry she seemed about the outcome of the trial.

"Hmmm..." Lindsay could almost see Max rubbing his chin. "She's just out of law school, what, three years? You know, some people can't take the pressure. Maybe she just doesn't like to lose, and wants to give you a hard time, even if nothing comes of it. Anyway, I wouldn't worry. Nothing will come of it."

"Thanks again."

"Sure thing, Lindsay. Say, while I've got you on the phone, I've got this question. Say you got a skeleton that shows indications on the ribs that the individual was stabbed, but you can't tell if the stabbing took place from the front or the back. Is there any other way to tell the direction?"

"Sure, the exit side of the cut on the bone will have a rougher edge than the entry side. You can usually feel it with your fingers. You have a skeleton you suspect of being stabbed?"

Max gave a little self-conscious laugh. "No, it's for a story I'm writing."

"I didn't know you're a writer," said Lindsay, smiling for the first time since she discovered what had been going on.

"I'm not sure my writing class knows either."

"I'd like to read it sometime."

"I might let you do that. Right now, what I've got going for me is authenticity. I'm having to work at the writing style."

"Sounds like everything's okay after all," said Sally after Lindsay hung up.

"Max seems to think so. I must say, I'm relieved."

"You must be good at your job if people are trying to destroy your credibility," said Emily.

"I like to think so," said Lindsay. "This is the first time anything like this has happened."

THE SUN SET AROUND 8:30. The darkness brought with it a loud chorus of tree frogs and crickets. Sally was out on a date with Brian, and Lindsay was alone. She opened the flap of the tent and lowered the mosquito netting to catch any breeze that consented to shift around the hot summer air. Lindsay had planned to read, but she saw the envelope of pictures the Lamberts had given her tucked into the bottom of her suitcase. She pulled out the photos of the three unfortunate cavers. "I don't know what they expect me to do with these," she said aloud, searching around among her things for a hand lens, finally finding it in the pocket of a pair of jeans. Using the lens, she scrutinized every part of the images carefully. Nothing revealed itself to her. She saw that the back of one skull was crushed, but that could have happened in the cave-in. She examined the hands for any signs of defensive wounds. Nothing. There was no way the pictures could tell her whether the cave-in was intentional or accidental. She returned the pictures to the envelope and picked up a book. She was still reading when Sally came back.

"Have a nice time?" Lindsay asked.

"Not bad." Sally smiled. "Not bad at all."

PIAQUAY LEARNED FAST. It did not surprise Roberto. The Indians had a facility with languages, perhaps because there were so many different ones and so much movement among the Indians. For several weeks Piaquay had learned basic vocabulary. Now he practiced conversation. He particularly wanted to talk to Roberto about the life of the Spaniards, as Roberto had taught him to call them. It had offended Roberto's sensibilities when he learned that Piaquay called him something akin to a devil.

Roberto Lacayo told Piaquay about how the Spaniards had been trying to colonize this new world and kept failing. Piaquay listened closely as Roberto told him how Ménendez had fought with the French, who were also trying to colonize the new world, how the Spanish town of Santa Elena had almost failed until Juan Pardo and the Governor Ménendez came with provisions and rescued it.

"Now tell me your story, Roberto," commanded Piaquay. "How did you come to be across the great water and live among us?"

"I was lost here about twenty-five years ago. That's a long time," he said almost to himself. "I was a poor man, and I wanted to marry." Piaquay's lips turned up very slightly. A man seeking to better his prospects and marry well was something he understood. However, when Roberto mentioned the name Hernando de Soto, Piaquay scowled.

"You have heard of him?" Roberto asked.

"The enemy of enemies. When I was a youth, he traveled through our lands, raping our women and massacring my people. You rode with him?"

"For a time," said Roberto carefully. "I was lost early in the journey, and I did not approve of all his acts." He grasped the beads on his belt. Piaquay knew that when he did this, he told the truth. "I was always faithful to Cristina when I traveled." Tears sprung unbidden to Roberto's eyes. "It was only when I realized that I would probably never be going home that I took a wife, and I was good to her."

"Where is your wife?" asked Piaquay.

"An epidemic swept through the village. It took her and my daughter."

Piaquay nodded. "The sickness took many in my villages, too."

Roberto could remember Cristina's face now. His time with Esteban Calderón had awakened his memory. It was an uncertain blessing. "I needed money to marry Cristina because she was from a good family. The only prospect I had of becoming rich was to come here and find gold."

"What is this gold?"

"It's a shiny metal the color of the sun. It's of great value there."

"We have no gold."

"I know. Believe me. I tried to tell them. On his first trip

to this new world, de Soto became rich in his travels to the south of here in the land of the Incas. De Soto returned home to Spain, but he believed that there was more wealth to find here in this northern land. I joined him so that I might have enough riches to marry Cristina.

"Cristina saw me off. I remember her excitement. She wanted to come, too. At that time Calderón was rich. He did not need to seek his fortune in La Florida. That is what we called the place where we were to disembark—the feast of flowers."

"How did you lose your way?"

"De Soto was going from village to village looking for gold. He heard a story about a village from a young Indian boy traveling with a group of Indian traders, and he sent me, Sancho, Ruiz, and the youth to the village while he continued westward." Roberto shrugged and shook his head. "The villagers were friendly at first, then they attacked. I was taken prisoner. For a long time I didn't know what happened to Sancho and Ruiz. First I was told they were dead, then that they escaped. I was kept as a slave for a long time, and gradually the village became my home, until the disease wiped out most of the people. I was allowed to move about freely by then. I explored on my own, made it to the coast, and saw the ship. It was a new expedition led by Juan Pardo. It was a remarkable coincidence that my old friend Esteban Calderón was on the ship. I became their interpreter, and they were going to take me back to Spain." Roberto fingered his beads.

"Does this Juan Pardo expect to find gold?"

"No. He would like to, but I don't think he expects it. He was sent to explore the land and secure it for Spain, and to discover what kind of riches the land does have. It's Calderón who seeks gold. I suppose his family wealth ran out." Roberto laughed. "He married my Cristina. He told me so..." Roberto stopped, staring out to nothing. He was struck with a thought like a blinding holy light that was so clear, he knew it was right. Roberto gripped his beads.

"Something ails you?" asked Piaquay.

Roberto said nothing, merely kept staring into his memory. He recalled the surprise and fear on Esteban Calderón's face when he had shown up, literally, out of the wilderness and into Captain Pardo's camp. He remembered the taunting way Esteban had told him of his marriage to Cristina, pretending he was assuring Roberto that Cristina had been well cared for. "She did not grieve long" were his words. He remembered that Sancho and Ruiz were cousins of Calderón. He arranged it. Esteban Calderón had always wanted Cristina. He told his cousins to find a way to get rid of me, and they left me.

Roberto slammed his fist into his hand. "¡Me dejaron!"

THE COUNCIL HOUSE was built like the domiciles, in the shape of a square with rounded corners, upright timbers anchored in the ground about two feet apart, sticks woven between the timbers, dried mud and clay covering all. The roof was slanted upward like the skirt of a woman and made from thatch placed on large roof timbers held up by pillars inside the structure. A hole in the peak allowed the escape of smoke from a central hearth.

Roberto was not allowed inside the council house, so he sat near the entrance listening for fragments of discussion he could understand. Piaquay and all the elders had gone inside the council house late in the morning after they had drunk the black brew and vomited. Roberto had tasted the concoction once. It was foul, but afterward he felt good and clear-headed. He heard them talking and arguing, but he understood little except that Piaquay had some desire and he had to persuade the tribe of its soundness. Piaquay was not chief now, Roberto knew that. The woman was chief. She despised Roberto, and it worried him. He was not sure why Piaquay relinquished his place to the woman Cacheci. It had something to do with the massacre. He had thought about running away, but he knew he could not get through the territory of Piaquay's friends without being caught. So Roberto listened.

"I HAD THE DREAM for three nights," Piaquay told the gathering. He, Cacheci, and the elders sat around the fire.

The men wore deerskin breechcloths. Some wore leather necklaces holding large round gorgets of shell carved with birds, serpents, or spiders. Cacheci sat on her heels with her legs tucked under her, unlike the men, who sat cross-legged. She wore a deerskin skirt from her hips to her knees. Her skirt was decorated with drawings to please the gods. Like the men, she wore nothing above her hips, and like the men, she had elaborate tattoos around her arms and legs and around each breast. Cacheci wore necklaces of shells and pearls. She had a handsome face, made all the more so by the flowerlike tattooing across her forehead and on her chin and cheeks. Some of the men wore turbans of animal skin around their heads. Others, like Piaquay, wore their hair long and straight.

"I dreamed," he continued, "that an eagle swept down to the lake and snatched a snake in its claws and rose to the heavens."

"A good omen," said the shaman, "but your war party would take you far and distant."

"The devils have spread across the land of our friends and our enemies," said Piaquay. "They are like the drought that takes the corn and leaves us but scorched earth."

"Will you return?" asked Cacheci.

"I don't know," answered Piaquay. "I know only that I must do this."

"We can't afford for you to take a war party of twenty," said an elder.

"The war party must be small," said Piaquay. "I will take my brother, Tesca, a young warrior to feed us, and the slave Roberto. Nayahti the trader wishes to go. That would be good. He knows the land through many chiefdoms."

"Four men is not the right number," said the shaman, who did not count Roberto. "Find two more to take with you."

"Then you favor this journey?" said Cacheci.

"Yes. His dream is a good dream," the shaman said to the new chief. The shaman turned back to Piaquay. "Be obser-

vant in all things on this journey. It will be dangerous. I'll give you new things for your medicine bundle. Don't allow your thirst for revenge to blind you to bad omens. Listen to your dreams. Return if they are not good. Take and keep a fire from this village, and read the crystal every morning.''

ROBERTO SAT in the deep shadows watching Piaquay and the braves dance in the flickering firelight. The way Piaquay danced with the bladelike war club was both elegant and fierce. The whoops and shouts of the braves sounded like a celebration, but Roberto knew better. His captors were deep in grief for their loved ones killed by Calderón. He understood that. Seeing Calderón again had brought to Roberto a longing for his family and for Cristina that had been numbed for years. The knowledge that Calderón had plotted his ruin lit an anger deep inside Roberto. He did not doubt that Calderón arranged his capture years ago, even meant him to die. Everything fit together like a giant puzzle that suddenly came together of its own resolve. Slowly, he rose and danced the war dance.

LINDSAY HAD SPENT four days at the Royce Site enjoying excavating and visiting with her friends, but she was also looking forward to moving on to the next place on her itinerary. She stood looking at the map spread out on the hood of her vehicle. She wore jeans, a T-shirt, and aviator sunglasses, her long red-brown hair in a ponytail and threaded through the opening in the back of an Atlanta Braves baseball cap. She was ready to go.

''Where to next?'' asked Sally.

Lindsay pointed to a spot on the map. ''Jane and Alan are digging a small campsite in a rock shelter not far north of here,'' she said. ''They think it may have been used by the Spaniards. This highway route,'' she traced her finger along the roads that led her to the next site, ''runs parallel to several routes that explorers might have taken. Interesting, huh? I guess a good route is always a good route."

"Good trails make good roads. Isn't that akin to 'central place' theory or something?" asked Sally.

"Yeah, I guess it is," Lindsay said, folding her map. "Well, I'll say good-bye. Thanks for the hospitality."

"Where to after Jane and Alan's dig?" asked Sally.

Lindsay grinned. "Derrick's Cold River Site."

"I'll bet you're looking forward to that," said Sally, grinning back at her. "Derrick's taking you dining and dancing, I imagine?"

"He said he has a special evening planned," replied Lindsay.

"Derrick's a special friend?" asked Emily, walking up to say good-bye.

"Yeah," said Lindsay, nodding her head. "He's my very best friend."

Emily stuck out her hand. "It was nice to meet you, Lindsay. I don't think we can ever agree about the burials of my people, but I still enjoyed talking with you."

Lindsay shook her hand. "Me, too."

Brian came over to say good-bye; so did Gerri and some of the others she worked with. She hugged Brian, then Sally. "Do you know where I can get gas and ice?" she asked.

"You'll pass Caleb's Grocery about ten miles on down the road," Brian said.

Lindsay drove away from the site and turned onto the road that went through a deep mountain forest. It was relatively early in the morning, and she had her window down while the day was still cool. A light fog still clung to the trees. It was going to be a good day for traveling—clear and bright after the fog burned off. She was smiling to herself as she traveled up the winding mountain road. As she reached over to turn on the radio, there was a sudden loud, sharp sound, like an explosion, and her Rover was suddenly swerving all over the road.

SIX

LINDSAY HEARD A car horn blaring angrily at her as she struggled to get the Land Rover back in her lane. She couldn't do it. The oncoming car swerved, missing her with such a narrow margin she felt its vibration as it passed. Now the direction of the Land Rover was toward the edge of the road and down the mountainside. Lindsay turned the steering wheel hard and stomped on the brakes. The Rover skidded to the edge and stopped. She tried to back away from the edge to get to a wider place on the side of the road a few feet ahead, but it wouldn't move. Lindsay took a moment to catch her breath before getting out. Her legs were weak, and she was still shaking from the near misses. She walked around the Rover and saw that not only was her left rear tire ruined, but her right front tire was just off the edge of the embankment.

"Damn," she said. It would have to be towed back onto the road. She started for her car phone when a pickup truck pulled in behind her and stopped. John West stepped out. His long hair, black and as shiny as obsidian, flowed over the shoulders of the brown shirt he wore.

"Having problems?" he asked, looking at the precarious position of her vehicle.

"I had a blowout," she said.

John looked at her and at her tire. "Are you all right?"

"A little frightened," she replied. "I swerved into the other lane and almost hit a car, then...well, you can see."

He went to the back of his truck and took a chain out of the bed. "I'll have to pull you away from the edge," he said as he proceeded to hook the chain to the rear of her Rover. He attached the other end of the chain to his truck, linking the vehicles together. He walked to the front of the Rover near the edge of the precipice and looked underneath the vehicle. He gave it a hard shove on the side, as if testing its stability. He grunted, looked up at Lindsay with a smile, raised an eyebrow, and said, "I don't think it'll go over the edge. Get in and try to hold it steady as I pull."

She did as he told her. The chain jerked as he started pulling but her Rover gradually moved away from the precipice. He unhooked the chain, and she drove slowly to the pull-off just ahead, her blown-out tire wobbling and bumping.

"I'll change the tire for you," he told her.

"I appreciate it." She gave him her key and he opened the back to get the spare and tools. He stood the spare tire against the side of the Land Rover and laid the tools on the ground.

"I'm lucky you happened along," she said.

"I didn't just happen along. Emily said you were going to stop at Caleb's. I was on my way to catch up with you there."

Lindsay watched him as he sat on his haunches beside her tire. She observed his tall frame, his long thighs and broad shoulders, how his raven hair flowed over his back, his very brown skin. He was like one of the skeletons fleshed out and animated. She squatted beside him as he jacked up the vehicle.

"Why were you trying to catch up with me?"

"I want to talk to you."

"Why?"

He took the lug wrench and began removing the lug nuts from the wheel. "You're the enemy. A strong enemy. I want to get to know you."

Lindsay was surprised. "I'm not your enemy."

John West stopped what he was doing and stared at Lindsay, as if trying to see inside her. "You're the most dangerous kind. One who speaks straight and persuasively. We Indians can have our say and convince your people that what you do hurts us, hurts our soul. Someone like you gets up and makes your side sound more wise. Many people will be persuaded by you and will agree with you because they think you will really do what is best for us, for our history, and for our future, and because they value what you value, and don't understand what we consider sacred.'' He turned and continued taking the nuts off the wheel. He removed the ruined tire and laid it down in the grass and put on the spare. ''At least they are ignorant. You understand what is sacred to us, yet it means nothing compared to your research questions.'' He said ''research questions'' the way some people would say ''profit.'' She supposed answers to questions were the profits of science.

''What is it you want?'' she asked.

''How does it make you feel to know that I hate what you do?'' he asked, looking at her, his black eyes glittering with his indignation.

''Frustrated,'' she answered.

He stopped, making no movements for several moments, then looked at Lindsay again. ''You feel frustrated? Why?''

Lindsay sat down cross-legged in the grass and took off her sunglasses. ''I'm not sure you would understand.''

''You think I'm stupid?'' he asked, returning to his work on her wheel.

''No. You know that is not true,'' she said.

''Tell me then,'' John insisted.

''It's hard to explain to anyone how I really feel about it.'' She hesitated. ''I'll try. The ancient villagers are not really dead to me. They are just not of my time. They can tell me things about themselves, and you want to stop them. I find it frustrating.''

As Lindsay spoke, it seemed that John West's movements as he bolted the spare tire in place became fast and jerky. He waited until all the nuts were in place and tightened before he spoke. He turned to Lindsay, still sitting on his haunches, his forearms resting on his thighs.

''They are dead. They lived once, and now they're dead. They don't talk to you. You examine the marks on their bones and make educated guesses about what their lives were like. But that's all they are—guesses.''

''You're guesses right, of course,'' Lindsay said.

He stood, reaching out to Lindsay, bringing her up with him. His hands were strong and firm as he gripped hers. For a moment he kept her hands in his, looking at her light skin contrasting against his brown. Then he let go.

"Thank you for changing my tire," said Lindsay. "Can it be repaired?"

"No," he said. "When it blew, it did too much damage."

Lindsay walked with him to his truck. He tossed the ruined tire onto the back. The sign on the side of his truck said: West Builders.

"Your business?" asked Lindsay, running her fingers over the sign.

"Yes. I make a living for my family and myself, and I'm not an alcoholic."

"I didn't think that you were."

"Then you are in the minority."

"I think you exaggerate."

"Get another spare," he said. "You shouldn't travel without one." He opened the door, ready to get in. "Follow me to Caleb's. He'll take the tire off the wheel for you."

"I don't want to be your enemy," she said as he closed the door.

"Then stop digging up my ancestors."

"Is there no compromise?"

"No. Tell me, Lindsay Chamberlain. What if my ancestors 'told' you that they want to be left alone? What if you found something that made you know that they do not want to be dug up? Would you stop?"

Lindsay was silent for a long moment. John watched her closely. "I would have to, wouldn't I?" she said finally.

"One of their descendants is telling you. As pure an American Indian as they are, I'm telling you. You say that to you they are not dead, just living in a different time. I'm living in this time, and I'm telling you."

Lindsay said nothing. There was nothing she could say: there was no argument to counter his. There was only this feeling in her heart of wanting to know about them.

"Think about it, Lindsay Chamberlain. At least do that," he said.

"I will." Lindsay laid a hand on the door between them. "Don't you want to know about them?"

"I know what I need to know."

"That isn't what I asked. Wouldn't you like to have the sites definitively connected to modern-day tribes?"

"We are connected. Who else are we related to?"

"You know what I mean. There are many tribes and many sites. Will you think about it?"

"Fair enough. It is also fair that I tell you that I won't change my mind on this." He started his truck, waiting for her to get in her Rover before he drove onto the road.

Lindsay walked to her Land Rover and climbed in. She had certainly made a lot of enemies in the past few months simply by doing her job. Maybe she was arrogant and manipulative. Maybe she should rethink her philosophy. Maybe bones didn't speak to her. Maybe she was wrong. She turned the key and followed John to Caleb's.

Caleb's was a combination grocery, garage, and gas station. Lindsay bought gas, filled her ice chest, and picked up a few snacks for the road. John took her tire to the mechanic on duty for her.

"Caleb has a spare tire that'll fit your Rover," John told Lindsay as she loaded up her supplies. "He's putting it on the wheel now. You need to get another one when you can, but this will do for now."

"Thanks," she said. "I appreciate your help."

John looked into her eyes for a moment, then at her Atlanta Braves baseball cap. He took it off her head and threw it into the trash. Lindsay stood openmouthed while John went to his truck and came back with a West Builders cap and put it on her head. He went back to his truck, climbed in, and drove off.

ESTEBAN CALDERÓN had fled the massacre, stopping only to pick up the men who guarded the provisions and the last two of the valuable pigs they had begun with. He had pushed his men hard, wanting to get far from the area, afraid that Pia-

quay might somehow send a plea for help to an ally village, that Indian reinforcements might attack and defeat his men in their weakened condition. Finally, Diego, an old family friend, had forced Calderón to stop and rest.

"The men can go no farther, estan cansados,*" Diego implored. "They need to heal their wounds. You are getting a fever, Don Calderón. We'll be safe here in these mountains. I have found a shelter. There is water nearby. We can camp there and be safe."*

The rock shelter was like a small cave, ten feet by twenty feet, with a stream nearby. Diego cleared a place toward the cooler rear of the shelter for Calderón to rest while the men, wounded, hungry, and irritable, made camp. At least the mountains were cooler, but the thick green flora everywhere and the damp humus smell were suffocating. The cries of the birds were strange and eerie to their ears. Indians signaled to each other by mimicking the birdcalls, so the Spaniards were never sure whether the cries were from birds or from their enemy. Diego made the decision to kill one of their remaining pigs. Good food would calm their nerves and make them cheerful or, at least, not mutinous.

CALDERÓN EXPERIENCED *more searing pain than he had ever known. He sat under the shelter of rocks on a bed of leaves and blankets, wheezing the thick air of the deep forest, tasting the foul taste of the weeping, infected wound in his mouth. He had lost nearly all his upper back teeth, some at the time of the injury, others one by one, pushed out by the inflammation. The only merciful thing about his injury was that the arrow had miraculously grazed only the top of his tongue, rather than severing it. The aroma of a pig cooking met his nostrils and brought with it a new wave of pain as his mouth responded to the memory of succulent meat. He groaned.*

Diego brought a fresh warmed cloth to lay over his face. Diego's old hands were deft and gentle. The warmth soothed Calderón enough that he could concentrate on his hatred. Sacrílego pagano, *he thought. These savages knew nothing of the value of gold and silver. They only knew to pound it into ornaments.* Salvajes, estúpidos. *Valuing their gold trinkets more than their own families. He showed them. He wasn't finished showing them.*

Diego brought him a drink, an opiate for pain, something he had learned from the Indians in his campaign with Pizzaro. "Toma," *commanded Diego.*

Calderón sipped the bitter drink as best he could. It was only a little better than the repugnant taste already in his mouth.

"Es malo," *rasped Calderón.*

"Necesitas cura de reposo," *said Diego.* "Rest."

The drink helped the pain, and made him drowsy, but it also gave him enlightenment. Eso es, *thought Calderón.* Es claro. It was Roberto. I should not have trusted him. Roberto gave the savages the wrong message in order to stop me, Esteban Calderón, from getting my treasure. That was it. I should not have told him I married Cristina. That was a mistake. Roberto knows where the treasure is hidden. He has lived among them so long. He wants it for himself. But he's dead now, dead and rotting on the ground. Or is he? *"Diego," he called out, and coughed.*

Diego rushed to his side. "¿Qué necesita, *Don Calderón?"*

"Roberto," whispered Calderón in his garbled speech. "¿Se murtió? *Did you see him die?"*

"No. He did not die immediately. He was injured. He is probably dead now."

"Vive," *Calderón whispered so lightly that Diego barely heard him.* El Sabe, *thought Calderón. "He knows where the gold is."*

LINDSAY BOUGHT a new tire in the next town before she resumed her drive into the mountains. The higher elevations brought cooler temperatures and some relief from the heat. She had turned off her air-conditioning and rolled down her windows to listen to the sounds of the mountains, the streams that flowed down the hillsides, the birds, the wind as she drove. She heard these things, but saw little of the holly, Cherokee roses, laurels, and magnolias that grew in great abundance in the mountains. Her mind was on the conversation she'd had with John West. She wondered if John would agree to having the burials excavated under his tribe's control or if his opposition was too deeply rooted in his religion. She didn't want to tell him she wouldn't stop excavating. She couldn't; she did not want to abandon the quest to discover as much as she could about the indigenous inhabitants of this continent. Maybe she could find a compromise.

When Lindsay crossed into the national forest, she pulled to the side of the road to consult the map Jane had sent her. In about a mile and a half she should come to the dirt road that would take her most of the way to the site.

Lindsay found the road. It had a chain across it with a sign that said the road was closed to the public. Jane's letter said to drive around the barricade. It was a tight squeeze, but Lindsay drove around and up the winding road. After five miles of rutted and washed road she spotted a university van, Alan's old '78 Chevy, and a couple of other vehicles parked under a grove of large trees. Lindsay pulled her Land Rover in between a Ford Explorer and a Jeep Cherokee. She slung on her backpack, hung the trowel on her belt, and started the two-mile hike up the trail to the rock shelter.

The three-foot-wide, well-worn trail inclined gently and steadily into the forest. She breathed in the fresh air. It smelled good to her—no odor of exhausts or industry, only the smells of clean earth and vegetation; no sounds but for the twittering of birds and the wind in the trees.

She stopped and took a swig of water and continued on, her hiking boots making a gentle crunching sound on the trail. After another half mile her legs and back began to feel the exertion. She stopped, adjusted her pack, and made a mental note to add a few hills to her jogging route when she returned home. She rounded a turn and came face-to-face with Grizzly Adams, or at least someone who looked like him, dressed in a dirty white T-shirt, cutoffs, and hiking boots. The shaggy brown beard and long hair made him look older, but Lindsay guessed he was actually in his mid-twenties.

"This trail is not open to the public," he said. "Can't you read?" He looked down at her belt and spied her trowel. He obviously thought her to be a pot hunter—here to plunder the site. She was opening her mouth to speak when he gripped her arm. "I'm going down the trail. I'll escort you back."

Lindsay pulled her arm from him, stepped back, and held out her hand. "I'm Dr. Chamberlain. I believe I'm expected."

He was taken aback for a second, then took her hand and shook it. "Oh, uh, yes. I'm sorry, Dr. Chamberlain, I thought you were here looking for artifacts."

Lindsay smiled. "I am, and please, call me Lindsay. Is Jane close by?"

"She's at the rock shelter," he said.

"I'll go check in with her. What is your name, by the way?"

"Gil Harris. I'm from the University of North Carolina."

"Glad to meet you," she said and continued on her way up the trail.

Nearer the site, Lindsay saw several more students scattered here and there, working in small excavations in the woods. The trail ended at a clearing below a rugged rock-faced bluff with a wide gaping hole in the side of the rock wall. The roof of the rock shelter was a weathered gneiss overhang that created a room about twenty feet wide and ten feet deep from front to back. Jane was inside near the rear of the shelter on her knees, working with her trowel. Lindsay saw that they had dug two intersecting trenches in the clearing outside the rock shelter. Each was about three feet wide and ten feet long, and a couple of students were working intently on something in one trench.

"Hey, Jane," said Lindsay, walking up to the mouth of the shelter.

"Lindsay, you're here!" Jane jumped up to greet her. "Did you have any trouble finding us?" Her blond hair was tied in a ponytail. Despite the fact they were working in heavy shade, Jane's long limbs were tanned.

"No, your directions were very good. What have you got here?"

Jane's blue eyes glittered. "Some really neat stuff. Digging is kind of hard with all this vegetation, but using a little logic, we've been pretty lucky. We're excavating most of the cave," Jane said, then pointed out into the woods. "We went over the area with a metal detector and found some interesting things. We're turning up some good refuse pits."

Lindsay laid down her pack by a tree and followed Jane inside the shelter. Against one wall were two wooden crates for transporting artifacts. Jane pointed to the boxes.

"We haven't found a large quantity of stuff, but what we have found is kind of neat: lead balls, iron crossbow bolt tips, ax heads, and what we think is the trigger mechanism for a harquebus. In the lower levels of the trenches we think we've found some Archaic stuff."

"Archaic and historic—nothing in between?"

Jane shook her head. "From the looks of the trench cross section, the shelter was subject to periodic flooding over the years."

"That's a neat collection of historic items. Where are you finding the things. In the cave or around it?"

"I'm excavating a cache of bolt heads in the cave right now. The musket trigger was found about ten meters away in the clearing outside the shelter. We found the ax by accident. Mike, one of the student workers, was taking a leak in the woods. He had his metal detector with him and did a quick sweep."

Lindsay smiled. "It would be interesting if that was how it was lost in the first place."

"Wouldn't it? We're finding some bones, too." Jane looked suddenly grim. "A couple of human teeth, bones of a left arm, and a right leg."

Lindsay raised her eyebrows. "Amputations?"

"We think so," said Jane. "We thought you could have a look."

"Sure. Sounds like a group of conquistadores resting up after a battle. Any indication of how many there were?"

Jane shook her head, but Lindsay saw a faint smile on her face. "Not yet, but we suspect around twenty." Lindsay was surprised that she could up with a number, but before she could ask a question, Jane pointed to a young dark-haired woman bent over an excavation just outside the shelter. "Over there we've found some bones of a pig in a fire pit. We don't know if it's a wild pig or domestic."

"I'll have a look. Who found this site?"

"That's fascinating, too. Gil Harris was the one who actually discovered that there may be something of interest here. Come over this way."

Jane had that smile on her face again as she led Lindsay into the cool, dark rock shelter. She picked up a flashlight lying beside her excavation and pointed it up at the gray ceiling of the shelter. Lindsay saw that over the years, people had marked their visitation with graffiti: their names, the dates they graduated from high school, who they loved, their philosophy of life in a sentence.

"Look closely up here." Jane pointed to an area with the flashlight. "It's overwritten with the name Tully Murdock."

Lindsay examined the area, squinting her eyes, then she saw faded dark letters. "Is that it? Is it written with smoke?"

Jane grinned. "Yes. It says: Diego Vázquez 1567. Neat, huh? Diego Vázquez was one of the conquistadores who was with Juan Pardo's expeditions."

Lindsay smiled broadly and examined the roof. The longer she stared at the gray ceiling, the more letters she could make out. "This is a nice surprise," she said. "You never mentioned anything about it in your letter."

"Then it wouldn't have been a surprise," said Jane. "We photographed it, then Alan digitized the picture and did some stuff with the computer to bring it out."

"I suppose you're searching the Spanish archives to look for information on this guy?" Lindsay asked.

Jane turned off the flashlight and they walked out of the shelter. "We've e-mailed Frank in France. He's going over to Spain when he can and have a look for us. We already know a little from Bandera's narrative."

"I can't wait to hear all about it. By the way, I met Gil Harris on the way up. He thought I was a trespasser and almost threw me out."

"Yeah, Gil's kind of territorial, but he's okay. Alan met him when they were both at UNC before Alan transferred to UGA. Gil's gone to get us some supplies. We use insect repellent around here like it was water or beer."

"How'd Gil come to find the site?" asked Lindsay.

"He's interested in caves and rock shelters. He's explored a lot of them."

Lindsay looked around at all the faces. "Where is Alan?"

Jane grimaced. "Jim took him to town to see a doctor. We're afraid he may have Lyme disease. He got that bull's-eye rash. We're infested with deer ticks. Which reminds me, you had better spray yourself down if you haven't already."

Jane took Lindsay to their camping ground, fifty yards or so from the rock shelter. "You guys are really roughing it, I see," Lindsay said, indicating the pup tents erected in a clearing.

"Sure are," said Jane, smiling. "It's sponge baths most days, unless you want to bathe in the creek a quarter mile away. We do that about once a week, the girls one day and the guys another."

Lindsay laid her sleeping bag in the supply tent. After making a hasty examination of herself for ticks, she sprayed her clothing and exposed skin with repellent. She tucked her hair under her hat and went outside to join the others.

Alan had returned. "Glad you made it to our hideaway," he said, greeting her with a peck on the check. Alan's normally tanned skin looked a little pale.

"How are you doing?" she asked.

He pushed a lock of dark hair away from his eyes. "Won't know until the blood tests are back, but the doc said I'm probably in for a round of antibiotics. But tell me, what do you think of our little site?"

"I'm impressed, I really am. You guys are doing a great job. I like the way they even signed their name to the site. That was considerate of them."

"Wasn't it, though?" said Alan.

"Jane said you had some bones for me to look at," she said.

LINDSAY SAT ON A wooden crate and used her hand lens to examine the bones that Alan showed her. "You don't need me to tell you that this humerus and femur were sawed off; the cross section is completely straight," said Lindsay.

"Yeah," said Alan. "Poor guys. No anesthesia." He wrinkled his brow in sympathy.

"Bring me one of the bones of the pig you found," Lindsay said. Alan brought two bones for her to look at. "It's domestic," she said after a close look. "No doubt about it."

"I wonder where they got pigs?" asked Jane. "I didn't think Pardo took pigs with him. Weren't they hurting for food at Santa Elena? Wasn't that one of the reasons Ménendez sent Pardo out, to ease the food shortage in Santa Elena by getting rid of a portion of the soldier population so they wouldn't have to feed them? Make them live off what they could extort from the Indians?"

"Yeah, that," said Alan, "and to inform the Indians they were now the subjects of Spain, and to find a good route from here to the Spanish silver mines in Mexico. But they must have had to take some provisions when they left Santa Elena or they'd have starved before they reached Indians who would feed them."

Lindsay examined the end of the pig femur while they talked, then picked up the human bone again. "They were sawed with a similar tool."

"Great," said Alan. "You mean those poor devils had to share medical equipment with the butcher?"

"Perhaps," said Lindsay, smiling. "Maybe their surgeon and their cook just had the same kind of equipment."

"Maybe the surgeon and cook were the same person," suggested Jane, smiling wickedly.

As the sun went down and it grew dark, the crew gathered in their primitive camp, built a fire, and ate buckets of Kentucky Fried Chicken that Gil had brought with him from his supply run. There was no moonlight. Illumination came from the campfire and Coleman lanterns. Some of the crew had put on long-sleeved shirts against the cool mountain air. Thousands of stars in the cloudless sky twinkled in the opening above the clearing. Tree frogs, crickets, and other night noises were as loud as they had been at Brian's site, but in the more primitive surroundings of the rock shelter, they seemed closer and louder just outside the circle of light. Alan unrolled a map and laid it on the ground. They all leaned forward as he traced his finger along a trail he had marked with a pen.

"On his second expedition," Alan said, "Pardo went this route, from Santa Elena, along the coasts of Georgia and South Carolina, through South Carolina and into North Carolina and Tennessee. According to Bandera's journal, at the town of Aboyaca, Pardo sent a guy named Estaban Calderón out to visit the town of Tipwan on the Zantee River, a tributary of the Chattahoochee. Calderón is reported to have had a skirmish with hostile Indians somewhere along his route, with major loss of life on both sides. Calderón lost seven men, and he is said to have killed perhaps forty Indians."

"That event would be consistent with the amputated limbs and lost teeth you've found here," Lindsay said.

"The crossbow bolts and musket trigger are from the kinds of weapons carried by the Spanish expeditionary forces of the period," Alan added. "Diego Vázquez is mentioned as a member of Calderón's party. This may be one of Calderón's camps."

"May be?" said Gil. "I'd say probably."

"De Soto also visited Tipwan about twenty years earlier," said Jane, taking up Alan's story. "From the description of his chronicler and from Bandera's report, we know that Tipwan is probably the Sarah Flint Site."

"If that's the case," said Brian, "it probably wasn't Tipwan people that Calderón fought. There was no indication of warfare and no battle wounds on any of the burials at the Sarah Flint Site, as I recall."

"No, there weren't," agreed Lindsay.

"Then who did they fight with?" asked Jane.

Lindsay peered at the map, which had triangles marking the probable locations of towns mentioned in various Spanish chronicles and squares for archaeological sites. She put a finger on the triangle labeled Calusa, several miles north of Tipwan. "De Soto also visited here," she said. "As I recall, the people at Tipwan told him that Calusa was a chiefdom with five wealthy villages."

"What are you getting at?" asked Alan.

"I don't imagine that the Spanish easily let go of the idea of finding treasure among the Indians. What if this Calderón had read de Soto's chronicles and either did not go to Tipwan, or went to Calusa after Tipwan?" suggested Lindsay, examining the map.

"But," argued Jane, "if I remember right, de Soto said that Calusa was the capital of the chiefdom, which meant it probably had a mound. There aren't any mound sites in that area that fit the description."

"Anyway," said Alan, "what makes you think that it was Calusa? It could be any village; it could be one not mentioned in anyone's account. We've got no site to match up with Calderón's skirmish."

"I think we do," said Lindsay. They all looked at her, surprised.

"Where?" asked Alan.

"Brian's site, the Royce Site."

"It doesn't have a mount," said Jane.

"It did. It was destroyed by landowners during this century, but the remnants are there." Lindsay told them about the massacred burials. "It's not that far from here," she said.

Alan raised his fists into the air above his head in a gesture of triumph. "That's great. That's fantastic! I'm going to visit Brian's site tomorrow. Wouldn't that be great if we can make a link between the Rock Shelter Site and the Royce Site?"

Lindsay got up and stretched her legs, leaving them making plans to visit the Royce Site and to e-mail Frank to hurry it up in Spain. She saw Gil Harris get up and stretch, and she walked over to him.

"This is a good site," she said. "You must be very pleased to have found it."

"I am. Almost missed it, though. Whoever that Tully Murdock is, he almost obliterated Diego Vázquez's name. I don't know why people have to deface every rock they come to."

"Marking their passage," said Lindsay. "If Vázquez hadn't, we might have never found this site, much less know any historical information about it."

"That's true enough, I suppose."

"Jane said you have explored some caves," she said.

"A few," he said. But Lindsay took the sound of his voice and the cock of his head to mean that he was making an understatement.

"Do you know other cavers?"

"Sure."

"Have you ever heard of a man named Ken Darnell?"

Gil looked down, trying to remember. "Sounds familiar—yeah..." He looked up at Lindsay. "Didn't he die, get killed in a cave-in? Yeah, I remember now. Met him a couple of times at the National Spelunkers conventions. Outspoken fellow. We went out drinking together once or twice. He was a real hot dog. Knew a lot about caving, but reckless. Kind of a daredevil, I thought. I wasn't surprised to hear he died in a cave. He a friend of yours?"

Lindsay shook her head. "His family asked me to look into his death."

"They suspect something?"

"The authorities didn't give them very much information about his death. I think they just want closure. Did you ever visit Hell Slide Cave in Tennessee?"

"Once. It's a dangerous and difficult cave to navigate. Is that the one he died in?"

"Yes. What's the cave like?" she asked.

"What do you mean?" he asked.

"The environment. Wet, dry...?"

"Damp, as I recall. I didn't go too far into it. As I said, it's a dangerous cave."

"If you remember anything else about Ken Darnell after I'm gone, give me a call?" Lindsay reached into her pocket and gave him a card with her car phone number on it.

"Like what?" he asked, trying to make out the writing on the card in the darkness.

"Anything odd or out of the ordinary," answered Lindsay.

"Sure, but that's all I know." He pocketed the card in his shirt.

After saying goodnight to the others, Lindsay went to her sleeping bag and turned in. She had a restless night filled with strange dreams. She awoke with stiff sore muscles and to a bloodcurdling scream.

SEVEN

A JOKE, LINDSAY thought at first. *Some guy put a snake somewhere for one of the girls to find.* But the scream continued, and she heard some of the crew run past the tent. She hurriedly got out of her sleeping bag, slipped into some jeans, and ran to see what the commotion was. The sun was just up, and the light was dim. The morning air was moist with dew and cold.

"What is it?" Lindsay asked Jane when she ran past.

"I don't know, but it sounds like it came from this direction." She pointed toward the trail that wound down around the hillside. They both followed other crew members who were hurrying in that direction. The screaming had stopped. Then more shouting—distressed, frightened shouting.

When Lindsay and Jane arrived at a rocky area beneath the bluff, they saw what had caused the distress. It was Gil. He lay among the rocks. His right leg, bent at the knee, was under him. His other limbs were at odd angles, draped over the rocks on which he lay. His head leaned to one side. Alan had climbed among the jumble of talus and was feeling for a pulse in Gil's contorted neck, but there was no doubt. He was dead. Already the miniature army whose job it is to reduce all dead things to dust had begun their work. Flies buzzed, settling on the body, ants assaulted from the ground. Lindsay smelled the faint odor of death that would only get worse.

"He's cold and stiff," said Alan. Lindsay heard sobs. As Alan moved away from the body, he brushed against Gil's left hand, which caught on Alan's clothes. Because it was stiff, the arm seemed to grab at him, and Alan almost stumbled. He cursed. As he climbed down, he inadvertently moved the rock over which Gil's left leg was propped. The lower part of the leg swung slightly and made Gil look animated. Someone gasped.

"We need to call the park ranger," said Lindsay. "Alan, you and Jim stay with the body. The rest of you go back to camp." Alan nodded slowly. They all had the confused look that people have when confronted with sudden death—that look that says, "But I just saw him last night."

Lindsay led the crew back to the camp. Jane fished in her knapsack and pulled out a phone, strangely out-of-place in this primitive setting. She dialed the ranger station, which Lindsay noted she had programmed into the phone, and told them to come, that there had been an accident, that one of the archaeology crew was dead. Several people looked shocked when they heard the word *dead*, as if saying it out loud made it official. Gil Harris was dead and would not rise off those rocks of his own volition.

After the call, they waited. At first in silence. Then one by one, they asked questions. What happened? When did he fall? What was he doing at the top of the cliff at night? It had to be at night, because they all saw him the evening before and they found him early this morning. It began to look sinister, and they all looked at one another and around them into the forest, still dark because the rising sun had not penetrated through the canopy. Lindsay tried not to show the anxiety she felt.

The agent in charge of criminal investigations in the national park arrived on an off-road motorbike. He was dressed in khaki pants and shirt and wore a gun in a holster and a badge on his belt. He had short brown hair and a clean-shaven face. Lindsay guessed him to be about thirty-five years old. He parked his motorcycle and approached the crew.

"Jane Burroughs?" he said.

Jane stood up. "That's me," she said timidly, as if she were about to be accused of something.

"You're the site director who called?"

"Oh, uh, yes, I am," she said, and came toward the man.

He held out his hand. "I'm Agent Dan McKinley of the FBI." He showed her his badge. "Where's the body?"

"This way," said Jane.

Agent McKinley told the crew to stay where they were and that he was expecting others and to send them along. Lindsay rose and followed the two of them. Dan McKinley stopped and turned.

"Are you morbidly curious?" he asked Lindsay. Neither his voice nor his expression was openly hostile, but his dark eyes suggested that he meant business.

"No...," began Lindsay.

"Then why are you following?" he interrupted.

"Lindsay is a forensic archaeologist," said Jane hurriedly. If that impressed the agent, he didn't let it show.

"There is something I would like to point out," Lindsay told him.

"Then please, join us," he said. They walked to the scene. Alan and Jim were there, standing as far as they could get from the body, talking to each other, neither looking at the corpse. Agent McKinley sent them and Jane back to the others after he had asked the usual questions: Who found the body? Had they touched it? Alan told him he only checked to see if Gil was dead, but that he did stumble over some of the rocks.

When they were gone, Agent McKinley and Lindsay walked over to the body, gave it a quick look, then looked up at the cliff. "You had something to say?" he asked.

"I saw Gil—Gil Harris, that's his name, last night around ten. He was found around five this morning. That's, at most, seven hours. However, rigor seems on its way to being well established throughout the body. That suggests a struggle that depleted the andescine triphosphate in his muscles, accelerating the rigor."

"You think someone gave him a shove off the cliff?"

"I have only made observations at a distance that are suggestive. Many things affect rigor."

"Anything else?"

"Yes. When Alan stumbled over the rocks, the left leg

swung at the knee. If it's true that rigor is vastly accelerated and has reached the legs, then the knee would be stiff, unless it was broken after death in some way, as in a fall."

"Let's take a look."

McKinley took a pair of latex gloves from his pocket and put them on. He tried to move Gil Harris's ankle. It was stiff. He did the same to the leg at the knee. It swung easily.

"Sure enough," he said. "It looks like the boy was dead for a while, then someone tossed him over the cliff. You observed all this from a distance?"

"Yes."

Dan McKinley eyed her. "Rather observant, aren't you?"

"Observation is how I make my living."

He smiled for the first time. "Tell me, what is a forensic archaeologist doing at one of these kinds of digs?"

"I mainly do prehistoric archaeology. I prefer it. But from time to time I am called on to look at bones that are not in an archaeological context. Right now, I'm supposed to be on vacation. I'm just visiting. I came yesterday."

They turned at the sound of approaching footsteps. The vanguard of the other army that deals with death, the human one, had arrived. It was their various jobs to ascertain the cause of death and to begin the process that would delay the microbes and insects and lengthen by centuries the time it took the body to revert to dust.

Agent McKinley questioned the crew members individually and separately about Gil Harris. Did he have any enemies? Was he suicidal? Had they seen anyone suspicious? Did anyone have any arguments with him? Who saw him last? All the answers were either "no," or "I don't know." Gil Harris was a normal archaeology student from the University of North Carolina who was interested in caves. He was well liked, enthusiastic about the site, and led what everyone believed to be a normal life. Lindsay, as it turned out, was the last person to have talked to him.

McKinley interviewed her last. They stood by his motorcycle while the crew gradually drifted to their archaeology tasks, mostly to keep their minds off the death of a fellow worker.

"What did the two of you talk about?" McKinley asked her, and Lindsay laid out the entire conversation before him.

"So, do you think there is any connection between Gil Harris and this Ken Darnell fellow?"

"I don't know. It would be a strange coincidence."

"Do you believe in coincidence?" he asked.

"Yes. Life's full of them," Lindsay answered.

Agent McKinley smiled again. "You're right, but it is interesting."

"I've gone over in my mind every nuance of his expressions as I talked to him, and there was just nothing about him that was suspicious."

"I see. Well, if you remember anything, give me a call." He gave her his card. "You're going to look into this Ken Darnell business for the Lamberts?"

"Yes. I don't expect to find anything. It seems to be a straightforward accident."

"Sounds like it, but if you find anything that connects with this, let me know."

"I will."

It was well into the afternoon before the crime scene people came out of the woods carrying Gil Harris in a body bag on a stretcher. The crew stopped what they were doing and stood silently as they carried the body past them and headed down the trail. Lindsay, Jane, Alan, and Jim exchanged glances. They had been through this before.

"Bad business, this," Agent McKinley said, looking around at the archaeologists. "Mainly my work with the Park Service has been to help the rangers look for poachers, looters, and grave robbers. I left Los Angeles for a quieter life." He shook his head. "Well, thank you, Dr. Chamberlain, for your help."

"You're welcome. I don't suppose you'll tell me if you found anything on the cliff or at the scene?" she asked.

"I'm afraid the information flows only one way: from you

to me. However, if you find out anything about the other thing, maybe then we can share."

"Look, the crew here need to be safe. If there's some maniac in the woods..." Lindsay hesitated, keeping her voice low so that none of the crew would hear. "Is there someone you could send?"

"At the very least, I'll have them checked on once a day. I'll try to spare someone more often. In the meantime, tell them not to go anywhere alone and to travel in twos and threes."

Lindsay nodded. Dan McKinley disappeared down the trail on his motorbike. The crew resumed their work. Jane and Alan came over to Lindsay.

"Was he murdered?" whispered Alan.

"I don't know," answered Lindsay. "Maybe. Agent McKinley said not to let anyone go anywhere alone. He'll have someone check in with you here every day."

"Who would do such a thing?" asked Jane.

Lindsay shook her head. She did not tell them about Ken Darnell. She really didn't believe that there was a connection.

EESTEBAN CADLERÓN would have a permanent lisp. Because of the lost molars, his cheeks were sunken. When the wounds to his face healed, he would have conspicuous scars on both his cheeks. His face, not a handsome one to begin with, had taken on a cadaverous look as the swelling went down. Already, behind his back, his men called him Calavera—death skull. *These realities, added to the fact that he was not any richer than when he arrived, made Calderón a perpetually irritable man.*

His cousins had told him another story from their travels with de Soto's expeditions. Another story of treasure, which he had dismissed as too fantastic but which now seemed more believable. His problem now was how to convince his men to continue along on his quest. Maybe he wouldn't need them. This quest was different. The treasure was smaller—it would not make him fabulously wealthy like de Soto—but it would do. He would travel northeast and catch up with Pardo. That would satisfy his men, then he could make plans of his own. He would need only a few men. Diego would be one. He could count on faithful Diego. Yes, that would be better.

ROBERTO LACAYO had never before been on a war party. He had not been allowed when he lived with his adopted tribe. This excursion with Piaquay was his first. He had, however, been on one hunting party and found this similar. On both, he observed that the Indians kept their bows strung most of the time, ready to use. They were fast with their bows. Roberto had seen an Indian get off as many as five arrows in the time it took a crossbowman to load and shoot one bolt.

Roberto had no weapon. Even if they had given him a bow, he couldn't have used it. That was one of the things he marveled at the most. The Indians were so strong. They could pull a bowstring back to their ear; Roberto could pull it only slightly, not enough to send an arrow anywhere.

The Indians were relentless and completely fearless in battle. If battles could be won on courage and strength alone, they would have won most of the engagements with de Soto. But battles are won by superior weapons and strategy, and the Indians had neither against the Spanish. Conquistadores on horseback with steel swords were simply too powerful. If Piaquay would listen, Roberto could tell him how to defeat Calderón when they met, but he knew Piaquay would not listen to him. Roberto would have to take his own revenge.

The war party trailed Calderón and his men. Roberto was amazed that they had found his trail so easily after so many weeks. But Roberto knew that Calderón was probably ignorant of how many hunting parties saw his passing, of how the animals fled when the noisy Spaniards made their way through the forest, of how much destruction of foliage was left in the wake of their passing, or how they really only had to follow horse droppings.

They traveled swiftly. Roberto was tired; he wished they would stop and rest. The Indians were quiet when they trav-

eled, another wonder for Roberto. They continually cuffed him on the shoulder for making noise. And every time he stepped on a stick and broke it, they made him carry the thing until the end of the day. After a while Roberto learned not to step on twigs.

When they stopped to camp, a young novice warrior prepared meals for Piaquay and the other braves. Roberto had to prepare his own food. He didn't mind. He was used to taking care of himself. He watched his captors closely, trying to learn their woodcraft, but frankly, there was much of their behavior he didn't understand—like why they never sat on the ground, but on logs or rocks, and never leaned against anything, whether sitting or standing. Maybe it has something to do with not being able to be tracked,*he thought. Even though he didn't understand the reasons, he imitated their behavior. Roberto wanted to escape. He wanted revenge against Calderón as much as the Indians did, but he did not want to throw in his lot completely with Piaquay. Roberto knew Piaquay's villagers hated him and blamed him for the deaths of their families, as they hated and blamed all Spaniards. They would kill him if that damn crystal Piaquay consulted every morning told them to. Also, Roberto only wanted revenge against Calderón, not against all of his countrymen.*

They stopped finally and quickly prepared camp. Piaquay usually lit a fire with coals from his village that he carried in a small clay pot in a wooden pack on his back. In this pack Piaquay also carried his crystal and other spiritual things. When they made camp, as usual he constructed a pedestal of rocks on which the wooden pack rested when he was not carrying it. But this time Piaquay did not build a fire.

Neither Piaquay nor the others had made any effort to teach Roberto their language. What he knew of it he had picked up on his own, but he understood that the reason they stopped now was that they had caught up with Calderón.

Piaquay took the crystal from his bundle. It was a large, long, clear, six-sided crystal with doe skin wrapped around the end that he held. Piaquay sat on a log and looked into the crystal and sang a chant to himself.

"They are going to leave soon," he told his brother. "I will go to their camp. You stay with the others."

Roberto approached Piaquay. "Quiero venir," *he said. "I want to see the bastard."*

"No," said Piaquay. "You make too much noise."

Roberto knew that arguing would be useless. He watched Piaquay go silently through the woods, quickly disappearing in the thick growth.

PIAQUAY PEERED at his enemy from the cover of the forest. They were making preparations to break camp. Roberto told him that they would probably try to find the Spaniard Pardo. Roberto called this Calderón his enemy, too. That was good, but Piaquay still didn't trust Roberto completely. It was hard to change from a bear to a wolf. Piaquay would follow the Spaniards. Like a ghost, he would curse their travels until they met up with Pardo. An idea was forming in Piaquay's mind. He knew the Spaniard Pardo would be going to Chilhaxul if Roberto was right. When Calderón met up with this Pardo, Piaquay would take the short way to the land of the Chilhaxuls.

AGENT MCKINLEY'S word was good. He or a ranger checked in on the archaeology crew every day. On Lindsay's last day he introduced Cal Barnett, a retired policeman and history buff, who was delighted to become a member of the crew.

"I appreciate this," said Jane.

"It's just a precaution," said McKinley. "I don't expect any trouble."

"But just the same," said Alan, "we'll feel safer."

"You leaving, Dr. Chamberlain?" he asked, looking at the backpack sitting at her feet.

"Yes, I'm moving on to another site."

"Keep in touch," he said, and Jane raised her eyebrows at Lindsay.

"I will," she said. McKinley left on his motorbike.

Alan's test for Lyme disease came back positive, and he was on a regimen of tetracycline. It sapped his energy, so he said good-bye to Lindsay at the site and didn't try the four-mile hike down to the parking area and back.

"Take care," he said, giving her a hug and a kiss on the cheek.

"You, too. Get plenty of rest."

Jane and Jim walked with her to the Land Rover. When they reached the vehicles, Lindsay put her backpack in the backseat and turned to Jane.

"Do you think we could have a dig next time where no one gets killed?" said Jim. "I'm having a hard time explaining to my folks that archaeology is a safe and wholesome occupation." They laughed.

"You guys take care," she said. She climbed into her Rover and drove off, watching them in her rearview mirror as they waved good-bye to her. Jim had his arm around Jane's shoulders. Lindsay had thought that Jane was dating Alan. She smiled at the sight of them, glad for a reason to smile, to offset the sense of dread that was beginning to gnaw at her stomach. Her vacation was not turning out the way she had planned.

Lindsay drove to Chattanooga and stopped at a motel. She could have driven on, but she was tired and was not sure she would continue her vacation as planned. The death of Gil Harris bothered her. Coincidences happen every day, true, but—but, that was it, that "but, what if," that kept gnawing at her.

Lindsay showered first, washing the residue of more than a week's digging and inadequate sponge baths down the drain. With a towel around her body and another around her head, she sat on the bed and called Derrick.

"Lindsay," he said, when he heard her voice, "I just heard about what happened at the site. How are you?"

"Fine. I'm a little worried about the crew at Jane's site. The Park Service did arrange for a retired policeman to stay with them."

"A policeman? The news said it was an accident."

"It may have been. But there's a chance he was murdered."

"What? Do they know who or why?"

"No." Lindsay told him about the Lamberts' request that she look into the death of Grace Lambert's brother. Then she told him about the conversation she had with Gil Harris before he died. "I don't know if they are connected. But I want to find out. I thought I'd come to visit your site a few days later than I originally planned, after I make a visit to the authorities in Ellis County, Tennessee, where Ken Darnell was found dead, and also pay a visit to Ken Darnell's wife."

The silence on the other end of the phone was more deafening than if Derrick were yelling at her.

"Derrick?" she said after several moments.

"What do you want me to say?" His voice was calm and even.

"That you understand."

"I can't do that. I don't."

"What do you mean?"

"I mean, I've been looking forward to seeing you. I thought you wanted to see me, too."

"I do."

"Lindsay, you're not a detective. People bring you bones, you identify them and give them a report. Better yet, stop the forensic thing and just be a plain ordinary archaeologist."

Lindsay smiled to herself. "Some people want me to stop doing that, too."

"Who?" Derrick asked. Lindsay explained about John West and his family. "Poor baby." Derrick's voice was softer. "Getting it from all sides, aren't you—and having a death at the site. I shouldn't argue with you over the phone. I'm sorry."

"You're right. I'll come see you first."

"No. This business will only be on your mind. Just be careful."

Lindsay's eyes started to tear over. She didn't know why, perhaps just a delayed reaction from the events of the recent past. "Derrick, I miss you," she said, hoping he could not hear the tears in her voice.

He did. "Are you okay?" he said.

"Yes. I miss talking with you."

Derrick hesitated before he spoke. "We're talking now."

"No, we're not. Not the way we used to."

"Things have changed between us. We love each other."

"Does that mean we can't be friends?" she said.

"I thought it meant we were better friends."

"Then trust me," she said.

"I do, Lindsay. I do."

"Then love me for who I am. You used to."

"I still do. The stakes are higher. I'll deal with it," he said.

Lindsay wanted to tell him about five-year-old Marilee. She started to, but then, she wasn't sure what that had to do with anything. Lindsay wanted to find out what happened to Marilee's uncle so that there would be no mysteries in Marilee's family and her mother could get about the job of raising her with no sad, dark, suspicious clouds hanging in the distance. She was being fanciful. At one time Derrick would have understood that.

"Lindsay?"

"I'm here. It has to do with a little girl I met," she blurted. "I want to do it for her. I know that sounds silly."

"No. I understand."

The old Derrick was back, the one who understood her without her saying anything. Lindsay wiped her eyes, and she told him about Jane's site and conquistadores camping, resting up from a battle, cooking domestic pigs, and losing their axes in the woods. When they said good-bye, she felt better.

When Lindsay was born, her family expected that she would be another celestial body in her family's scholarly galaxy, so she had a lifetime of expectations that she would be nothing less than stellar. The pressure they applied was gentle because it did not occur to them that she would be less than what was expected, and they assumed it had not occurred to her either. However, gentle pressure over many years still had force behind it. Lindsay wondered if that was why she resisted serious relationships. She wanted no expectations of her other than that she would be herself and she would decide who that was.

Lindsay looked at the time. It was early enough to call Susan and check on things at home. She dialed her number. A man answered.

"Dr. Chamberlain's residence."

Lindsay was taken aback for a moment. "This is Lindsay Chamberlain. Is Susan there?"

"Oh, Dr. Chamberlain, this is Paul Gitten, Susan's brother."

"Is she all right?"

"Yes, she's fine. She moved Mandrake to her place. He's fine. She told me to tell you not to worry. There's been a few reporters and some trespassers, and she just wanted to get Mandrake out of the way. You know, in case anyone left the gate open or anything like that."

"I see." Though Lindsay was not sure she did. "It must have been serious for Susan to be worried."

"Not serious, just several minor incidents. Judd, you remember my brother Judd?" Lindsay said she did. "He and I wanted to do a little fishing, so we're keeping an eye on the place. Susan didn't want it left alone."

Susan was very conscientious, one reason Lindsay liked to have her look after her place. She knew how to see to things.

"I hope this isn't an inconvenience for you and your brother."

"No, not at all. Like I say, we wanted to do a little quiet fishing. Don't worry about anything here. Judd and I can take care of anything."

"By trespassers, what exactly do you mean?"

"She heard things at night, like someone creeping around the outside of the house. You know Susan. She has no imagination, so there was somebody there." Lindsay smiled to herself at Paul's description of his sister. It made her wish she had a better relationship with her own brother.

"Did they do anything?"

"Nothing much. Didn't get a chance. We think it was some of Denny Ferguson's relations. They're all riled over him getting convicted and having to run off. They're bad-mouthing you pretty bad."

"Yes, but they've been doing that all along. Do you think it may be Denny himself?"

"No, I imagine with a death penalty hanging over his head, so to speak, he's hightailed it out of the state. His whole family has always been no good. They look for excuses to harass people. Right now, you're it. It'll blow over. In the meantime, while you're gone, we'll take good care of your place."

"I appreciate it, Paul. I'm sorry it's so much trouble."

"No trouble. Judd and I never liked the Fergusons. We went to school with some of the older boys. None of them's ever been any good. Don't like reporters much either, so I guess we can take care of all of them."

Lindsay smiled again. "What do the reporters want? I can't imagine I'm that interesting a news item."

"Denny's lawyer's kind of keeping the whole thing in the news as much as she can. Anytime there's a slow news day, the reporters come over here. I don't think there's much to it. The last time, one called on the phone wanting to know something about a killing at a site you were working on."

How news travels, thought Lindsay. Paul didn't ask Lindsay what it was about, and she didn't volunteer any information.

"Thanks for taking care of my house," she said again.

"No problem. You take care, and don't worry. We have things covered here."

She hung up the phone. Her mind turned to Gil Harris, wondering if his death was connected to the unfortunate Ken Darnell, if Grace Lambert was right, and Ken's wife, or someone, had killed him. Lindsay put on her nightshirt and lay down to a restless sleep. Tomorrow she would drive to Ellis County and talk to the authorities in person about the death of Ken Darnell.

EIGHT

THE ONLY CORRESPONDENCE the Lamberts had received about the death of Grace's brother came from Tucker Prescott, the coroner of Ellis County, Tennessee. Lindsay doubted that Tucker Prescott would answer any questions from her if she just walked in off the street, so she had asked the coroner of her home county to fax her a letter of introduction. Dressed in a beige blouse, light brown skirt, and matching jacket, and her hair up in a French twist, she drove to the Ellis County coroner's office.

The office was in a small white house next to a large red-brick steepled courthouse. The reception area was freshly painted white with robin's-egg blue trim around the windows, the floor, and the ceiling molding. Someone had hung lace curtains. A table by a window held freshly cut flowers in a white hand-painted vase. A woman in her mid-fifties with gray hair wearing a pink polyester pantsuit was sitting behind the desk, typing. Lindsay waited by the woman's desk. When she came to the end of a paragraph, she looked up at Lindsay and smiled.

Lindsay held out her hand. "I'm Lindsay Chamberlain, a forensic anthropologist." She handed the woman the letter of introduction with her card paper-clipped to it. "I don't have an appointment, but I would like to see Tucker Prescott."

"He's not in at the moment. He's due back soon, if you'd like to wait." The woman pointed in the direction of three wooden hardbacked chairs against the wall. Apparently, they discouraged people from waiting very long.

"Thank you," said Lindsay, and took a seat. The woman resumed her typing. "Did you do the china painting?" asked Lindsay, gesturing to the vase. "It's very nice."

The woman stopped typing and gave Lindsay a broad smile. "Yes, I did. I do quite a lot of china painting. It's very relaxing. I'm not a great artist, but it passes the time."

"Oh, I think you have captured the irises very well. You must grow them." Lindsay had a policy of always, whenever possible, making friends with the gatekeepers of the world.

The woman's smile grew broader. "Thank you. Yes, I do grow them. It was so nice of you to recognize it. Mr. Prescott shouldn't be too much longer. He makes a trip down to the drugstore every day at this time. He never stays more than thirty minutes. He left, let me see...," she looked at the round school clock on the wall behind her desk, "about twenty minutes ago." She went on to tell Lindsay about Mr. Prescott, how her mother taught him in school and he was such a bright kid, and that it was a shame he couldn't finish his medical degree because of the quota system. Lindsay listened politely.

This time, Tucker Prescott stayed thirty-five minutes, if his secretary was accurate, for he came strolling in the door fifteen minutes later. Lindsay allowed the secretary to tell him he had a visitor and introduce her before she stood and held out her hand.

Tucker Prescott was in his early thirties, Lindsay guessed. He was heavyset in a way that made him appear chubby. He had dark hair and probably should shave twice a day to appear clean shaven by the late afternoon. He was dressed in a white, short-sleeved shirt, navy-blue pants, brown shoes, and white socks. He had no wedding ring, which confirmed the words of her great aunt Margaret that sprang into her mind: "No decent woman would ever let a man out of the house dressed like that."

"Lindsay Chamberlain," he said, as if trying out the name. "What can I do for you?" He gestured into his office. Lindsay entered and he followed, closing the door.

His office had not been recently painted. It was covered in inexpensive brown paneling, scratched and worn with age. His desk was not an antique, but it was old and as worn as the walls and the same color of brown. He gestured to a chair, the same kind of hard chair that sat in the reception area. The only new piece of furniture in the room was his Naugahyde executive office chair. A degree hung on the back wall, a B.S. from the University of Tennessee. In this county the coroner was an elected official, just as in Lindsay's home county, and was not required to have an advanced degree.

"Thank you for seeing me," she said. "Miles and Grace Lambert asked me to find out what I can about the death of Grace's brother, Ken Darnell."

"I pronounced the death an accident." Tucker Prescott swiveled slowly back and forth in his chair. He studied Lindsay as he tapped his pen on the desk, letting his finger slide down the shaft, then turning it over and repeating the process.

Lindsay chose her words carefully. "You were the only official kind enough to give them any information at all. That's why I came to you. The Lamberts know very little about his death. Mrs. Lambert loved her brother and feels a need to know more. Is there anything you can tell me?"

He shrugged. "I am aware that Mrs. Lambert thinks her brother was murdered. There was absolutely no evidence that supported that. He was a caver who made a mistake. We get our share of caving mistakes in this region. I understand there were some bad feelings between Mrs. Lambert and her sister-in-law."

"Who identified the bones?"

"Is there some suspicion that the bones were not Ken Darnell's?"

"They haven't expressed any." Lindsay smiled. "When a body has been skeletonized..." She searched for words that wouldn't offend him. "I'd like to know the identification process, so that I can explain the entire procedure to the Lamberts. Understanding how things are done will help them understand why the death was declared an accident."

"There was no question of the identification. I am very careful about those things," he said, as if he hadn't heard Lindsay or didn't believe her motives. "The Lamberts themselves identified the jewelry as belonging to Darnell. The wife identified the clothes. I sent the bones to the University of Tennessee to Nigel Boyd. He used dental charts. I believe there was also a broken left arm in the Darnell case. Dr. Boyd said that there was no doubt about any of them."

"I know Nigel. He is very good."

"Then you can put their minds at ease that no one got away with murder in this county."

"Do you happen to have any close-up pictures of the bones?"

"No. The sheriff probably has them."

"Was Ken Darnell well known here?"

"No. He just happened to get killed in one of our caves. He picked the most dangerous to explore. As I said, we are not strangers to caving accidents. Karst topography, they call it. It's what we have here. There's Hell Slide, where Darnell and his two friends were killed. There's the Grand Serpentine, Bone Cave, and, of course, Cumberland Caverns in the next county. We've got dozens in this area. People come from all over to explore 'em, and some of them are either unlucky, stupid, or both." He stopped moving his chair and looked straight at Lindsay. "I got a call the other day from the FBI. Wanted to know if the name Gil Harris surfaced in connection with Ken Darnell. Now that I think about it, the FBI agent may have mentioned your name."

"I see. Were you able to tell him anything?"

"Just what I told you. The guy died through misadventure. Never heard of a Gil Harris."

Lindsay could sense that she was not going to get any more information from Tucker Prescott. She thanked him for his time and went back to her motel. She changed into more comfortable clothes and stretched out on the bed to think. She knew Nigel. He was very competent. He would have examined the bones thoroughly, and if he didn't find anything suspicious, then there probably wasn't anything to find.

She dug out her address book and found Nigel's office number. He did not answer his phone. She left a message and her motel phone number, then decided to get something to eat and try him again later. First, however, she tried Derrick. She let the phone ring until it turned over to the answering service. She left him a short message with her phone number.

Lindsay walked to a restaurant across the street and had a salad. Though she hadn't eaten since breakfast, she had no appetite. *What,* she wondered, *is making me so restless.* The image of Marilee appeared unsummoned in her mind. She had seen a bookstore about a block away. She thought that after she ate she would look there for some books for Marilee.

Lindsay returned to her motel room with three books: one on Native Americans, one on archaeology, and one on identifying rocks and minerals. The archaeology book came with its own miniature "dig"—a box with some "artifacts" buried in plaster for a child to unearth, as if at an archaeological site. When she laid them on the bed, she wondered how she was going to explain to Marilee's parents why she'd bought so many gifts for her, especially since she didn't get any for Joshua. Lindsay wasn't sure she could explain it to herself. She could deliver them, she thought, when she brought back Joshua's Spanish knife, all cleaned up. She could also fib and tell Marilee's parents they were on sale really cheap. She couldn't pass them up, but didn't know who she could give them to, and thought of Marilee. "That is stupid," Lindsay said aloud to herself. "I probably should just save them for Christmas and give them to Derrick's youngest brother." He was about the same age as Marilee and would enjoy them. The phone rang in the middle of her thoughts, and she picked it up.

"Just what the hell do you think you are doing?" The voice was so full of anger that for a moment Lindsay didn't recognize it.

"Kelley? Is that you?"

"What are you doing to my aunt? You have her thinking now that Ken may still be alive somewhere."

"What? I've done no such thing!" exclaimed Lindsay.

"No? Then why did the coroner of Ellis County call and

explain to her that no matter what Dr. Chamberlain's suspicions, it was Ken's remains he had identified?''

"He did that? When?'' asked Lindsay.

"About an hour ago,'' said Kelly

"He completely misrepresented what I said to him. I voiced no such suspicions.''

"Then why did he call?'' asked Kelley.

"I don't know. It was a very cruel, irrational, and unfounded thing to do.''

"Then you really didn't tell him you doubted the identification of the bones?''

"Of course not,'' said Lindsay.

Kelly was silent for a moment. When she spoke she seemed calmer. "Aunt Grace doesn't know what to think.''

"May I talk to her?''

"I don't want you to upset her further.''

"I won't.''

"Just a minute.''

Grace Lambert came on the line. She did not seem as upset and confused as Kelley described, just puzzled. "Hello, Lindsay. Kelley told you about the strange call we got?''

"Yes, and I'm so sorry. When I talked to him, the identity of the remains was not an issue. I don't know why he thought it was.'' Lindsay suspected that simple paranoia on his part made him think he was hearing something different from what she was saying to him.

"I had kind of hoped—''

"I know. I asked him who identified the remains so that I could talk to them about any marks that might indicate what happened to Ken. As it turned out, I know the person well, and he is very competent. I'll talk to him, unless you would like me to stop altogether.''

"No. Please continue. Please. I want to know everything I can find out.''

"All right. Bear in mind, there may not be much to know.''

"I know, but I'll have tried everything I could to find out what happened to Ken. I have to do that.''

"Very well. I'll keep in touch."

The phone rang immediately, just as Lindsay hung it up. When Nigel said hello, she realized she had hoped it was Derrick.

"Lindsay, love. Great to hear from you. How about coming over to England? I'll take you over to Paris, and we can fly back to the States together."

"You're in England?" said Lindsay.

"Visiting the folks, catching up on my culture," he said.

"Sounds nice, Nigel. How are they?"

"Good as ever. You still seeing that Derrick fellow?"

"Yes."

"Rats."

"He's kind of mad at me at the moment."

"Great, there's hope. Why's he mad?"

"I kind of stood him up to do detective work."

"Uh, oh, I see his point already. You mentioned something about a Ken Darnell case?"

"Yes. Do you remember it?"

"Didn't do it."

"You didn't. But the coroner—"

"They contacted my office about it, but I wasn't available."

"Well, I wonder why Prescott said you did?"

"Probably knew I was out of town and couldn't deny it. I've worked with Tucker Prescott occasionally. We have a mutual dislike for each other. He's a paranoid beggar. Flunked out of med school and tells everybody it was the quota system that knocked him out—too many women and foreigners trying to be doctors these days, a man just doesn't stand a chance, it seems."

"He believes that?"

"I don't think he does, actually. I think he's just trying to save face, and that's a hot button for a lot of folks. Gets him sympathy."

"Do you know who identified the bones?" asked Lindsay.

"No, sorry, I don't."

"Sorry you had to call me all the way from England for nothing," she said.

"It's not for nothing when I get to hear your lovely voice. How about it? Paris is beautiful this time of year."

"It's tempting, but I'll have to pass." She heard Nigel sigh. "I'll come to Knoxville sometime and take you out to dinner. Goodnight."

"I'll hold you to it," he said.

Lindsay thought briefly of calling Tucker Prescott at home and telling him what she thought of his lack of professionalism. But she could imagine his bureaucratic mentality concocting some paranoid reasoning, blaming her. It was best to ignore him.

Lindsay hung up and tried Derrick's number again. He didn't answer.

She would talk to Jennifer Darnell, then go to Derrick's site and forget about Ken Darnell. Lindsay put the gifts back in the sack and got ready for bed.

PIAQUAY LOOKED out over the valley at the village of Chilhaxul. It appeared peaceful. He surveyed the landscape as far as he could see from his high mountain perch and saw no sign of the coming Spaniards. He had left the trail of Calderón days before the Spaniard was to catch up to Pardo and took the trail to Chilhaxul. He had expected to arrive before them.

Chilhaxul was located at a bend in the river. From this vantage it looked much like his village, except for the seven mounds. Chilhaxul had enemies to the north and west, Piaquay knew. Evidence of this was the tall wall around the village made from timber covered with dried clay, guard towers, and a moat connected to the river surrounding all. Inside the wall the houses, the wall-less shelters, and the plaza were like those in his village. This would be a town the Spanish would like, for the soil was rich and corn grew well. Chilhaxul was the main village of at least eight other lesser villages. It was powerful. It was a good place for Piaquay to seek allies for his plan.

"SOME HAVE SAID they are turtles because they live inside a hard shell," said a young man sitting on his haunches, scraping the shaft of an arrow with a piece of flint.

"No," said another, taking one of his arrows, rolling it in his hands and looking down the shaft. "They are bears. They are lazy and have much hair covering their bodies. I've seen them."

"I believe," said a younger man, sitting cross-legged, watching his friends, "that they are Uktena or the water cougar. I have heard their odor is foul and they bring death. They sometimes walk on four feet and sometimes two."

"They are none of these things." The three young men looked up to see a stranger in their midst. "I am Tesca, brother of Piaquay of Calusa." He squatted down beside the youths. "The creatures you speak of are men. They come from a place where all men are hairy and wear metal to protect them in war. They stink because they do not bathe. They are men," he repeated. "They rule because they have the four-footed beasts as servants, or they are the servants of the four-footed beasts who rule. I do not know. They care for the beasts and feed them as an apprentice prepares and serves food to a warrior. The beast in return carries them on its back. When they fight on the back of the beast, they are invincible. When they fight on the ground, they are weaker."

"How do you know these things?" said the youth, who was straightening his new arrows.

"They came to our village, took our women and children, and said they would kill them unless we gave them much wealth. We did, but they killed them anyway."

"And you took revenge?" asked one of the youths.

"We're on a war party now."

"You're far from home," said another youth. "Can you not find them?"

"We can find them. They have to be approached with care. They have magic that can kill people from a distance." Tesca had the attention of the youths. They all sat down, cross-legged, to listen to the stranger. "They have two ways they

kill from a distance. They have invisible warriors that they send to weaken a village. This sometimes takes many seasons. When a village is weak, they come and ask for food because they cannot feed themselves, nor can they hunt animals of the woods. Maybe they have to promise the beasts food to get them to carry them; I don't know. But when you give them corn, they also take the women and children. There is another weapon they use then. It is long and looks like a thick hollow reed. It's not a reed, though; it's made from something like copper, but harder and black. This weapon is so heavy, they cannot lift it and must support it with a stick stuck in the ground.'' Tesca showed the braves with gestures how they used the weapon. ''When they command it, it vomits fire and smoke, spitting a gizzard stone made of itself. If this stone hits you, it rips the flesh like the point of an arrow and must be dug out. You either die or suffer much pain.''

''That's a terrible weapon,'' said one of the youths, in awe.

''It is. But it is a weapon that tires easily and must rest before it can spit again.''

''And you say these are men?'' they asked.

''This is Piaquay, who comes from the village of Calusa to the south of here,'' announced a brave entering the council house of the elders Chilhaxul.

The men who sat in the council house were not unlike the elders of Piaquay's village in dress and manner. Their language, though similar, was not Piaquay's, but he understood it and could speak it after a fashion. Though there were similarities, there were also many differences between this tribe and Piaquay's as well. The differences were subtle taken by themselves, but taken together they were such that Piaquay would not have felt at home here. He ignored any discomfort he felt and walked in the midst of the group.

''I am here to talk about the strangers in our land,'' he began.

''You know these men?'' asked an elder.

''You do not? Do you not remember the man Hernando de Soto?'' asked Piaquay.

"We heard of him. But none from our village saw him. The villages to the east and to the north of here know of him."

"They are the same. Not the same man, but the same tribe."

"Why have you come?" asked the eldest, whose long hair was silver.

"These men massacred my people, killed my sister, my nephew, my wife, my infant daughter. I want to avenge their deaths. These are men who kill women and children as easily as they kill other men. I want to drive these people from our land back to their own."

"Why have you come to us?"

"They are coming here. They will ask that you bow to the rule of their leader, accept their gods, and give them food to eat."

"How do you know they come here?"

"I have a slave with me, a captive. He is one of them but has lived here many seasons. He knows the villages they visit. We must drive them out of our land," Piaquay repeated. "I will tell you what I think we should do."

NINE

LINDSAY SAT IN the motel diner, drinking a cup of coffee with a road map in front of her. She decided to drive to McMinnville and interview Jennifer Darnell, Ken Darnell's wife. She debated with herself about calling before she left. Her polite upbringing told her to call—after all, the woman had lost a husband. But the emerging detective said to wait until she was in McMinnville—don't give her much time to collect her thoughts. Her polite self won out.

She was taking a drink of coffee, and a shadow crossed her map. She looked up to see a man and a woman standing beside the table, both thin as rails, looking to be in their late twenties or early thirties. The man had a mustache and Vandyke beard. His dark hair was long in the back and shorter on the sides and top. He wore faded jeans and a green-and-white-striped shirt. His short-sleeved shirt revealed scratches and bandages on his arms. The woman had on a pink flowered housedress that buttoned up the front. Long, thin, light-brown hair wisped about her face, and bangs hung just past her eyebrows, running into thin rimmed glasses.

"Lindsay Chamberlain?" said the man.

"Yes."

"My name's Clay Boshay. This here's my sister, Lorinda Hillard."

Hillard, thought Lindsay. *That sounds familiar.*

"Do you mind if we sit down and talk to you?" he asked.

"It's about my husband, Blaine," said the woman.

Blaine Hillard, thought Lindsay. That's right. One of the men killed with Ken Darnell. "Sit down," she said.

"Thanks." Lorinda slid into the booth opposite Lindsay

and her brother slid in after her. She put her purse on the table and fiddled with the strap as she spoke.

"Martha said you was a real nice lady. Martha—Tucker Prescott's secretary—she's the cousin of a friend of mine." At the sound of Prescott's name, Lorinda's brother gave a derisive snort that his sister ignored. "She said you're investigatin' Ken Darnell's death."

"Yes," said Lindsay.

"Then I want you to look into Blaine's death, too." She snapped open her purse. "I can give you a retainer."

Lindsay put a hand on the purse. "I can't take money," she said smiling at her.

"You work for free?" asked Clay, clearly not believing it.

"I work for the University of Georgia as a professor. I get a salary for that, and I also do consulting with the state on forensic work. I'm not a private detective. I'm looking into Ken Darnell's death as a favor for a friend."

"Then we want to be your friend," said Clay, "because there's something fishy about Blaine's death."

Lindsay raised her eyebrows, as did the waitress who had just come to the table to ask if Clay and Lorinda wanted anything. The two newcomers ordered coffee. Lindsay ordered a glass of tea and waited for the waitress to leave before she said anything.

"How do you mean?" she asked.

"Blaine and me was married five years. We got two babies. Lily's four now and Holden's five. Now, Blaine was a bit of a dreamer, but he wasn't stupid. He'd not go off caving without telling me or somebody where he'd got to. And he'd take care of his family."

"How do you mean?" asked Lindsay.

"Blaine had insurance. He worked with Clay at Tooly Construction Company. We got fifty thousand dollars when they found his—him. But we found out he'd taken our savings and become a partner in Darnell's sporting goods store. See, he had this idea of offering tourists wilderness trips in caves that most of the public don't go in and down wild rivers, things like that. The Darnells really liked the idea. Blaine always wanted to be in business for hisself. He was real excited about. We talked it over, but I didn't know he'd already done it."

"Anyway," said Clay, "it seems Jennifer Darnell took out more insurance on Blaine. Something about..." He looked down at the floor trying to think of the term.

"Key person insurance?" supplied Lindsay.

"Yeah, that's it. The bitch—pardon my French—got half a million dollars on Blaine. Now, if he was going to insure his life for that much, then he'd see that his family got at least some of it."

The waitress came with the tea and coffee. Again Lindsay waited until she was gone before she continued. "Wasn't the insurance company suspicious of having to pay out such a large sum of money shortly after the policies were taken out?"

"They tried their best. But, see, that's where she was smart. It all looked normal." Clay tapped the table with his finger. "It seems she had the policy on her husband for about a couple of years and the one on Blaine for a little over a year. Blaine had made all these plans. They'd even booked people for the trips. Then him and Ken disappeared, and they didn't find them for two years. The woman's nothing if not patient."

"As wife of a partner, don't you have some share in the business?" asked Lindsay.

Both of them shook their heads. "I can't believe that Blaine would sign a contract like that, but he did, initialed every page of it. It was notarized and everything," said Lorinda. "We've seen a lawyer, talked to the sheriff, the insurance company, everybody we can think of. They all say it looks suspicious, but there is just no evidence she's done anything wrong."

"Did the coroner have this information when he pronounced the death accidental?" asked Lindsay.

Clay made a derisive noise. "The coroner—he's so stupid he couldn't pour water out of a bucket if the instructions was written on the bottom of it."

"Martha says he has to be careful. He can't just accuse folks," said Lorinda.

"He didn't have to accuse anybody; he just didn't have to be so—well, I didn't come here to re-argue old stuff," said Clay. "Just to ask you if you'll have a look into Blaine's death."

"You wouldn't happen to have any pictures of the remains?" asked Lindsay.

"Sure. I had a devil of a time getting them from ol' Prescott, but I got 'em."

"Do you know who identified the remains?"

"Sure. Blaine's—what you call him, Lorinda?"

"Orthopedist," she said. "Blaine had a bad knee. Football injury."

"Yeah, that's it, orthopedist. Dr. Ballinger, Olin Ballinger. He replaced Blaine's knee or something. Anyway, he recognized his own work."

"I see. Did he look at the other skeletons as well?"

Clay shrugged. "I reckon."

"Has he ever done this kind of identification before? Would he know how to look for bones damaged by knives or bullets?"

"Don't know that either. I think all the coroner wanted to do was identify the bodies. He thought it was pretty clear what killed them. But you know, rocks can fall on you when you're dead just like when you're alive."

"You can tell if a person's been shot or something even if there's only...uh...bones left?" asked Lorinda.

"Sometimes. Tell me about his disappearance," said Lindsay.

"It was on a Friday," said Lorinda. "He didn't come home from work. I remember he'd been tellin' me all week about a surprise for me and the kids, but he wouldn't say what. He was like that. A kid when it came to surprises. He told me to go out and buy the most expensive dress I could find. That Saturday night we were going to a party." Lorinda stopped speaking and her mouth quivered very slightly.

Clay took up the story. "We know now that Jennifer Darnell," he said her name in a mildly haughty voice as if perhaps

Jennifer had used that tone with him, "had planned a party Saturday to announce Wild Journeys, Inc., an offshoot of Everything Sporting—that's their store. She had to cancel the party when Ken and Blaine went missing, but again that's where she was so smart. Anybody who watches *Unsolved Mysteries* knows that's where people get tripped up and bring suspicion to themselves. They don't make plans they're supposed to, and the police thing, *aha,* they knew the person would be dead and not really need the tickets to Rio, so they didn't buy them." He leaned forward, emphasizing his point. "Jennifer was smarter than that. She followed through with all the plans, incorporating Wild Journeys, planning the party, hiring caterers, sending out two hundred invitations, the works. The police were so dumb, they fell for it." He sat back in his seat, as if he had proved his point.

Lindsay didn't say what she thought—that perhaps the woman was innocent and that you couldn't use her having done all the right things against her. Instead she asked, "Do you have any physical evidence, or did anyone overhear her say something that was incriminating?"

"No," said Lorinda. "Nothing. But what I couldn't make people understand was that I knew my husband. I know he didn't tell me about investing our savings—they always throw that into my face every time I try to tell them anything—but that was a surprise, a present. You can have secrets in a marriage, but that don't mean you don't know each other. Blaine would not have cut us out of that much money. He wouldn't have. He had dreams for the kids, things he wanted for them." Lorinda reached in her purse and drew out a Kleenex and delicately blew her nose.

"May I have a look at the pictures of the remains?" asked Lindsay.

"They're in the car. I'll get them," said Clay.

"No, I'll do it," said Lorinda. "I need to stop by the ladies' room."

After Clay let Lorinda out of the booth and watched her disappear into the hallway that led to the rest rooms, he leaned forward and said to Lindsay in a conspiratorial whisper, "You know, you can look at the bones anytime you want."

Lindsay eyed him, puzzled. "They've not been buried?" she asked hesitantly.

He shook his head and looked around to be sure the waitress was not coming and no one was listening, then continued. "They have a family plot on their property. See, Blaine's father had these—what you call it—grandiose delusions for the family. He was also in construction. He built one of them marble buildings in their private graveyard."

"A vault?" asked Lindsay.

"Yeah. Can you believe it? Anyway, ol' Blaine's in there."

"Well," said Lindsay carefully, "if I find anything in the pictures, we may need to get an exhumation order."

"I'm telling you, you don't have to dig him up. He ain't buried, and he ain't in a public cemetery. Just let me know, and me and Steven—that's his brother—will get you in."

Lindsay had a vision of herself in the dead of night carrying a lantern, breaking into a crypt with the guy sitting across from her and his brother-in-law. She could just see the headlines. "Let's hope it doesn't come to that."

Lorinda returned shortly and handed Lindsay a large folder tied with a blue ribbon. Lindsay untied the ribbon, opened the folder, and glanced at the contents. It must have been hard for Lorinda to look at the picture of the bones, knowing they were her husband's. Lindsay wondered if, like Grace Lambert, she simply did not look. She closed the folder.

"Can I keep these a while? I will need time to give them a thorough looking over."

"Sure," said Lorinda. "We're just glad to have somebody listen to us."

"Did you know Ken Darnell?" asked Lindsay.

Both Lorinda and Clay shook their heads. "Not well," said Lorinda. "He was mainly a friend of Blaine's."

"Did Blaine ever mention any trouble Darnell and his wife might be having?"

"No," said Lorinda, 'but he wouldn't. Blaine really didn't

notice things like that, and he wasn't much for talking about personal stuff with people."

"What about the other man who was killed—who was he?" asked Lindsay.

They shook their heads. "We didn't know him," said Clay. "He was a friend of Ken's. I don't think he was a partner or anything."

"I think the guy's name was Roy Pitt," offered Lorinda.

"So, you'll look into it?" asked Clay.

"I can't promise anything. I'll do my best," Lindsay told them.

"We really do appreciate it," said Clay. "Like Lorinda said, it's a relief just to have somebody listen to us."

On her way back to her room, Lindsay stopped to put the photographs in the motel safe along with the ones the Lamberts had given her. They were evidence, as far as she was concerned, and she treated them as such. Her telephone was ringing as she was opening the door to her room. She raced to get it. Grace Lambert's voice was on the other end.

"I heard on the news about the death at an archaeological site," she said a little breathlessly. "It said that you were there."

"Yes," said Lindsay, going over in her mind how much to tell her.

"That must have been terrible for you," she said.

"It was very unpleasant for all of us," replied Lindsay.

"I don't suppose you have had the time to do much investigating since I spoke to you."

"Not a lot, but I did talk to the wife of one of the men killed with your brother. I didn't learn anything definitive, but, like you, she has her suspicions." Lindsay heard a sharp intake of breath. "Don't make too much of that. I haven't seen any hard evidence of anything yet. She was able to give me some good photographs of her husband's remains. I haven't examined them yet."

"So I may not be overreacting to my brother's death, after all," she said.

"I don't want to mislead you in any way," said Lindsay, carefully picking her words. "It's true there are things about the accident that need to be answered. It may be that when I find the answers they will be completely reasonable."

"I understand," said Grace, but Lindsay could tell by her voice she was anticipating that her worst fears would be true—that her brother was murdered.

Lindsay cautioned her again to not expect anything unless the evidence justified it. After she got off the phone with Grace, she dialed Jennifer Darnell's number. A housekeeper or a secretary answered. Lindsay told the woman her name and asked to speak to Mrs. Darnell.

"Just a moment," said the voice.

Lindsay thought it odd that the woman did not ask what she wanted. Gatekeepers usually do. It's their job to guard the gate. Lindsay suspected that the woman already knew her name and was expecting her call.

"This is Jennifer Darnell."

"Mrs. Darnell, I was wondering if I could talk to you. Perhaps in a restaurant or park? It's about—"

"I know what it's about, and I really don't care to talk to you."

"I understand that your husband's death is a painful topic. It's painful for your husband's sister also. I won't take up much of your time."

"I have no obligation to talk to you. What is your connection to any of this?"

"No, you don't have to talk to me. I have no authority, whatsoever. But I just want to know what happened so I can tell Grace and her family."

There was silence—a full thirty seconds of silence.

"Do you know where Gilby's is?"

"I can find it," she told her.

"Meet me there in two hours." Click.

Lindsay put on the suit she wore to meet Prescott, and after calling the restaurant for directions, she drove to McMinnville, arriving in the parking lot twenty minutes early. She sat in her

Land Rover for a few minutes, going over in her mind what she wanted to confirm—discover—from Mrs. Darnell. Truthfully, she wasn't sure. Jennifer Darnell was not going to admit to murder. Lindsay didn't even know if there had been a murder. So what did she expect to discover from the dead man's wife? Did she expect Jennifer Darnell to incriminate herself during Lindsay's clever interrogation? Lindsay smiled to herself. Not for the first time, the reality that she wasn't a detective occurred to her with harsh clarity. She didn't really know what she was doing if she didn't have a pile of bones in front of her.

She reminded herself, however, she didn't have to solve the case. She only had to look at the available evidence and render an opinion. It would be up to the authorities to take any necessary action. Lindsay took a deep breath and got out of her vehicle.

It was an elegant restaurant—linen tablecloths and napkins, silver, china, and crystal goblets on the table. The wallpaper was a deep red with black and gold Victorian floral designs. The carpet was also a deep red, the color of a good red wine.

Jennifer Darnell was exactly on time. Lindsay had chosen a table in the far corner of the restaurant and sat facing the entrance. The hostess was ushering a woman toward her, a small, trim woman who knew how to dress. Her apricot suit went well with her dark hair. Jennifer Darnell was also very pretty. She had large blue eyes, a small nose slightly pointed, and a small oval face with a fair, what some call a peaches and cream, complexion. Her hair came to her chin and turned under slightly. It was smooth and slightly puffed around her head, not stiff with spray but soft and shiny.

"You must be Lindsay Chamberlain," she said.

"Yes. Thank you for coming." Lindsay held out her hand. Jennifer hesitated a moment before she took it. An emerald circled by diamonds glittered on her finger in the soft candlelight. She had well-manicured nails, polished with a color that matched her suit. Her hand was cold and her handshake firm.

"I almost didn't come," she said, sitting down opposite Lindsay.

"I know dragging all this up again must be painful, and I debated about whether or not to contact you," said Lindsay. "I only want a little information to tell the Lamberts."

"All right. To start with," she said, "I didn't kill my husband or his friends." Lindsay opened her mouth to speak, but Jennifer interrupted. "Don't deny that's what you want to talk to me about. I know what Grace thinks. She never liked me from the beginning."

"Why not?" asked Lindsay.

Jennifer shrugged. "I don't think it's me, really, I don't think anyone was good enough for her precious brother." She shook her head. "Grace was so blind."

The waiter came to take their orders. "I recommend the Chateaubriand," said Jennifer. "It's their house specialty." Jennifer ordered the house steak, marinated mushrooms, and a bottle of the house wine for both of them. She gave the menus to the waiter and turned her attention to Lindsay. "I hope you like red meat."

"That's fine," Lindsay said. "You sound angry with your husband."

"I am. Just when our life was starting to get good, he goes and gets himself killed, and his family blames me."

"Not the whole family, and I really believe it is the mystery surrounding his death that makes them suspicious."

"What mystery?" Jennifer Darnell asked.

"It's not a mystery to you, because the authorities kept you informed. But the Lamberts weren't told very much. It's hard for anyone to lose a loved one and not be able to say good-bye to the body. Death is such a dreadful thing. The family must be convinced not only that it has happened, but that it was somehow an understandable death and the soul is at peace. That's what viewing the body does for families. Because Ken was found so long after his death and because the authorities were not forthcoming, it was not possible for the Lamberts to reach any closure."

"You sound like an anthropologist," Jennifer said.

"I am. I majored in anthropology." The waiter brought their salads and dark bread on a cutting board. They ate in silence for a while. Finally Jennifer said, "What is it you want to know?"

"Just the chain of events."

"I'm sure Grace told you I was married before. My husband was a lot older than me and had money. I can't say that security wasn't one of the reasons I married him. But he was also a smart man, and that was important to me, too. I'm not a bimbo. I read a lot." She looked up from her salad at Lindsay, expecting to be challenged. "He died of a heart attack. It wasn't a suspicious death, or even unexpected. I inherited quite a bit of money. A lot of it went to pay off debts, but I was left well off."

The server brought the steaks and poured the wine. Jennifer took a sip. "This is good wine. I've never had a bad bottle here."

Lindsay took a bite of her steak and sipped her wine. She hoped the food and wine would loosen Jennifer's tongue some more. So far she was very cooperative.

"How did you meet Ken Darnell?" asked Lindsay.

"A party. Halloween, of all things. I was Cleopatra and he was Zorro." Jennifer smiled. "In the beginning he looked rather dashing, but as the evening wore on the temporary dye he used to spray his hair black began to run. It was very funny. He was charming and asked me out." Jennifer stopped and again smiled, almost to herself. "I didn't recognize the blond lanky guy who showed up at my door the next day until he pulled his mask out of his pocket and put it on. Ken was really a funny guy then. That's why I fell in love with him. I didn't kill him."

"I'm sorry for your loss."

Jennifer shrugged. "Life goes on. I've met someone else and we're hitting it off. If that seems heartless, I'm sorry. Ken shouldn't have gone into a cave as dangerous as Hell Slide."

"Why was he there? Do you know?"

"He was checking out a place for our new venture."

"Wild Journeys?"

"Yes."

"Were you in sporting goods before you married Ken?"

Jennifer shook her head. "No. That was Ken's dream, but I was glad to make it come true. Harold—he was my first husband—and I knew people socially who had ties with the Olympics. There are thousands of hopefuls out there, all needing equipment. We started out as mostly a mail-order place. We branched into mountain-climbing, camping, fishing equipment—we had the best and developed a market through friends of Harold's. It turned out I was good in business. Ken and I were successful. We had just expanded and moved to McMinnville when he disappeared."

"Where did you get the idea for Wild Journeys?"

"Ken and a friend of his came up with the idea. Actually, I thought it was pretty good. They were going to put together tours anywhere from a day's outing to a week through caves, or white water, anything adventurous. Advertise it as getting back to the days when men explored dangerous places."

"And Hell Slide Cave was supposed to be one of those places?"

"No. It was on private property and known to be dangerous, but Blaine Hillard—that's Ken's friend—thought it would be perfect for the more adventurous tours. I was against it and I thought that was the end of it. Now Hillard's wife thinks I murdered Blaine and my husband, too."

"Why?" asked Lindsay.

Jennifer looked at Lindsay. "I can't believe you haven't talked to them."

"I have, but I want to hear your story."

"I see."

"I'm not trying to trap you. I just don't want to throw other people's accusations at you."

"That's very considerate of you."

"They are suspicious because of the large amount of insurance," Lindsay said.

"Look. When we decided on this venture, a lot of money up front had to be spent—advertising, equipment, insurance for the customers, deposits on hotels. There were a lot of things to take into consideration. If anything happened to Blaine or Ken or any one of us, and we couldn't carry out the plans, these things still had to be paid for."

"Mrs. Hillard thinks that her husband would have named her as beneficiary for a large amount of the money."

"Not bloody likely." Jennifer chewed a piece of meat while staring at Lindsay. "I bought the policy. It was for the business. Taking care of his family was Blaine's responsibility. He could have bought insurance at the same time, but like a lot of men who like excitement, Ken included, Blaine unfortunately didn't think anything would happen to him." She pointed a fork at Lindsay. "I had a financial adviser telling me how to protect myself and the business. If I hadn't gotten insurance on Ken and Blaine, I'd be stuck with a lot of bills and people would be calling me a poor businesswoman instead of a murderer. Yes, I came out far ahead with the insurance money. But I'd rather have my husband back."

Jennifer stopped and took a breath and a sip of wine.

"What can you tell me about the day they disappeared?" asked Lindsay.

"Not a lot. We were planning a party Saturday evening. The last time I saw Ken, it was Friday afternoon and he was waving to me, going out the door of our store. He just said he'd be back in a while. He never came back. Saturday morning I called the sheriff. I found out that Blaine was missing, too. I figured they were together, but I had no idea where. We looked everywhere we could think of."

"No one thought of Hell Slide Cave?"

Jennifer shook her head. "They weren't supposed to be there. It didn't occur to me. Like I said, it was on private property, and Mr. Lafferty is very hard on trespassers. I thought they had maybe gone rafting, working the kinks out of the first tour coming up, perhaps drowned. It was the only thing I could think of."

"What about the cars?"

"They took their off-road bikes and left them parked just inside the cave entrance. They apparently boarded up the cave behind them so Mr. Lafferty wouldn't know they were there. It's rough terrain, hard to get to, and he keeps the entrance to the cave boarded up."

"Were there boats missing?"

"Boats?"

"You said you thought they might have gone on the river."

"Oh. No. But Ken was buying the equipment for the tours. I thought he might have rafts that I didn't know about."

"Who was the third man?"

"Roy Pitt? He was a friend of Ken's. I didn't know him. Ken was going to hire him as a guide, I think."

"You've been very open," Lindsay said.

"Yes, I have, and I'll tell you why. I have a new man in my life, and I don't want him to start believing I'm some kind of black widow. I want all these accusations to stop."

"How long have you known him?"

"What?" Jennifer snapped.

"The new man in your life. How long have you known him?"

Jennifer sighed. "I met him before Ken died, if that's what you're asking. He was a business associate, and that was all. I know Grace thought I was having an affair, but I wasn't. I understand one of her busybody relatives saw us together once. It was business. But it's not just business now. I really like him. Ken is gone, and I have a right to be happy." She put down her fork and knife and picked up her napkin, twisting it in her hands. Lindsay could see anger burning her face. "Ken shouldn't have gone into that damn cave and not tell me where he was going. How does Grace think I felt, wondering where he was, wondering if he was somewhere hurt and needing help? Ken was reckless and stupid, and he died for it." Her hand shook as she took a drink of water.

"Thank you for answering my questions."

"Will you tell Grace to leave me alone?"

"Since there is no evidence that he was murdered, much less by you, she'll have to. Do you, by the way, have pictures of his remains? I know that is a rather—"

"No, she doesn't." Both looked up at the sudden intrusion. A man sat down at the table. He was a handsome man: black hair, dark eyes, straight nose, square jaw, evenly occluded white teeth. His hair was short and professionally styled, and his tweed jacket, Armani shirt, and slacks appeared new. He looked polished, as if he never wore old clothes. He also looked as if he worked out regularly. "That's a cruel request, don't you think?" He had a smooth Midwestern accent.

"Unpleasant, yes," said Lindsay, "but not cruel. Suppose someone did kill Mrs. Darnell's husband. I'm sure she would be the first to want the murderer caught."

"But someone didn't. Many professional people have looked into it."

Lindsay and the newcomer stared at each other for a moment.

"This is Craig Gillett, my friend," Jennifer explained.

"I'm sorry if I seem insensitive," said Lindsay. "I'm only trying to find out some information about Ken Darnell for his sister."

"Jennifer said she was going to tell you everything she knew. I hope you're satisfied with that."

The waiter brought a small folder with the check and discretely put it on the table. Lindsay reached for it, but Craig Gillett slid it out from under her hand.

"I should pay," said Lindsay.

"Yes, you should," said Craig. "However, it will be high, and since I don't believe this is either university or state business, it will probably come out of your pocket, so I will pay for it. But don't count on any more goodwill from us. Jennifer deserves a life."

"Thank you for your cooperation," Lindsay said to Jennifer. "Under the circumstances, it was more than I expected."

"Please tell that to Grace."

"I will."

Gillett paid the check, and they walked out of the restaurant. Lindsay watched him put Jennifer into her car, then get into his own, which was parked beside hers.

Lindsay drove to the motel. She entered her room, slipped out of her shoes, and had started to take off her clothes when she heard a knock at the door. Through the peephole she saw Craig Gillett standing outside her room.

TEN

A LONG TIME ago, the Sun became angry with the people of earth when she saw them squinting their eyes in her direction. "I'll teach them to make ugly faces at me," she said and became very hot, sending them fever and disease. The Little Men who sometimes helped the people saw what the Sun was doing and said she must be killed.

The Little Men turned two men into snakes, an adder and a copperhead, and told them to bite the Sun when she visited her daughter who lived in the middle of the sky above the earth. They hid near the daughter's house, ready to strike the Sun, but she was too radiant and blinded them.

The Little Men then turned a man into a large winged snake with crystal scales that sparkled like crackling fire and horns that grew out of his head. In the middle of the snake's forehead there was a dazzling crest that sparkled like a bright star. The bright crest was called Ulunsuti. The snake was called Uktena, the Keen-eyed. The Little Men also turned another man into a rattlesnake to help Uktena kill the Sun.

Uktena and the Rattlesnake went to wait near the Sun's daughter's house, but the Rattlesnake was so excited that he raced ahead of Uktena and bit the daughter when she came to the door and killed her instead. The Rattlesnake became confused by his mistake and raced back to the people without waiting for the Sun. Uktena followed angrily. In his anger and frustration he became dangerous. If a warrior simply looked at him, Uktena would cause him and his whole family to die.

Many warriors tried to kill Uktena, but their arrows and spears could not pierce the hard scales. There was, however, a special place on the Uktena's body that was vulnerable. A great shaman found it and killed Uktena and took his crest.

It was a great crystal, transparent except for the blood-red center.

The crystal gave the shaman great power, the power to see into the future, to always have a good hunt, to make it rain whenever the shaman wanted. Even each of the thousands of scales of Uktena had power. The big crystal that was his crest, however, was so powerful that the shaman had to keep it in a cave, wrapped in a deerskin and placed in a clay jar and fed the blood of animals.

ESTEBAN CALDERÓN reread the story his cousins, Sancho and Ruiz, had written down during their visit with de Soto. A young Indian boy they had met told them the story. Esteban had said that it was a foolish story, the tale of a savage and backward people, but Sancho kept pushing the map at him and pointing at an X, tapping his finger on the place for emphasis.

"We heard this story again at another village. An old man knew where the cave was. He said his great-great-grandfather was the one who killed the Uktena. He showed us the cave in return for an ax and a knife. Don't you see, Esteban? Read the story! It's diamonds they are talking about. One large diamond and thousands of smaller ones. It's diamonds. Diamonds, Esteban. A king's ransom in diamonds."

"You know this?" Esteban had asked.

"Yes. They are waiting there in the cave."

"If these," Esteban had gestured at the diary with Ruiz's notes, "are so powerful to the Indians, why did the old man trade you the knowledge of the cave for a mere ax and a knife? Tell me that!"

"Because only the owner, the old man's great-great-grandfather, could go into the cave and use the crystal. After he died, no one could use it. That's what they believe."

"This is a map to the cave, Cousin," Ruiz had said. "It is very accurate. You know Sancho can draw a map that is so accurate you can find your way in the dark. Find the diamonds and bring them back."

ROBERTO UNDERSTOOD the language of some of the people visiting in the town of Chilhaxul, the large Indian village that welcomed traders from all over the land. As he wandered through the village, looking at the various wares to be traded, he met a few Indians from his adopted tribe. They were not from his village, however, for he didn't know them, but they had the same dress, same tattoo designs, and spoke the same language. Roberto discovered from them that the chiefs of several neighboring chiefdoms were traveling to Chilhaxul for a meeting called by Piaquay. Filled with apprehension, Roberto stationed himself outside the council house, pretending to be working on a piece of clothing for his master. He listened to the translator inside the house and discovered that the Indians were planning to attack the Spanish when they came to the village of Chilhaxul.

Roberto gazed around the village and realized that the women were readying themselves and the children to leave. They were placing dried food into leather bags, collecting the children who usually were out running and playing at this time, giving them things to carry.

The warriors would wait until the Spanish were settled in the village, sitting and talking to the chiefs before they attacked. They planned to kill the leader first, then the soldiers.

As much as Roberto wanted to kill Esteban, he could not allow his fellow Spaniards to be massacred. And truthfully, he admitted to himself, he did not want any more of the Indians he had lived with and who took care of him to die. However good their plan was, the superior weapons of the Spaniards would fell many of them. He had to do something. If he escaped to find Pardo and his men, he reasoned, Piaquay would come after him and probably kill him on the spot. But Roberto had an idea. He rose from his place by the council house and went in search of Cocunae, a young Indian trader who was from the same region as Roberto's adopted people.

He found Cocunae trading a sack filled with rose-colored chert to a brave in return for a sack of freshwater pearls. Cocunae had the chert spread on a piece of doeskin, showing the prospective buyer the fine quality of his wares. Yes, Roberto smiled to himself, Cocunae was the right choice. Traders were different from other Indians. Roberto thought it was for the same reason that explorers were different from others of his people. Traveling to exotic places, seeing different customs, he reasoned, made traders and explorers develop a different attitude about the world. It is often a larger view, one more receptive to possibilities. Roberto was counting on that being true with Cocunae. Because Cocunae was young and because he was a trader, perhaps Roberto could talk him into helping. When the brave left, Roberto sat down in front of the young trader. It would have been very bad manners to start the conversation before they got their clan alliances declared, so Roberto did not begin with his business.

"Do you know the Tuco clan of the town of Chichwee?" he said.

The youth nodded. "But not for a long time. My father's father is of that clan."

His father's father, *thought Roberto.* Cocunae is no relation to the Tucos then, because they recognized relatives only through their mother's side of the family. *Too bad; if he were a relative, that would have been easier. However, being a member of the clan of his father's father was not without some bargaining influence.*

"Most were taken by the sickness," said Roberto. "Tuco is my clan. My wife was a Daymah."

The young Indian nodded. "That is my people."

Roberto smiled. This was good. "I know how you can get a metal ax from the Spanish," he said, knowing that a Spanish ax was a valuable resource for the Indians. "Not only can you get a metal ax from them, but you can also send them away from this place."

"How?" Cocunae asked.

"The chiefs are planning a surprise attack on the Spaniards when they come to this village. You see the women and children already leaving." Roberto gestured across the village. "If the warriors attack, Spaniards will kill many warriors with

their metal axes and swords and the metal-reeds-that-shoot-fire-from-long-distances. Then they will hunt down the women and children and make them slaves. You, too. They will make you a slave, or kill you. Their weapons are too strong, but the chiefs do not understand this. It is better that the Spanish go away and leave everyone in peace.''

Cocunae listened patiently. The Indians were very patient people who both spoke at great length and listened well. If one was to communicate with them, one must do the same. Cocunae had not asked him what this had to do with him or how this knowledge would get him an ax. He assumed that Roberto would get around to it. He would only ask if Roberto failed to make it clear when he finished. Roberto knew all of this, so he spoke clearly and laid out all the nuances and alternatives of the situation.

''So,'' continued Roberto, ''you must ask to talk to Captain Pardo. Talk only to him. That is important. First, you must tell him that you have information that you will sell for an ax. That is the Spanish way and that is what he expects from someone who bargains with him. When he says yes, then you must tell him to avoid this place so they won't be attacked. If Pardo should ask you if you swear allegiance to the king and His Holiness, simply say yes. That is part of the Spanish ceremony. Then he will give you the ax.''

Roberto stopped speaking and waited for Cocunae to respond. Roberto did not hurry him or ask if he understood or try to further plead his case. He simply waited.

''I will go,'' Cocunae said finally. When these Indians made up their minds, they were brief.

ESTEBAN CALDERÓN pondered his cousins' story and their carefully drawn map as he lay on his cot at Fort San Marco, waiting for Pardo. He dug in his sack for the papers, carefully unrolled them, and reread the story and reexamined the map. He put his finger on the mark for Fort San Marco, where he was now, and traced the route to the X. It was not that far. When he was strong, he would take Diego and a couple of men and go to the cave. The Indians in this place were more friendly. He would be safe. Yes, he thought. He would go home a rich man.

Fort San Marco was a twenty-meter by twenty-meter enclosure made from tree trunks anchored into the ground. The Indians built two houses inside the fort—one for the soldiers and one for the officers. The houses were also built with walls of upright tree trunks woven with limbs and twigs and covered over with a thatch roof.

The Indians helping build the fort marveled to one another how the Spanish couldn't seem to do anything for themselves. The Indians had to build them houses and store up food for them. They speculated on what housed the Spanish where they came from, deciding they must have slaves who did everything for them. The irony that this fort they were helping build was designed to keep them and their kind under the control of the Spanish chief, whoever he was, was not lost on the Indians. What the Indians did not understand was how the Spanish planned to hold possession of the fort with only a few men after the main garrison left.

Esteban lay in a small open-front cell of a room inside the structure that was to house the officers. He was reasonably comfortable. His mouth was healed to a point that it was not quite so painful. He lay, making plans, thinking what reason he could give Pardo for another foray out into the wilderness. A mine, *he thought.* A mine for the Crown. *He would tell Pardo he had heard a story that was sufficiently credible that he felt compelled to check it out. Yes, that would work. He would tell him that his cousins had heard of this mine also when they had traveled with de Soto.*

Diamonds are much better, *he thought.* Much better. Gold is heavy. *He would have had a very difficult time taking gold home without anyone knowing.* But diamonds, there are many ways to hide diamonds.

"Diego tells me the Indians were very hostile," Juan Pardo said to Calderón. He sat down on the end of the cot to talk to Calderón.

"As you can see, he speaks true," said Calderón, as clearly as his damaged mouth and tongue would allow.

Pardo shook his head. "De Soto reported they were barbaric. I have found them more cooperative, but..." He gestured, leaving the thought unspoken, but hinting that perhaps he, more than either de Soto or Calderón, was suited to the task of dealing with the Indians.

"I fear I have not your skill," said Calderón, willing to put Pardo in a good mood if it helped his cause.

"Sometimes skill is lost on heathens," said Pardo magnanimously. He stroked his beard. "I am glad to have you back, Esteban, but I am disturbed by the desertion of so many good Spanish soldiers. I can't fathom why they would leave in the night—and with a horse. I have visions of an army riding aimlessly through these dark forests. What could they be thinking?"

"I don't know, my captain. I only know that many disappeared, deserted from camp during the night. We searched for Indians, thinking they were following us, picking us off one at a time, but we saw no evidence. No. I fear many of my men went mad."

"Curious," replied Pardo.

"It is my belief they will show up at Santa Elena with excuses or entreaties for forgiveness."

"I hope you are right."

"My captain," began Calderón. "I heard a story from a young Indian. It is one I have heard before from my cousins, Sancho and Ruiz, who traveled with de Soto." Calderón related the story he concocted, adding evidence of his invention as he went along. At the end, he made his request. "I will need only a few men. My old friend, Diego, and a couple of others. We will travel avoiding the towns. I believe I can find this mine for His Holiness and His Majesty."

"How far from here do you think it is?"

"A day and a half," answered Calderón.

"Do you think you are sufficiently recovered for such an undertaking?"

"I am recovered enough. I can finish healing at Santa Elena when our task out here is done."

Pardo consented. "Find this mine and catch up with us. Tomorrow we are traveling to a town called Chilhaxul. It is large, and they have an abundance of food, I'm told. Meet us there."

LINDSAY PUT THE SAFETY LOCK on her door and opened it to the width of the bar. "I'm surprised to see you here," she said to Craig Gillett.

"Can I come in? I'd like to talk with you," he said, curling his fingers around the door.

"I'll meet you in the coffee shop downstairs," Lindsay told him.

"What I have to say is private," he said.

"Then choose one of the tables in the rear. I'll be down in ten minutes."

"Look, Dr. Chamberlain, I haven't come here to hurt you."

"I'm glad to hear it. I'll meet you in the coffee shop in ten minutes."

He removed his hand and stepped back. "Very well. I'll see you down there."

Lindsay closed the door, put on her shoes, and ran a comb through her hair, wondering what he wanted and what it was about him that put her off.

He was waiting in the coffee shop in a rear corner booth. Lindsay sat down opposite him. A steaming cup of coffee already sat in front of her.

"I took the liberty of ordering you a cup of coffee," he said.

"I'm sorry, I've had my limit of caffeine today. But thanks for the thought."

"Aren't we just a little paranoid today?" he said.

"Mr. Gillett, I think you're taking things a little too personally. When I travel I have certain rules I always follow. One is never letting men I don't know into my room. And I always restrict my coffee drinking. It is you who are being a little paranoid." She pushed the coffee away from her.

He smiled tightly. "Perhaps you're right."

"What did you want to talk to me about?" she asked.

"Jennifer has been through a lot. She hasn't been able to get much peace from everything that has been going on in her life."

"And?"

"And I want you to stop this stupid investigation."

"There would seem to be little left to investigate. And as for Mrs. Darnell, I only spoke with her briefly over dinner, so she hasn't had to deal with me very much."

"Now that's naïve. She has to worry about what you are trying to do."

"I'm simply trying to find the truth. That should be a comfort, not a worry," said Lindsay.

The waitress came to take their orders. "Just coffee," said Gillett in a clipped tone that made the waitress take her leave. "The Lamberts and you seem to think Jennifer has not been touched by all these accusations. The authorities have asked her the same questions, had the same suspicions. She is not an insensitive woman. It has been very trying for her. It has to end sometime."

"Are you Jennifer's financial adviser?" asked Lindsay.

"What?" He seemed puzzled by the change of subject.

"She said she had a professional advising her about things like insurance. Is that you?" Lindsay asked again. Lindsay, looking into the face of this man with his charming white-toothed smile, thought that he would also have a motive to get rid of Ken Darnell, and he would be more capable of the task than Jennifer. They could be in it together, or she could be completely ignorant of his involvement. If there was an "it" to have been involved in. So far, she hadn't found any evidence that what happened to Ken was anything other than an accident.

"I have advised her on occasion," he said carefully.

"What is your business, exactly?" asked Lindsay.

"I buy sporting goods for teams."

"Teams?"

"I didn't come to be interrogated," he said, eyes narrowing.

"No. You come to interrogate me. However, since Jennifer was so cooperative, I thought perhaps you would be also."

"I am a liaison between foreign teams—baseball, soccer—and companies that sell equipment. I met Jennifer and Ken through a mutual friend of her late husband."

"I see. What did you think of Ken?" Lindsay asked.

"He was all right. Reckless—too reckless, as it turned out," he answered.

"Do you know of anyone who might have wanted to kill him?" asked Lindsay.

"No. I don't believe anyone wanted to or did. It was a tragic accident. These murder rumors are simply fueled by other people. I'm sure it's been hard on the Lamberts since Mrs. Lambert's brother disappeared. They want to blame someone. That's natural. Blaine Hillard's family is just plain greedy. Look, I only came here to ask you to drop this. There's nothing to find. It was an accident. If the authorities found nothing, why do you think you can?"

Lindsay said nothing. There was nothing she could say that wouldn't sound arrogant.

On the way back to her room, Lindsay got the envelopes from the motel safe. In her room she undressed, put on her robe, and stretched out on the bed with the photographs. She looked first at the ones of Blaine Hillard. There were pictures of the front and back of his skull, as well as his full skeleton laid out anatomically. On the whole, not bad, but she wished she had more. She wished she had the bones.

Most of the bones of Blaine Hillard were still articulated, as Lindsay would have expected. The skull still had a scalp of hair, not a full mass but fine wisps. Thin pieces of dry parchment skin were stretched over bone here and there. She took a hand lens from her purse and began a slow, careful examination of the bones in the photographs. The first thing she observed was that Blaine had his right ninth rib on backward, or rather, upside down. She smiled to herself. The skeleton of Blaine Hillard had two left ribs that were supposed to occupy the ninth position. One had been placed upside down to make it a right rib. The bones were commingled. This seemed to be a pretty obvious error. She wondered why it wasn't caught. Perhaps because the person identifying the bones was only interested in identity, since cause of death seemed fairly straightforward, or perhaps because the examiner was not a forensic specialist.

Starting at the first rib, she began examining them one by one. After finding one out-of-place bone, she couldn't be confident now that others weren't, so if she found anything, she might not know which person it belonged to.

Lindsay found nothing on the ribs except rows of parallel grooves, indicating the bones had been gnawed by rodents. She was mildly disappointed. Ribs are a good place to find evidence of knife and gunshot wounds. She examined the long bones and joints. Blaine Hillard's surgeon appeared competent. The repaired knee joint looked good.

After looking at everything she could on the bones that were visible, she turned her attention to the skull. The back of the head was crushed and most of the skin was gone on the lower part of the skull. Probably the falling debris from the cave-in had crushed the cranium, but she examined it closely several times with the lens. Abruptly, she stopped at an injury on the right upper part of the occipital. Just jutting out from a crushed portion of the skull was a depression fracture that looked to be hook-shaped. It could be part of the injury from the rock fall, or not. It was hard to see in the photograph. But it looked suspiciously like the depression that the end of a crowbar or a similar weapon would make.

Lindsay stared at the picture for several minutes, trying to find more clues around the site of the wound. She jumped when the telephone rang.

"Hello," she said into the phone.

"Lindsay Chamberlain?"

The voice was familiar. "Yes, this is Lindsay," she said.

"This is John West. I tried your car phone, then your house, then Susan Gitten. She gave me your motel number."

"I'm sorry you had to call so many places. What can I do for you?"

"Nothing. I need to tell you what I found in the back of my truck. I would have called sooner, but it didn't occur to me. Because of the land settlement, we have enemies we didn't have before, and I thought it was one of them. But I couldn't figure out how it got in the bed of my truck without making a hole anywhere. It was as if it had dropped from the air. Then I remembered your tire, the one I tossed into my truck, and I realized what it must be."

"What did you find?" she asked.

"A bullet. I believe someone shot your tire, Lindsay Chamberlain."

ELEVEN

LINDSAY DIDN'T SAY anything for a moment. She gripped the receiver and nervously glanced at the door to make sure she had locked it. "A bullet?" she whispered.

"I don't know that it came from your tire, but I don't know where else it could have come from. I went along the highway where you had the flat and looked for bullet casings or some other evidence. I found nothing."

"Who would have shot at me?"

"Who are your enemies?" he paused, then added, "Besides me. I don't kill my enemies; I take them to court. Or lecture them to death." Lindsay smiled. "Emily tells me you have had trouble with a man you convicted with your testimony?"

"Yes," Lindsay said, "that could be. His family is very angry. But—" She hesitated, then decided to confide in him, mostly because she was alone and he was on the other end of the phone. "At the next site I went to after I left you—a conquistador camp," she added, so he would know it was not an Indian site—"one of the crew was murdered."

He was silent a moment. "Hmmm. A coincidence?"

"I don't know." Lindsay told him about the Lamberts, about the skeleton in their field, about the cavers who were killed, and about what the Lamberts asked her to do.

"So, Rabbit, your curiosity's got you stuck to a tar-man." He chuckled. Lindsay knew he was not referring to the Joel Chandler Harris story, but to Indian lore from whence the story originated. "Sounds like you need greedy wolf to get you out," he said.

"Do you know one who'll take my place?"

"I know one who might cut you loose and let you walk away," he said.

He sounds like Derrick, thought Lindsay. "I have only one more person to talk to, then I'll be finished."

"I hope that's not prophetic."

"I didn't mean it exactly like that." She laughed. "Besides, if it is Denny Ferguson or his family, my walking away from this won't help."

"I talked to the FBI about the bullet," he said.

"FBI?" she asked.

"You were in the national forest when you had your accident. The FBI has jurisdiction. I don't know what they will do, but they know about it."

"Thank you."

"You're welcome. You're a high-maintenance kind of girl. Your boyfriend must have his hands full."

Lindsay didn't know if he was trying to make her mad, make her defend herself, or just take her mind off her fear. Perhaps all of the above. "He probably believes he does."

"Are you alone now at your motel?" he asked.

"Yes."

"Has anything happened while you have been in Cave City?" he asked.

Lindsay hesitated. Craig Gillett's coming to visit her would hardly be considered in the category of something that happened, but it felt like it, the way he looked at her with his dark eyes, the way he wanted to come into her room. There was something frightening about him. She hesitated a little too long and John spoke again.

"Something has happened."

"No, not really. Just the boyfriend of the prime suspect came to see me. I talked to him in the coffee shop. He just kind of gave me the creeps is all."

"Why do you do this?" he asked.

"I don't know. I just like the Lamberts and wanted to help them. I plan to talk to the guy who identified the skeletons, then give everything I have to the Lamberts and to the police."

"I would stick to that plan. Well, Little-Rabbit-who-digs-up-my-ancestors, I'll say goodnight. Keep your door locked. Do you have a pencil?''

''What? Yes.''

''Write down my phone number. If you need anything, give me a call.''

She wrote down the number John West gave her, thanked him again, and rang off. With the phone back on its cradle and the room silent, Lindsay felt very alone. Every footfall past her door made her edgy. She double-checked the lock on the door, then went to take a shower.

This is silly, she thought as she soaped herself. *The bullet may have come from somewhere else. It may have fallen out of something else he put in his truck, or someone may have shot at him and he just didn't see the bullet hole.* Then she thought about the rumors that had begun about her, the things that had happened at her house. A thought struck her like a bullet and she stood letting the warm wash over her. All the things that had happened were events that should make her want to go home—the attack on her reputation, the calls and visits to her home. Someone wanted to scare her into going home. If she didn't, what then? Would they escalate to something more dangerous? Was that what the bullet was, an escalation? What about poor dead Gil Harris? Where did he fit into this? Tomorrow she would call Agent McKinley and talk him into telling her what he had found at the crime scene.

Lindsay awoke to the ringing of the telephone. She looked at the clock—almost 1:30 in the morning. ''Hello,'' she said.

''Lindsay, sweetheart. Is everything all right over there?'' It was a voice filled with concern.

''Derrick? Yes, fine. Is everything okay with you?'' She was wide-awake now.

''Yes. I got an interesting call from someone who calls you Rabbit and thought you could use some comfort from someone close,'' he said.

''John West called you?'' she said.

''Yes. He had quite a time finding my number. He was

sufficiently worried about you that he went to Brian's site at midnight to get it,'' said Derrick.

"He told you about the bullet he found in his truck?'' she asked.

"Yes, and that you had a visitor who frightened you. Lindsay, I'm really worried about this.''

"I know, I'm sorry. I'm worried enough now that, after I tell the orthopedist who identified the bones that he commingled them, I'm leaving this alone. I've been shot before, and I didn't like it. I've done all I can do here anyway.''

"I'm glad to hear it. Do you want me to come over?''

"No. It's too far for you to drive tonight. I'll be fine. I'm sorry you're worried. It's not certain that the tire was shot, anyway.''

"Just don't do any more investigating. You have a lot of people who care about what happens to you.''

"John is just trying to get on my good side so I'll stop digging up his ancestors,'' she said.

"I'm glad he was concerned enough to track us both down. I don't like thinking about you alone in a motel room,'' he said.

"I'm fine. They have good locks on the door.''

"I love you, Lindsay. Take care of yourself.''

"I am. I love you, too.''

"Call if you need me.''

It took her a while to get back to sleep. She stared into the darkened room, dimly illuminated by the night-light in the bathroom. Her eyes focused on the lamp sitting on the left side of the dresser. It had been on the other side. She remembered thinking that it was in a bad place because it would interfere with opening the television cabinet to the right of the dresser. She hadn't moved it because she hadn't wanted to watch the TV. The maid? No. She remembered that it was there after the visit from the maid. But someone had moved the lamp. Why? To open the TV cabinet. Why? To search it. When? When she was out of the room. Lindsay thought about that. Thought about when she was out of her room and when she saw the lamp. It had to be when she was having dinner with Jennifer Darnell. But it could have been before that. She was in and out often. Lindsay got out of bed and checked to be sure she had locked her door and got back into bed. It was a while before she finally fell asleep wondering who had moved the lamp in her room.

ROBERTO'S SCHEME WORKED. *Pardo changed his plans and began his journey back to Santa Elena. Piaquay took the news well that the Spanish were not coming to Chilhaxul. If they were running away, then perhaps they would go home. That was all he wanted from them. But he did not surrender his plan of revenge on Calderón. The news that Calderón was planning an expedition of his own filled Piaquay with satisfaction. The news was brought to him by Cocunae, who did not mind pleasing both sides of harmony could be preserved and his own interests were maintained, and who also had learned early that information is as much a tradable commodity as deerskins.*

Cocunae told Piaquay the story of the Uktena. Piaquay knew it, of course, or rather, a variation of the story, but he listened patiently while the young trader unfolded his narration.

"So Calderón goes to find the cave where the Crest of the Uktena is kept?" said Piaquay when Cocunae had finished. Cocunae nodded.

"Then I will follow," said Piaquay.

SANCHO WAS A GOOD *mapmaker. Still, it was harder to find a small location such as an entrance to a cave than it might seem at first. Calderón was tired. So were the few men he took with him. Pardo had denied him horses. Calderón cursed him. It was not his fault so many of his men deserted him and took the horses. They were cowards.*

The mountains were cooler now—too cold at night. The trees grew so close together it was hard to travel through the forest. Calderón and his men thought they saw Indians at every step they took, but it was always a bird taking off from a limb or a deer running in the woods or a rabbit.

"Tell me again," asked Diego, "how Sancho was able to draw the map when he had never actually gone to the cave?"

"You doubt my cousin's map, mi amigo?*" said Calderón.*

"I don't doubt his skills. I am just curious," replied Diego.

"He explained it to me. He visited a village just beyond the ridge we are on now. It was there that they heard the story. He got the teller to take him near the place where the cave is, but he would go no farther. They are superstitious, you see."

"Yes, I see, but how—" Diego was impatient.

"The teller of the tale told him exactly where it is. Most everyone in the village knows. But they will not go there. We find the village, and we find the cave."

Diego was still skeptical. "Caves can be very large. How will we find the way?"

Esteban smiled. With his damaged face, his smile had a decidedly evil twist. "It will be marked." He said no more.

But Diego continued to question. He did not relish entering a village on foot with only Esteban and a few men and no way to send for reinforcements. "How friendly are the Indians there? Did he say?"

"Friendly. He said they are friendly. They think us Spanish to be gods," replied Esteban.

They came out of the woods into a clearing that was once a cornfield, from the looks of it, but it was overgrown with weeds and pine seedlings. Beyond the field was what was left of the village. The houses looked as though they had long since fallen in. Calderón and his men walked through the deserted Indian town. Only the sounds of birds could be heard. Here and there lay a broken pot. A torn, vermin-eaten basket blew across their path. The inhabitants were gone and had been for a very long time.

Calderón was disappointed, though he said nothing. He was counting on getting someone from the village to take him to the cave. Now he would simply have to locate it himself with his map, he thought as he sucked in his breath and mentally strengthened his resolve. He always had to depend on himself. Everyone around him was unreliable. This was nothing new.

"We'll stop here and eat. It's a good place to make a camp before we proceed. There are no savages here to bother us."

They found a fallen structure with its walls still standing and firmly set into the ground and cleared out a place to sit and built a fire. They took off their heavy armor and ate a meal of roasted corn and dried deer meat. It tasted good in the cool air.

"This isn't so bad," said Diego. "Nobody here to bother us, good food, a place to sleep." The others agreed. It wasn't so bad.

PIAQUAY, ROBERTO, Tesca, Nayahti, two braves, Quanche and Minque, and Kinua, the young warrior apprentice, stood looking at the place where Calderón had camped. The Spaniard and his men had given them a clear trail to follow. Even though they had several days' head start, Piaquay had gained on them every day.

"They will come back to this camp," said Roberto. "We could wait for them."

"No," said Piaquay, "we will follow."

After much shifting and meandering the trail ended at the mouth of a cave that was concealed under a profusion of vines and ferns. The clumsy passage of Calderón and his men was evident.

"This cave is taboo," said Tesca. "We will be bewitched if we go in here."

"This may not be the cave of the Uktena," said Piaquay. "I will go. The rest of you, stay and wait for me."

"No, brother, bewitched or no, I will go with you. The others can stand guard."

Nayahti gathered reeds and tied them together. In his travels he had experience in caves and knew how to make torches. "You will need many of these," he said. "When you use half of them, you must come back, whether or not you have found the enemy.'' He put the torches in the deerskin sack in which he carried food. ''Piaquay,'' he continued, ''mark your trail. It is easy to become lost in caves. If you do not come out by the time you should be out of torches, I will come and follow your marks.''

Piaquay smiled at his friend. Traders are always practical, *he thought. When Piaquay listened to Nayahti speak, it reminded him of his father's brother, also a trader, who told him many times, ''Keep your medicine bag, but sharpen your arrows.''*

''Be watchful,'' Piaquay told the others.

''I will go with you,'' said Roberto. Piaquay looked into his eyes. He had known Roberto would ask this. Revenge against Calderón burned in him, too. ''You can trust me,'' Roberto continued. ''I won't betray you. Only Calderón.''

''Very well. Come. But it will be hard. Caves are the trails to the underworld. They are always hard.''

LINDSAY AWOKE ABRUPTLY at 6:00 A.M. Her eyes went immediately to the lamp, as though it might have moved in the night. She got out of bed and turned on all the lights and began looking through her things to see if anything was missing. Nothing. Nor did she find anything else moved. Perhaps she just imagined—no, she had not, she knew that. She opened the cabinet and looked at the television. It sat there like a blind Cyclops, oblivious to anyone who might be staring at it. Nothing seemed amiss. She closed the doors.

What then? She was not missing money. She never traveled with jewelry. Her gaze fell on the envelopes with the photographs. It had to be them. They had been in the motel safe. If they had not, would they be gone? Her mind went to Craig Gillett and Jennifer Darnell. Could it have been him? Was that why Jennifer had been so cooperative, keeping Lindsay busy while her boyfriend searched her room?

Lindsay stood, contemplating the possibilities, when the phone rang. It was Derrick, checking on her. She decided to wait to tell him about someone being in her room. After all, she reasoned, she wasn't completely sure there had been anyone. It might have been the maid. That was the problem with everything about this case—the uncertainty. Were the cavers murdered or not? Did someone shoot at her or not? Was someone in her room or not? One thing was certain, however: Gil Harris was dead. And he knew at least one of the people who died in the cave. She hung up after assuring Derrick that, following her talk with Dr. Olin Ballinger, she would be off this case.

She looked at the photographs again. She saw nothing that she hadn't seen before. She got out the ones the Lamberts had given her, separating out the ones of the bodies where they were found in the cave. She scrutinized them with her hand lens. She could see nothing unusual, but the bodies were under rocks and were clothed. She looked at Ken Darnell, the only skeleton whose skull had rolled away from his body. He had been lying on his back, and when his head came loose from the neck, it rolled away, a common occurrence in skeletons. Then she saw it—it was staring her in the face. She looked at the neck, then the hands. Unlike the other two skeletons, Ken's hands were mostly disarticulated and there was hardly any skin left on the skull. The three bodies either had not decomposed in the same place or had decomposed at different rates. Why hadn't Dr. Ballinger mentioned that? Surely he'd noticed it. He must have.

Lindsay put the photographs back in the envelopes and got dressed in jeans and a shirt. She was sure she wouldn't be able to see Dr. Ballinger until after 9:00 at the earliest. She took the envelopes to the motel clerk and put them in the safe, then went to have breakfast. She planned on a leisurely breakfast to make up for all the nervous energy she had used up being frightened last night, then to return to her motel room, dress up in her suit, and go camp out on Ballinger's doorstep. Perhaps she should see the sheriff first. She would decide that over coffee.

Lindsay walked into the coffee shop and sat in a booth near

the window. When the waitress came, she ordered scrambled eggs, bacon, toast, and orange juice. She took a newspaper from the counter to read while she waited. She didn't wait long. In about ten minutes the waitress brought her order and a fresh cup of coffee. Lindsay lingered over each bite and sipped the coffee as she read the comics. She finished and looked at her watch. It was only 8:30. She paid her bill and left the coffee shop.

As she walked across the lobby past the schefflera plant and past the door to the parking garage, the door burst open and two men jerked a hood over her head, held her mouth, dragged her out the door, and shoved her into a vehicle. Lindsay kicked, tried to scream, but couldn't. She tried to bite the hand that held her mouth, but couldn't. The air under the hood was suffocating, and the fabric tasted awful. It wasn't until she heard the car door close that one of the men cursed. She thought she recognized his voice, but he was yelling. Lindsay continued fighting, then felt something hard, like a rod or a gun, push against her head.

"Now stop fighting, or I'll blow your brains out here and now," a voice whispered.

Lindsay stopped kicking. "Who are you?"

"It'll be easier on everyone if you don't know," he said.

"What are you going to do?"

"Just take you to someone who wants to talk to you, so calm down. We'll take you there, you'll have your talk, we'll bring you back. You won't have seen our faces, so we can let you go. It's as simple as that, so just relax."

Lindsay did, but in order to think. She didn't believe him. Everything she had ever heard about attackers said they lie; they want you to cooperate so they will tell you anything. But she didn't know what to do. Think. They didn't have her tied. Why? It would be easier for them to tie her, so they must have a reason not to have done it. No rope? If they had gotten a sack to put over her head, they could have gotten a rope. No ligature marks? There would be bruises. But maybe bruises that could not be accounted for in an accident?

She was in a van. She deduced that from the sound of a sliding door closing and the fact that there seemed to be a lot of room. *A van. Who owns a van? Archaeology students? Damn, anyone can own a van.* She didn't remember anyone involved in the investigation who owned one. Any of them could; certainly Jennifer Darnell could. She owned a store. It would have a van.

But she was thinking about the wrong things. Knowing who it was wouldn't help her get away, and getting away was her first priority. She couldn't count on anyone having seen her abduction. She thought about snatching her hood off and making a run for the door, the driver, or a window. Window—there probably were no windows in the back of the van. Truthfully, she was afraid of getting shot. She had been shot before by a kidnapper, and she didn't want it to happen again. *Damn, shouldn't there be a limit to the number of times a person can get kidnapped in a lifetime?*

"What do they want to talk to me about?" she asked.

The question seemed to surprise her captor. She thought she felt him jump. He was not accustomed to this. Was that good or bad? Maybe that meant it would be harder for them to be cold blooded.

"You'll find out. Just keep quiet."

They turned off the road, and the highway noises were gone. There were a lot of turns, but this was a mountainous area, and almost any road off the main highway was winding. But that was good. She knew wooded areas. If she could get away from them, she knew how to find her way out of almost any woods. Lindsay tried to think of things in her favor, things that would make her more optimistic. Then she wondered if maybe she should have made a run for it when they were in traffic. Now they were in a less populated area, and she heard fewer and fewer cars.

"Don't think about making a break for it," the man whispered, as though he had been reading her mind. "You must be thinking about it. I would be. But don't. We don't want to shoot you, but we will."

They don't want to shoot me because they don't want a bullet hole in me, she thought. She would wait until she was outside to pull the hood off her head and make a run for it. Yes, that is what she could do. Lindsay was a good runner and she knew woodcraft. She felt better with a plan. A line from *Tremors,* one of her favorite movies, ran through her head: "Running's not a plan. Running's what you do when a plan fails." She almost laughed. She was getting giddy. Was it the lack of oxygen or the natural progression of the psychology of her circumstances? *Sorry, Earl,* she thought, *running's the only plan I got.*

The van stopped. She felt the gun at the back of her head. She heard the driver's door open, then the side door slid open and someone climbed in. She was grabbed by both arms and hauled out of the van. The ground she walked on was soft, like a wooded area. She felt brush against her legs and heard the soft crunch of forest litter. She was trying to decide when to make her move, but both men held her tight. Maybe someone did just want to talk to her. *No!* she thought sternly to herself. *Don't believe the lie.* She kicked the leg of the captor whom she thought had the gun. He yelled and let go of her arm. She struggled with the other one. He wrapped his arms around her, pinning both her arms against her.

"Stop it," he whispered. "Don't make this any harder than it is. He told you he didn't want to shoot you. Now stop."

Lindsay stopped. When he relaxed his grip she ran free while trying to get the sack off her head. She pulled it off just in time to avoid a tree. She ran as fast as she could, but the man caught up with her and tackled her to the ground. She could see the entrance to a cave like a yawning mouth before her. Boards had been torn from the entrance and thrown aside. There was no doubt in her mind which cave this was. She saw one of her captors carrying a backpack. He was dressed in coveralls from a window-cleaning company, and he had a ski mask over his face. She thought of Denny Ferguson. The man also had latex gloves on his hands. The other man, the one holding her pinned to the ground was probably disguised the same way. They were not even going to let her know who was killing her. She struggled, but the man was too heavy on top of her.

"Come help me," he yelled. "She's damn strong."

The man dropped the backpack to the ground and came over. He wore hiking boots. She flinched, ready for him to kick her in the face, but he didn't. He put the gun against her temple.

"Get up. No more trouble or we'll end it here."

She rose. The other man helped her up while telling her to put her hands behind her head and lace her fingers. She complied. The first man held a gun on her while the other one got the backpack. He was dressed exactly like the first one. They could have been identical twins for all she could tell.

They marched her into the cave. It was damp, earthy smelling, and very cool. "Put on this backpack." They handed it to her and again she complied.

"Now keep going." They prodded her and turned on flashlights.

Lindsay understood their plan now. While investigating the cave where the accident happened, she would have a tragic accident herself. She would be found with caving equipment, and there would be no unexplained bruises if she was found before she decomposed. It would be as tidy as the last one was supposed to be. John West was right. She was stuck on a tar-man, and no wolf would be along that she could entice to take her place.

They walked through a short corridor into a chamber with rubble piled here and there and against the walls, away from the center. It smelled musty and damp. This was the place it happened last time. One of the men, the one without the gun, walked over to retrieve some equipment stashed behind rocks. The other set his flashlight down and dug in his pocket with his free hand. Lindsay was standing between the two men. With one rapid motion she reached and grabbed the flashlight and swung it hard, hitting the man on the temple. The other one turned and started for her. She ran through an opening deeper into the cave. Suddenly, after a few slippery feet she was sliding down a slick surface. It was like a water slide with a thin sheet of water. Instinctively, she clutched the flashlight. She slid for an eternity, the walls of the cave a mere kaleidoscopic flicker as the light of the flashlight illuminated her passage like a strobe. Then she was in the air, but only for a second. She hit something, slid farther for several moments, then rolled off onto the ground, rolled again, and stopped. She lay there, numb, afraid to move. There was no sound but her heart beating furiously in her ears. The flashlight was still on, and she moved the light around the chamber. She saw a beautiful cascade of stalactites with stalagmites growing up to meet them. The long water slide was like a lava flow. She couldn't see the top, even with the light. She heard a mild explosion and a vibration. After several moments, debris came sliding down the flow. Lindsay realized they had sealed the entrance to the cave.

TWELVE

IT WAS DARK, pitch black except for the small circle of light produced by the flashlight reflecting off the ground and a distant wall. Lindsay stood up on shaky legs. She could stand. Her legs weren't broken. She took a couple of steps. They weren't sprained, but she limped slightly from sore joints. Lucky. She set the flashlight down and felt her arms and sides. Her clothes were torn. She felt numb in places, but she believed she was unhurt. She took the flashlight and looked around the chamber, more methodically this time. The walls curved upward to form the domed ceiling. Roughly twenty by twenty, the chamber was like a cathedral—alien and beautiful.

She walked to the base of the flowstone. *This must be the Hell Slide,* she thought. Aptly named. She shone her light toward the top of the slide again, but couldn't see it because of the way the flow curved. She traced the light down the slide and caught her breath. The slide was interrupted partway down by a gap, an abyss. The chasm was a few feet across and the slide started again. That must have been when she was airborne. As if on skis, she had leaped across the crevasse and slid to the center of the earth.

Lindsay felt a heaviness on her back and realized she was still wearing the backpack. She took it off, opened the flaps, and began taking inventory of what was in it. There was a trowel—her own trowel—and three nutri-bars, also her own. When did they get her trowel and her nutri-bars? There were batteries—batteries, she hadn't thought about batteries. She looked at the flashlight as if it might treacherously go out at any minute. She would have to conserve the batteries. No light. No life. She clutched it and turned off the switch and was plunged into absolute darkness. She looked around her for anything, any pinpoint of light anywhere, any reflection, any shining thing. Nothing. She wondered if blind people were in this kind of darkness. The darkness was like a thing itself, substantial, smothering. Her situation hit her like a solid object slamming her body, knocking the wind from her, catching her throat. She was lost in a way few people are ever lost, buried alive in the bowels of the earth, and no one knew where she was—no one, that is, who wanted her found.

"Oh, God," she choked, "please, don't let this be true." She started to cry—a desperate, frightened crying that echoed throughout the cave. If her crying were heard by anything, it would have sounded like a dreadful mourning of a lost spirit. Lindsay cried as she had never cried before, a gut-wrenching sobbing that made her stomach heave. Never had she been this frightened or felt this hopeless or been this lost.

She lay in the dark for a long time, hiccuping from her crying, pain creeping into her body, replacing the numbness. She thought of Derrick, wishing he would come to her rescue. She thought of her family, never to know what had happened to her, their lives ruined by her disappearance. Then she thought of Harley Davidson.

Harley, her seventh-grade boyfriend—her first boyfriend—had been named by parents who loved motorcycles and had spent a big part of their youth on one. He had not been her parents' choice of a boyfriend for her, but Lindsay had liked him.

Unlike his parents, Harley didn't like motorcycles. His passion was caves. He loved caving. Mammoth Cave was his favorite place in the world. He talked to Lindsay all the time about caves and caving. She learned from his friends that he was a pretty good caver.

There was a place he'd had to show her: a cavern covered in gypsum blossoms—white crystal florets made when water seeps into the dry passages and evaporates, leaving behind the deposit of gypsum. It was beautiful. They'd had to drop into the cavern using a rope, but it had been worth it. Harley had been good with the rope, she remembered. He'd also brought a couple of friends to stay outside and wait for them. Harley had always said that caves are safe if people are safe.

When they'd returned to the surface, their parents had been waiting for them. Lindsay had never seen her mother and father so angry. Neither had spoken to her on the way home. That event prompted her father to tell her that a life with Harley was not what they were raising her for and that she had to stop seeing him. Her mother, often sympathetic to Lindsay in disagreements with her father, was not sympathetic on the matter of Harley Davidson. They argued, but in the end Lindsay had done what she always did—obeyed her parents. But for a month, every evening when her father came home, he had been greeted with the song "Leader of the Pack," a song about a girl whose father made her stop seeing her motorcyclist boyfriend. Despondent, he had a wreck and was killed rather dramatically. After a month Lindsay's father had asked her to please stop, that someday she would thank him. She'd told him she would never thank him, but that she would stop playing the song. Harley had grown up to be a lawyer and was currently running for the state senate in Kentucky. Lindsay had framed the announcement when she had seen it and sent it to her father.

Now, Lindsay wished she had paid closer attention to Harley when he'd talked about caves, which he had done so incessantly that often she hadn't paid attention to what he said, but simply listened to his voice. She tried recalling his voice now.

She sat up and turned on her flashlight. She continued the inventory of things she had with her. There was a pencil and paper, a tape measure—all belonging to her. Her kidnappers had packed some aluminum foil, a waterproof case with matches, candles, an extra bulb for the flashlight, and a magnifying glass—she wondered what that was for. The cache cheered her. There were a lot of useful items. She thought of Clay talking about how Jennifer Darnell planned things as if they were actually going to be carried out. That was Jennifer's genius. Lindsay wondered if this was her work. Were they going to kill her, crush her skull, and place her in the cave? Make it look as if she had gone there to investigate and some of the debris fell on her and killed her? Tragic. But then what was an amateur doing in a dangerous cave where experts had been killed? Foolish girl. But at least she had taken the right caving things with her.

Anger washed over her, momentarily covering the fear. She turned her attention back to the inventory. There was fishing line and her own pocketknife. They had taken several things from her motel room after all, and from her Rover as well. Lindsay knew what most of the things were to be used for; she remembered Harley talking about them. She remembered him getting things ready for their foray into Feather Cave. Whoever had prepared her death backpack was a caver.

Many caves had several entrances; this one would, too, she told herself. Lindsay took off her belt and threaded it through the handle of the flashlight. She buckled and further secured the belt by tying fishing line through the buckle and one of the belt holes. She couldn't afford to lose the light. She put the belt over her head and around her shoulder so that she carried the flashlight more or less under her arm.

"Okay," she said to herself. "That will work." Her own voice sounded strange to her ears. Too breathy, too shaky. *Be calm,* she told herself. Her hands shook as she worked.

She repacked the backpack and put it on, securing the straps around her waist. She looked at her watch. It was broken. She almost started to cry again.

"No," she said aloud. "I'll get out of this. I will. The watch is not important."

She started by shining the light on the ground around her. She examined the slide again, looking for a way up the flowstone. It was steep and slick. The chasm she had flown across was too wide to jump. She walked carefully to the wall of the chamber, watching where her feet would go on each step. Caves have a lot of drop-offs, Harley had told her. She made her way carefully along the circumference of the chamber, looking for a way out. She was almost in despair again when she found the entrance to a large opening. It was across a chasm, but it was damp and probably slippery. If she fell here, she would become wedged between the narrow walls of the crevice, where she would die—suffocate from slipping deeper between the narrow walls or from dehydration and despair. The prospect terrified her. *I can't,* she thought. *Oh, God, I can't.*

She thought of the famous death of Floyd Collins in a Kentucky cave. It was a horrific story that everyone in Kentucky knew. It happened in 1927, but even small children could tell you the story today. A newspaper reporter had crawled near the spot where Floyd was wedged, and the whole nation had watched through his newspaper reports the sad and lonely death that took days. But she wouldn't be another Floyd Collins. There was no one here to see her die.

She raked her fingers through her hair. "What am I going to do? Damn, what am I going to do?" She heard the words echoing in the cave and realized she had said them aloud.

What if I get across to the opening and it's a dead end? Then what? She said this silently to herself.

Lindsay shone her light into the opening. It looked like a passageway. The walls were limestone, scalloped with small, scale-shaped indentations. Lindsay tried to remember her geology. Small scallops, fast water. The passage was narrow. That fit also. Narrow passages, fast water. This passage had been shaped by fast water flowing through it. Then did that mean it was probably not a dead end? Yes. She remembered now. The steep side of the scallops were upstream. The steep side was away from her. That meant the water flowed in her direction. That also meant that the passage went up. Didn't it? She couldn't tell from her vantage point, but she was filled with hope. If she could find passages that led up, she would find a way out.

It wasn't a far jump across the chasm, she told herself. *Just do it. If you're going to get out of here, you're going to have to be confident and unhesitant. Don't look down.* She looked down. She thought about becoming wedged between the narrow walls of the crevasse. Already she was suffocating. She couldn't do it. Again she examined the walls of the cave for another, more accessible, opening. She found herself back at the one hole that she could find leading from the cavern.

"You have to do it." The voice echoed in the chamber again, like some spirit, not herself. "You have to do it. Dear God, please help me," she prayed. She stepped back and leaped, landing hard, falling forward, catching herself with another step and slipping. She fell again, but not hard. *Oh no, the light.* What if she had broken the light? She pressed the switch off, then on. The beam of light reflected off the wall. *Be more careful,* she told herself. *Be more careful.*

The passageway was narrow and gently curved. It did go upward. She felt confident. She was moving, going up. She turned a curve and was again slapped with desperation. The way was blocked by breakdown, huge boulders fallen from a collapsed ceiling. She nervously examined the ceiling above her head. It looked stable. She looked again at the boulders blocking her path and tears stung her eyes. She wanted to sink to her knees. Instead she shone the light around the breakdown and the walls of the passage.

She found one small opening to her right. Her flashlight revealed a rocky passage that led downward at a very steep angle farther into the depths of the earth. Tears dropped on her cheeks. Her head hurt. Should she go back, she wondered, and look for another opening? What if she had missed a different passage? It was so dark, she could have missed a passage hidden behind a stalagmite, or breakdown or—

"No," she whispered. These emotional ups and downs and insecurities could end her life as surely as the hazards in the cave. If she was going to save herself, she was going to have to reach some equilibrium within herself. She sat down and turned off the flashlight.

The darkness engulfed her like a thick, suffocating blanket. She closed her eyes. She fought the panic rising in her by thinking about how people in other desperate life-threatening situations had survived. How, in the most dire circumstances, the most hostile environments, people had survived. The Eskimo, the African bushmen, the Indians of Terra del Fuego—even Bruno Bettelheim in Dachau. People who lived and survived in the most severe circumstances had one major characteristic in common; she knew that. They learned and understood their environment to an extraordinarily high degree, and they faced their fate with courage.

The path might lead downward for a while, but she would find a passage that led up to the surface. She would bring to the front of her mind any knowledge she had learned from Harley or her geology classes that would help. She would be alert for dangers or signs that an opening to the outside was near, like pack rats that live in caves but have to get to the surface for food. She would do these things, and she would get out of this cave, and when she did, she would find whoever put her here and… She turned on the flashlight, took a deep breath, and started down the yawning throat of the passage.

CALDERÓN LIT HIS TORCH and stepped into the entrance to the cave, motioning for the others to do the same. Finally, *he thought. Finally he was on the brink of getting the riches he deserved.*

They entered into an underground room and quickly found the one passageway that led off of it. Calderón searched the walls for the sign that his cousins had told him he would find. But there was so much wall, and the light was so dim. There! There was the mark, carved into the wall. It was true, then. There was treasure here! He was at the right place. He rubbed the symbol with his fingers as if by touching it, it would tell him more.

"This is it," he said. "This is the way."

It has to be, *thought Diego.* It is the only way. *He was, after all these years, becoming weary of his old friend. Perhaps he was getting old and simply wanted to go home. Perhaps he wearied of Esteban because he knew that he would not share the treasure—much of it anyway. Diego, of course, expressed none of his thoughts. He simply followed Esteban Calderón down the passage.*

PIAQUAY, TESCA, and Roberto lit their torches and entered the cave. The first chamber was small and littered with rocks. Footsteps in the fine dirt led to a winding narrow passageway that sloped gently downward. It is so winding, *thought Piaquay.* This must be the path where the serpents slithered out of the underworld. *He listened for the conquistadores, but heard no sounds except his own footfalls. He stopped and listened again.* Quiet. *It was then that he saw carved into the rock the shape of a hand with an eye in the center. The symbol of the ability to see into the future. Were the devils following this sign? Did they know of it?* Yes, *he answered himself. There were many willing to trade these devils information for the hard metal axes and knives they carried.*

The passage suddenly opened onto a large cavern with a vaulted ceiling. Piaquay looked up and thought he saw the stars. He blinked and looked again.

"The sky?" asked Roberto to no one in particular. "No, some kind of shining stones." What a place is this, *he thought to himself.*

After what seemed like several leagues the passage forked. Piaquay knelt, holding his torch over the ground, looking for tracks or some kind of disturbance that marked recent passage. The cave floor was rocky, but he saw arrangements of pebbles that indicated shuffling feet had passed. He examined the walls of the entrance to the passage. Again, the sign. They were following the sign. He led the way down a steep passage strewn with large boulders. The way was more difficult. They had to weave around the large stones, squeezing between some and climbing over others. His torch burned low, and he stopped and lit another one, then proceeded, listening, always listening. His heart beat faster at the thought of avenging the deaths of those he loved and removing these evil demons from his land.

The rocky passage opened into a cavern so large their

torches lit only a short distance. It was colder here. Wind blew from somewhere. Another entrance? Carried on the wind he heard a cry. He listened. Was it the demons he followed or something else, or simply his own imagination?

"We must split up here and follow the walls to look for a passage," he said.

It was Roberto who found the opening. Piaquay checked for the mark before he led the way into yet another twisted passage. We are getting close, *thought Piaquay, as he followed the winding route to the room of the snake.*

The passageway Esteban Calderón followed terminated at a great stone. In the flickering light of his torch he saw an ancient carving of a serpent with wings, horns, and what looked like rays coming from a large crystal in the middle of its forehead. Calderón's heart raced as he stood before the stone. He touched the engraving, tracing it with his fingers.

"This is it," he whispered. "This is it. Move it, move the stone." He held the torches as his men gathered around the stone and pushed. It was heavy. "Harder," ordered Calderón, "harder."

The men grunted and groaned as they pushed on the heavy boulder.

"It's no use," said Diego, but just then the stone shifted.

"It's moving. It's moving. Push harder. Put your backs into it."

The stone moved little by little, revealing a dark opening.

LINDSAY THOUGHT that she had been climbing downward for hours. She wished her watch hadn't broken. She knew that with no objective markers the passage of time could be deceiving. Her legs ached. Her head felt as if it was in a vise. She tried to think of nothing but each step as she picked her way through the rubble. With some footsteps, rubble loosened and boulders lid down the passage. When that happened, she stood still and prayed. Surely this shaft wouldn't go down forever. When she reached the end of it, she would reward herself with a piece of the nutri-bar in her pack. She was thirsty. Water, she hadn't thought of water. Surely, there would be water somewhere. Maybe she would find an underground stream or pond. But maybe it was a dry cave and she would die of thirst, maybe the batteries would run out, maybe... She stepped on a rock and started another slide.

"Oh, please," she whispered. "I'll pay attention, I promise."

The sliding stopped and she continued. Just ahead, the tunnel curved. As she reached the curve she realized that it wasn't as steep. Suddenly she stepped out of the narrow sloping passage into a large chamber. She sighed with relief. Rest. She would rest here.

She shone her flashlight around the chamber. It was huge, bigger than an airplane hangar. In fact, the entire Atlanta airport would have fit. *There could be a hundred passages leading from this room,* she thought with dismay. *Don't think about that now,* she told herself. *Rest.* She walked a distance from the shaft she had emerged from to get past the rubble that had accumulated in front of it. She sat down on a large boulder, breathing heavily. She was dead tired. The batteries. She switched off the light. Darkness. It continued to surprise her how utterly black dark could be.

Lindsay took off her backpack, then switched on the light again. She pulled out a candle, matches, and a piece of the aluminum foil. She put the foil around the candle to catch the melting wax and stood it up by supporting it with rocks. She lit the candle and turned off the flashlight. There was a surprising amount of light, and it shone all around on the rocks and floor, not just forward like the beam from the flashlight. It was comforting. She unwrapped one of the nutri-bars and broke off a fourth of it. She took a small bite and chewed slowly, savoring it.

She could use the candle in some of the passages. It would save the batteries. That was a joyful thought. Lindsay finished the allotment of food and rewrapped the rest, tucking it safely in the backpack. She was exhausted. She wondered if she should try to sleep. How long had it been since she became lost? An hour? Two hours? Three? A day, even? In a place where nothing moved, no daylight, no shadows, it was hard to tell how fast time was passing. No, no sleep now. It was better to make as much progress as she could while she was still in good condition. She still had to locate water. And she was at a much lower level than when she entered the cave. She had to find a way up. She stood up and put on her backpack. She would travel close to the wall so that she could look for a passage and take the first one that led up. This would get her out. Always go up. Then she had a thought. This is a mountainous area. There might be an entrance to the cave at a lower level. Of course, how stupid of her. Any tunnel might be a way out. Which one? *No,* she thought. *Don't confuse yourself. Going up is a good plan.* She needed a rational plan or she would just be wandering around in the cave. She took the candle and walked from the center of the chamber to the rocky wall. It seemed like a long distance. She watched for signs that animals had been here, but saw none. There were more signs of life on the moon, she thought.

Lindsay found a passageway quickly. It led upward to a dead end. She retraced her steps and followed the wall until she found another passage. She used the candle to light the way. She wound her way through the tunnel and emerged into another large room as big as the one she left, from the looks of it. She switched on her flashlight and shone it around. She let the light linger on several rock formations that looked familiar. It was the same room. She had circled about and gone nowhere. All that time and energy wasted! She used the flashlight to try to find another passage, shining it along and up and down the wall. She walked a long way, looking. Nothing. She shone the light behind her and out into the cavern. She had a sense she had reached the other side of the room and was going along the opposite wall. Like space curving back on itself. At this rate, she would be back to the steep tunnel she had descended from. She felt as though she was in the far reaches of space, cut off from time and humanity. But the terrible reality was that time did pass; her body felt the effects of gravity, stress, and the lack of water, and it would get worse as time went on. *Don't think about that,* she chided herself. *Push on.*

She came to another tunnel. It occurred to her that she should have been marking her trail in some way, that she should have been making a map of her travel through the cave. *Mark it how? Smoke. Smoke from the candle.* She would mark her progress with an X in smoke. Her next rest stop she would draw a map as nearly as she could remember, but she had no idea how to judge distance. Harley enjoyed mapping the caves he explored. She wished he had taught her how.

Lindsay smoked a large X beside the opening and entered the passage. It was a wide tunnel that led upward. *This is good,* she thought. The candle was burning low, and she thought she could make better time now with the flashlight. She constantly swept the beam of light from the floor to the walls and, when she thought of it, to the ceiling. Caves are three-dimensional. It was like traveling in space—the path she needed to take could be up or down, as well as left or right.

Lindsay walked at a comfortable pace for what seemed like miles. She didn't know how long. She wondered if she could fix the watch. She desperately needed a sense of time. If only she could make the hour hand work, that would help. She was thirsty. She wondered if people really drank their urine to conserve water in their bodies. The thought repulsed her. That was good; maybe she wasn't that desperate yet. Surely, she would find water soon. She didn't think she could pee, anyway. She stopped abruptly.

There was a choice to be made. Three separate passages opened up before her. *Damn,* she thought. She didn't want to have to make a choice; she wanted to be lost in a linear cave. She shone her light into each tunnel and took the one that had the steepest angle up. Go up, that was her plan; always go up.

She walked only a few feet when she came to a ninety-degree turn and another choice of three. Again she took the high road. Again and again she was met by choices of either two or three ways to go. She was in a maze. "No, please, no," she whispered. "Don't make this so hard." She wanted to sink down and cry. Maybe she should sleep now, she thought. Maybe with a good hour's sleep she would feel better. Sleep on what? The hard cave floor? That would make her feel great when she awakened. Instead, she lit a candle and smoked an arrow on the wall of each passage she took. She needed a compass. Why couldn't her kidnappers have given her a compass in the pack? *Don't cavers carry them? Damn them, damn them.*

She came to a passage that went on for several hundred feet with no turns, no choices. Maybe she was out of the maze. Harley had said something about mazes. *What? What?* She couldn't remember. "You have to know what kind of cave it is in order to explore it safely," he had said. "The arrangement of the passages depends a lot on how the cave was formed." Great, what type was this? *Chemical dissolution.* Like a neon sign, it flashed in her head from a long ago geology class. Caves formed through chemical dissolution had almost all types of passage structures. Impossible to predict, at least for her. Would nothing break her way? Lindsay came to an abrupt stop. The floor of the cave disappeared just in front of her. She shone the flashlight into the void. It might have been the Grand Canyon. A dome pit, a vertical shaft that went up and down, stretched out before her. It was so big she couldn't see the other side. She couldn't even see the bottom. She threw a rock over the edge and listened and counted, but she never heard it hit. She shone the light above her. She saw no ceiling. She stepped back, sank to the floor, and cried.

THIRTEEN

"HURRY," SHOUTED CALDERÓN. "Hurry!" The men cursed and pushed the stone. It slowly ground aside, unblocking the opening. "Stop!" he said. "I can fit through. Stop!"

Gladly the men stopped pushing on the huge boulder and stepped back, leery of the gaping black hole revealed by the shifted stone. Calderón, however, was not so timid. He rushed through the opening and fell into a chamber below, dropping all but one torch.

Calderón stood up, holding the torch out so he could see. At first he saw nothing. He stepped farther into the chamber and, suddenly he saw a myriad of tiny reflections of his flickering torchlight. "It's here! It's here!" he shrieked. "Thousands of diamonds! Thousands!" His exclamation brought the others rushing into the chamber with their torches.

The additional light revealed pots of sparkling gems sitting on a stone slab that resembled a stage. In the center stood a large earthen jar incised with the winged serpent. The men sucked in their breath. Calderón approached the treasure, his eyes flashing with excitement. He was thinking about how he could keep all of it. His eyes shifted from the pots filled with gems to the tall jar.

"This is where the large stone is," he said.

He took out his sword and broke the jar. A large bundle of deer hide fell to the floor. Calderón rushed to it and began cutting through the leather straps that held it together. "Bueno Dios," *he exclaimed as the unfolded hide revealed a large faceted crystal as clear as cleanest water. "Look, look Diego." He held it up for him to see.*

Diego, however, was not looking at Calderón. He held his torch over one of the jars of gems and ran his fingers through them. "Está cuarzo, necio! *It's only quartz. Not diamonds.*

Quartz!" He threw a handful and they scattered over the floor of the cave.

"What are you doing?" cried Calderón.

The other men examined the crystals. "Diego's right. They're not diamonds at all. They're worthless," said one of the soldiers, spitting on them.

"Fools!" cried Calderón, "Don't you think I can see through your scheme? You want them for yourselves. But they are mine." Calderón was barely intelligible with his damaged mouth and his excitement.

"You are an idiot!" Diego cried. "Why I have followed you this long, I don't know. You can have these worthless pieces of glass if you want them. I'm leaving this place and making my way back to Santa Elena."

"Go, then, go! I can carry these myself."

As Diego turned to go, he felt a pain in his leg. He looked down, puzzled at the arrow sticking out of his thigh. The soldier beside him was felled with another arrow. Diego looked up and saw two Indians, bowstrings drawn back to their ears. Arrows flew through both of the other soldiers and through Diego. He lay on the floor, his sword lying too far away. His harquebus and matchcord were outside the chamber by the stone. He heard Calderón screaming.

"No, no! Get out of here! You won't take my treasure!"

Diego saw Roberto walk through the entrance behind the Indians. So the old madman was right all along. Roberto was in with the Indians.

Calderón was backed up against the wall, holding the crystal to his bosom. "Roberto, I knew you had survived. So you, too, want this treasure?"

"This is no treasure, you fool. Don't you know quartz when you see it? No, I don't come to take anything from you but your life, like you tried to take mine."

"What?"

Piaquay and his brother listened. Piaquay intended to allow Roberto his say before he finished the devil Calderón.

"It took me a long time." Roberto rapped his head with his knuckles. "But I finally figured it out. You sent your cous-

ins, Sancho and Ruiz, to kill me so you could marry my Cristina."

"No, I—I'll share, I'll share the diamonds."

"There are no diamonds." Roberto picked up Diego's sword and advanced on Calderón, who stubbornly clutched his "diamond" and slid his back against the wall of the cave trying to get away from him. Roberto raised his sword. Calderón cringed. The sword hung in the air, ready to strike. Piaquay looked at Roberto.

"I can't," said Roberto. "There is no satisfaction in killing a madman." He dropped the sword to his side.

Piaquay took an arrow, raised his bow, and pulled back the string in one fluid motion. He did not hesitate to shoot into Calderón's breast. Piaquay turned as his enemy sank to the floor.

"Come," he said to Roberto.

"Where is the other one?" asked Tesca.

Piaquay looked to the spot where Diego had lain wounded, but was now gone.

"Diego," said Roberto. "Where did he go?"

As LINDSAY CRIED, she wondered how much water she was losing through her tears. Mingled with the sound of her own sobs, she heard another sound, easing into her mind. She didn't know why she hadn't heard it sooner. The cave had been so silent, but there was now a white sound in the background. *What?* She listened. *Water?* Was it water? Lindsay rose and walked to the edge of the gorge. She listened and shone the light where she thought she heard the noise. She saw glittering flashes in the beam. It was water flowing from a hole in the wall of the cave, and it fell—fell to who knows where in the darkness below.

It was a small waterfall. But a trickle would be all she needed to drink from. It was to the right, she guessed, about thirty feet. Just above the fall, about twenty more feet, was a wide opening. Lindsay could see the scalloping inside the walls of the opening where water once flowed long ago.

The wall of the cavern was rocky and almost vertical. A

rock climber could climb it. The thought came unbidden into her head. A rock climber would have no problem climbing it. She was not a rock climber, but she was strong. Lindsay made it a point to be strong. Archaeology was tough, hard work. But if she fell, she would fall into the rocky shaft and die, or maybe just fall to—where?

Lindsay didn't want to die. She didn't want Derrick and her parents to always wonder what had happened to her. She wanted to get married and have a family one day. She wanted to find whoever did this to her. She wanted to yell at her parents for making her break up with Harley. She wanted to live.

She was still in good shape, she reasoned. Tired, but in good overall shape. As time went on, she would deteriorate, become weaker, dehydrated, disoriented. She was also losing body heat. It was only a matter of time until she developed hypothermia in the coolness of the cave. She couldn't go back and start over. She had to do what she could to save herself while she still had strength, while she still had light from her flashlight. A rock climber could make the climb, but she had never done that kind of thing before.

Lindsay stepped back into the cave. She took off her backpack and sat with her back against the wall. She fished for the rest of her nutri-bar and ate it slowly, thinking.

There are enough handholds and footholds.

But what if they are unstable?

I will fall.

What if I can't make it up the side of the shaft?

It's not that far, no more than fifty feet altogether. A rock climber could make it.

But what if I can't?

I can climb down. Down must be easier than up.

But down is longer and deeper into the earth.

There will be passages along the way.

What if I just can't?

I can't stay here forever. I can't start over. I can't backtrack.

Why?

I just can't.

Lindsay closed her eyes, then snapped them open. *No. Don't do that. Don't close your eyes, you'll fall asleep. Do what you have to do now, or don't.* Lindsay rose and slung her backpack over her neck and shoulder. Cavers preferred to carry their packs by their side. She remembered that now. It could get caught if it was carried on her back.

She walked to the edge, again staring into the void. *Just do it. Do it. Do it. Don't think about it, do it. Please help me decide. Please help me do it.*

She took a deep breath. Her light hung around her neck and under her arm, and she could aim it where she needed it. She had become good at that. She would need both her hands for climbing. She would manage. She could do it. It was possible for a human to do this. She remembered a story she'd heard in graduate school about a geology student camped near a volcano. The volcano erupted unexpectedly. It was later calculated that in order to outrun the lava flow to safety he would have to make it in world-class time. He was not even a runner. He made it. Humans can do superhuman things when they have to save their lives. She could do this.

Lindsay turned her back to the void and slowly put her foot on the first rock along the precipice.

PIAQUAY SHONE THE TORCH around the entrance and walked out to the passage. He saw neither Diego nor his torchlight. But Diego couldn't have gotten far. Piaquay's torchlight showed dark stains on the ground. The Spaniard was bleeding. Piaquay followed the stains. Roberto and Tesca followed him. They reached the large cavern of a room and saw the glow of a torch behind a pile of rocks.

Roberto saw the silhouette first, the long rod of the harquebus resting on a rock. "Duck!" he shouted and pushed Piaquay just as a blast of light flashed and a deafening sound erupted.

The noise echoed throughout the chamber. Then another sound came like thunder rolling in the distance. First, there was a groan, then a cracking sound, and suddenly rocks, dirt, and boulders were falling from above. Roberto thought he heard a scream, but wasn't sure. He held on to his torch and tried to get as close to the cave wall as he could. The dust choked him and stung his eyes. It seemed like an eternity before the noise stopped. Then there was utter silence. Roberto lifted his torch. Dust hung in the air like a dense fog. He felt a hand on his shoulder.

"Are you injured?" asked Piaquay.

"I don't know. I don't think so," answered Roberto.

"Tesca!" shouted Piaquay. He was answered by a groan. Piaquay picked up his burning torch from the cave floor and followed the sound. Tesca was half buried under large boulders. He had been shot in the chest. Piaquay knelt beside him and held his head. Roberto knelt and crossed himself.

"Go," whispered Tesca. His voice was raspy and weak.

"I won't leave you," said Piaquay.

"Dying."

"I won't leave your body here."

"You have to. You live. Is my wish, my brother. Old coyote got his way...closed the door on me... You leave."

"I will not leave you here to die alone." He stroked his brother's brow. Tesca's breathing slowed until each breath seemed like the last. Finally his body went limp.

"Help me pull him out," said Piaquay, laying his torch on a rock and taking his brother under the arms.

"You can't get him out," said Roberto.

"I won't leave him here."

"You must." Roberto laid a hand on Piaquay's shoulder.

Piaquay shook it off. "Take the rocks off him."

"There are too many, and they are too heavy. Please, my friend, honor his last wish."

Piaquay struggled with his brother, then tried to remove the rocks himself. It was an impossible task. Roberto watched helplessly, then tried to get him to stop.

"You will tire yourself and won't be able to get out of the cave."

Piaquay ignored him.

Roberto picked up the torch and went to examine the pas-

sage they had used into the cave. He found Diego first. Only his hand was visible from under the pile of rubble.

"Old devil," he whispered.

"We have to get out of here," he shouted, turning and racing back to Piaquay, who stood looking down at his brother's lifeless body. "We have to get out of here. There might be another cave-in. Please, let's find a way out."

Piaquay looked at him a moment as if he did not understand him. "The way is blocked?" he asked at last.

"Yes."

"I thought there was a wind in here when we entered. There must be two openings. Perhaps there is another way out." Roberto thought that Piaquay seemed very calm. Roberto wanted to scream at him. Piaquay examined the collapsed entrance.

"You are right. We cannot leave by this way. I'll get the other torches," said Piaquay. "There will be another way out."

Piaquay found the sack of torches and slung it over his back with his bow and arrows. He and Roberto examined the chamber. There was another passage. Piaquay took his torch and made a circular pattern of smoke at the opening to the tunnel.

"Why are you marking the passage?" asked Roberto. "Nayahti can't possibly come after us. The way is blocked."

"This is for the spirit of my brother. He will recognize the sun and know it is us. He will follow," Piaquay said.

The passage was the same kind of sinuous, pockmarked passage as the ones they had come through. Maybe it will lead to the surface, thought Roberto. He was almost sick with the fear that rose from his belly and stung his throat.

The passageway terminated at a black pit. Piaquay tore off a piece of Roberto's shirt, lit it, and dropped it over the side of the pit. They saw only a flash of light reflected from the rock bottom before the torch went out. Piaquay held out his torch, looking at the edges of the pit. It wasn't wide, and there was a ledge that led to the other side.

"We can go here," he said.

"No," said Roberto. "I can't."

"You will go or you stay," said Piaquay calmly.

"No, I can't."

"Then stay." Piaquay started to step out onto the ledge.

"Please," Roberto pleaded. "Please don't leave me here. I would cross the ledge if I could, but I'm afraid."

Piaquay looked into Roberto's eyes. Eyes of the enemy, but of one who had saved his life and one who had suffered as much by the hands of his own people as Piaquay had; one who had taught him the language of the Spanish, and one whom he had traveled with for a long time.

"I will not leave you. What is it you fear?"

"Falling."

"Don't fall."

Roberto almost laughed. He guessed it was that simple for Piaquay. "A fear does not have to be reasonable. It is just there. I could not work on the masts of ships because I was afraid of the height."

"If I held on to you, would you be afraid?"

"If I fell, so would you."

"Neither of us will fall if you do what I say." Piaquay held out his hand. "The ledge is wide. Don't look down, and ask your God to make you forget that there is a pit. See only a road." Roberto took a deep breath and listened to Piaquay's voice. "It is the only way out. Can you feel a breeze on your face?"

"No."

"I can. Come." He took Roberto's hand and stepped out onto the ledge. "Keep your eyes on the passage across the way. Hold the wall with your other hand. Walk behind me."

Piaquay led him as if leading a child. Roberto inched along, shuffling, barely lifting his feet. They reached the passage, but the opening was high, almost out of reach.

"I'm going to let go of your hand," Piaquay said. "Stand there and don't take your eyes off the opening. It's freedom. And don't close your eyes, or you will lose your balance."

Piaquay hopped up to the opening in an easy leap. He turned and held a hand out to Roberto. Roberto eased over to him and took his hand. Piaquay pulled as Roberto climbed up into the passageway. He scrambled away from the opening and collapsed with his back to the wall, breathing heavily.

"See how easy it was?" said Piaquay.

Roberto closed his eyes and fingered his beads. "Ave Marie, gratia plena, Dominus tecum..." *he whispered.*

"Come," said Piaquay. "We must leave this place."

Roberto followed Piaquay down the passage. He did not feel this breeze that Piaquay felt or understand why he went in the direction he went or follow the passages he did. He wondered briefly if the deaths of Piaquay's family were driving him mad. Perhaps he, Roberto, was a little mad, too. He had thought revenge against Calderón would make everything right. Perhaps it would have meant more if Calderón hadn't been insane. But Cristina was still lost to him—lost forever. He realized that now. He could have no life with her. No family. What would she say of his stretched earlobes, his exotic tattoos? What could he do in Spain? He followed along after Piaquay, sad and very lonely. There was nowhere he belonged now. He had no home.

FOURTEEN

LINDSAY CLUNG TO the wall of the void, close to panic. She wanted to look back, to go back, but she couldn't maneuver the flashlight. She was committed. No turning back. Thirty feet to the water. Forty to the passage. Thirty feet. Just thirty feet. But she didn't have to go to the water. She had to go to the passage. *Yes, the passage. How many feet? More than ten, less than twenty. What is it? Something like sine of alpha equals—equals what—"a" over the hypotenuse. Is that it? So, how far is it? I must be going insane, trying to do higher mathematics while suspended over a void. It doesn't matter how far it is, I have to do it.*

Don't think about falling. Don't think about being tired. Think of the method. Shine the light to look for a foothold for the left foot. Try it carefully. Lift yourself up. Feel for a hold for the right foot. Try it carefully. Reach up to find the handholds. Move diagonally up toward the passage. Move on the hypotenuse. $a^2+b^2=c^2$. *That's it.* She could do that in her head. *What is the square root of 2500?* She placed her foot on a narrow jutting rock. It slipped. The surge of fear was like an electric shock. She groped for another foothold and held tightly to the rocks with her hands and fingers. *Pay attention.* She found a firm toehold and slowly lifted herself. Her muscles strained. Her hands hurt. This was hard; too hard. *Fifty feet—the hypotenuse is fifty feet. Pay attention or you will die. Left foot, right foot, left hand, right hand. Do it, do it. Wait.* She stopped her climb. The water was loud and distracting. What if the stones were slippery near the water? *Feel the holds before you commit,* she told herself. *You can do this.*

Despite Lindsay's efforts to climb in a diagonal toward the passage, she climbed more or less up. She reached to find a hold with her left hand. It slipped, scraping her nails and the tips of her fingers. Her hand hurt. She shook it and reached again for another hold. She climbed up two more feet. She was almost level with the passage. Adrenaline rushed through her body. She put a foot on a rock and put her weight on it. It slipped. Her body banged against the wall, almost knocking the breath out of her. She hung by both hands, sick with fear, trying to catch her breath, searching for footholds. Her fingers were numb.

She found a solid place for her left foot, then her right, and just stayed there, afraid to move. *It's not that far now. What if the passage is a dead end? No. Don't think about that. Just climb.* She searched for hand- and footholds to the left of her toward the passage, inching her way, straining her muscles.

There it was, almost within reach. She reached for the ledge of the passage, groping for precious footholds. *Don't go too fast now,* she chided herself. *Don't make a mistake now; you are almost there.* She pulled herself up to the ledge and hung by her elbows and forearms as she pushed with her toes. The rocks were slippery. She pulled herself and climbed and finally crawled into the passage. Relief came like a drugged high. She lay in the passage, catching her breath. Slowly she stood and shone her light down the passage. It was open. Small, but open. She thought she would faint from the joy.

Water. Now for the water. She had had an idea while she was perched out on the wall above the water. A clever idea. She fashioned a cup from a piece of aluminum foil. She fished in her pocket for her handkerchief. Great Aunt Maggie thought all well-bred women should carry handkerchiefs, not tissue, and she kept Lindsay well supplied. Lindsay thought it quaint and rarely used them, but often carried one in her pocket anyway. She took fishing line from the backpack and tied it to the handkerchief. She lay on her stomach at the edge of the opening and lowered the handkerchief down into the running water, then hauled it up and wrung the water into the foil cup. *Clever,* she thought. She sipped the water, holding it in her dry mouth, delighting in its sheer wetness. It was cool, tasteless, and refreshing—the way water should be. It was heavenly. She lowered the handkerchief several times until she collected a cupful, took out a nutri-bar, and ate half of it while sipping water. A feast. A reward.

Lindsay leaned back against the stone wall of the passage and closed her eyes.

PIAQUAY AND ROBERTO came to two tunnels. The choices were not good. Both were small and littered with rubble.

"This way," said Piaquay.

"Are you sure we can get through?" said Roberto.

"Yes. Come." Piaquay marked the passage.

Roberto felt sorry for Piaquay. He knew the loss of his brother must hurt him deeply. The marking of the tunnels to show the way for his dead brother's spirit seemed so melancholy. Roberto wanted to comfort Piaquay, show him his deep appreciation for not leaving him in the cave to die. Roberto had seen the compassion in Piaquay's eyes, a sight he would never have thought possible. But other than convincing his countrymen to go home and telling the French and the English to stay away—that the land across the ocean belonged to another people—Roberto could do nothing for him. So he followed in silence.

The way was difficult. The passage was a narrow tunnel. It had a steep incline and was strewn with loose rock that shifted with every step. In some locations they could only move forward on their bellies.

"There's an opening ahead," said Piaquay.

He hurried through and dropped to the floor in a large cavern. Just then the rocks began to shift and fall.

Roberto screamed. "I'm stuck!" he yelled.

Piaquay leaned the lit torch by the wall and climbed back into the passage. He grabbed Roberto by the arms and pulled hard while scrambling backward. Roberto yelled, partly from fear, partly from being pulled over the jagged rocks. He tumbled out onto the floor of the cave.

"Thank you, my friend. That is the second time you saved me. I will say a special prayer for you."

Roberto hurt from head to foot. He saw that Piaquay, who was mostly naked, was cut and bleeding. He wondered if any of the cuts were on the elaborate tattoos, then wondered why that came to his mind at a time like this.

"Are you injured?" asked Piaquay.

"Yes. No. I don't know. Let's keep going. I can walk, and I want to get out of this place," he said.

The torch was burning low, and Piaquay lit another one. It was the last. They continued onward.

Roberto saw the filtered light first and yelled, ran toward it, and fell on his knees in the daylight outside the cave.

"You have done it, mi amigo,*" he said. "You found the way out."*

Piaquay looked at the crystal he held in his hand. "It was the powerful scale of the Uktena," he said softly.

"What? What was?" Roberto looked at him, puzzled.

"This is the scale of the Uktena. Not as powerful as the crest, but the crest could only be used by the owner. The scales, however..." He dropped the crystal into a pouch.

"You mean you were following that damn crystal to get us out of the cave?" Roberto stood facing Piaquay, balling his hand into a fist.

"Of course. How else could we know the way?"

"I thought you knew where you were going! I followed you because I thought you knew what you were doing!"

"I have never been in the cave. How could I know the way out?"

"I don't know. I thought it was a talent that Indians have, like your ability to track."

"We learn how to track from our mothers' brothers. They don't teach us how to travel through caves."

"But a crystal! We might not have gotten out! We could still be wandering around in that cave!"

"But we are not. We are here. And now we must find Nayahti and Kinua. We are finished with Calderón. I can go home."

Roberto raised his eyes to heaven as he and Piaquay went in search of their comrades—Nayahti the trader, and Kinua the apprentice warrior, and the braves Quanche and Minque.

They had to walk two hours to find them, taking a trail to the village and backtracking to the cave.

"We are relieved," said Nayahti when he saw them. "Kinua and I heard the thunder in the mountain. We went in the cave to look for you and the way was blocked. Where is Tesca?" Piaquay gave Nayahti and Kinua a long narration of the events in the cave. Roberto shifted impatiently throughout the story, understanding it mostly because he knew what had happened.

"So the devils are dead?" said Nayahti.

"They are dead, and the others are retreating back to their village on the coast, but I learn as I talk to Roberto that the devils across the water have many clans that fight over what the others have. I fear that more will come."

Piaquay turned to Roberto. "You are welcome to come and live with us."

Roberto looked at him, wondering if the Indian had some sense that allowed him to see his doubts about returning to his people in Spain.

"I'll walk with you for a ways, if I may, and decide what to do on the journey. Right now I'm very tired."

LINDSAY JERKED AWAKE. She felt panic, but didn't know why at first. Then she saw her flashlight. It was on. She had been asleep. *Oh, God, how long have I been asleep? Please don't let the batteries be dying.* She lit a candle from her bag and turned off the flashlight. *How could I do that when I've been through so much? How could I leave the flashlight burning?*

In the glow of the candlelight and with trembling hands she made preparations to continue her journey. There was no way she could carry water. The best she could do was wet the handkerchief again and carefully wrap it in the aluminum foil, creasing the edges tight. She put it gently in one of the side pockets of her backpack.

The way through the tunnel was tight. She had to crawl on her hands and knees most of the way. Her legs cramped as she tried to stoop and walk and keep her knees off the rocky floor of the cave. The passage was narrowing the farther along she went. She tried not to worry about that. She tried to keep focused on going forward. The passage made a sharp incline upward. Although it was hard traveling, it gave Lindsay a sense of optimism. Abruptly, with the next step, her head peeked out into a chamber and, like a little mouse, she scrambled out a small hole onto the floor of a large room. The hole she emerged from was next to a wall cluttered with breakdown.

Lindsay turned on her flashlight and extinguished her candle. To her horror, the light flickered and went out.

"Oh, no. Oh, no. Oh, no," she whispered. "Please, God, no."

She sat on the floor and fumbled in the darkness with her pack, found the matches, and relit the candle. *What now? Batteries, I have extra batteries,* she remembered with relief. She grabbed them out of the pack and opened the back of the flashlight. They were the wrong size. Her heart sank. She started to cry.

Maybe it's the bulb. She found the extra bulb and unscrewed the front of the flashlight case and then the bulb. The new bulb fit. She screwed the cap back on the flashlight and pressed the button. The light came on brightly. She sighed with relief and quickly gathered the things back into her pack.

Lindsay shone the light around the chamber. It looked like many she had been in and was about as large as her house back in Georgia. She walked, shining the light, looking for a passage, and came to a large pile of breakdown. The beam from her light rested on a hand.

It startled her at first, but she saw immediately that it was mummified. She kneeled, examining it with her light. It looked like a male hand. That was all she could tell. Caught in a cave-in, she thought. She didn't tarry. She rose and began looking for a passage. She saw an opening on the other side of the chamber. She almost ran to it. She had to hurry. She had no idea how long the batteries would last.

As she approached the entrance, the beam rested on a head. She flinched, then walked over to it. The dryness of the cave had mummified the body. It was that of another male who had been caught in the cave-in. It lower half was covered in rubble. She knew from the earspools and tattoos that this was an Indian. The skin under the tattoos was better preserved. Lindsay put the age to be the Mississippian period. *Odd,* she thought, *I didn't think that the Mississippians used caves.* Then she realized this was the first fleshed-out Mississippian Indian she had ever seen. She wished she had a camera. The Indian once had a head of long hair. There were still many locks left. His chest was damaged. She examined it with the beam. *Rodents? No, the gnawing would have been more extensive. He was shot,* she thought. Lindsay looked back over toward the other body. She couldn't afford to tarry, as interesting as the puzzle was. She hurried through the passage. *Slow down,* she said to herself. *I can't slow down. I don't know how long the batteries will last.*

She did slow to a comfortable walk. Suddenly she was brought up short when her beam rested on a large engraving of a winged serpent. It was very similar to the many she had seen carved on shell and copper gorgets. This one, however, was about three feet long and about two feet tall and was carved into a large stone. Beside the stone was another opening. She gave the carving a brief look as she passed and ducked into the cave. She found more mummies. Two lay close together and had pieces of wood protruding from them—arrows. They were dressed in smooth dome-shaped crested helmets and fabric clothing. She recognized the helmets as sixteenth-century Spanish conquistadores! Neither wore armor, she noted. One was shot through the neck, the other in the side and in the leg. Two oval shields stood against the wall. The remains of burned torches lay near their hands. Their swords were still sheathed. She was in the midst of the archaeological find of the New World! And lost.

Farther ahead in the small room was another body, dressed like a conquistador, with his back against the wall. His arms clutched something to his breast. Lindsay gently moved the mummified fingers and revealed a large quartz crystal. The unfortunate man had been killed by an arrow to the chest.

The man was surrounded by pots filled with quartz crystals.

She picked up one and stuffed it into her pocket. *I'm a pothunter,* she thought. A large broken clay vessel lay amid what looked like the remains of a hide of some sort. It reminded her of something, maybe some story. She couldn't remember.

It looked like the conquistadores had been caught stealing. Lindsay wished she had the leisure to investigate further, but she had to get out. She looked for an opening, but there was none. She had to backtrack out to the cavern. What if the room was sealed? What if she had come to a dead end? What if her end was here with this dead Mississippian Indian and the Spanish conquistadores? Ironic end for a southeastern archaeologist.

No, she wouldn't think like that. She went out to the main cavern and searched for an opening, shining her light over the walls. She found one, not large, but it was an opening. She walked through it, ducking her head, then backed out, shining the light around the entrance. There was a round dark smudge about the height of her head. She touched it with her fingers, then rubbed it. A faint gray soot came off on the tips of her fingers.

"Smoke," she said aloud, but didn't linger. She went back through the passage. It was small, with the now familiar scallops and tight curves indicating the fast passage of water. It was not a long passage and ended at a pit.

"Oh, no," she said aloud. "Not another canyon. I can't do it. I can't."

She almost collapsed, defeated. She was so tired. She very carefully took out the foil she had wrapped her wet handkerchief in, opened an end, and carefully squeezed a few drops of water into her mouth. It was so good. She wanted to drink more. Instead she resealed the foil and put it back into the pocket of the backpack. She picked up the flashlight and looked at the canyon.

It was a pit. It didn't rise as high as the gigantic shaft she had already climbed, and it wasn't as deep. Moreover, there was a ledge wide enough to cross and a tunnel almost on the other side of the pit. Lindsay took a deep breath and stepped out onto the ledge. It wasn't nearly as scary as the last one.

She walked slowly and carefully to the other side. Near the entrance to the passage was the same round patch she had seen before, smoked onto the rock. *The passage is marked.* Lindsay clapped her hand to her mouth. *The way out is marked.*

Don't get too excited, she told herself. *It could be only these two or it could mean something else entirely.* But she couldn't suppress the optimism, and she enjoyed the feeling. Lindsay entered the passage recharged. It was similar to the last and sloped gently upward. Before long she came to a choice. She could continue to go forward, off to the left, or to the right. She shone her light around the entrance to each opening. There it was. The sign on the passage to the left. She walked onward, almost racing, ignoring aching muscles and hurting joints, stinging cuts and scrapes. Lindsay stumbled a few times, but caught herself before she fell. *Slow down. Don't make a mistake this late. You've come too far.*

She was in a maze again, she realized, but each passage was marked. She hardly considered any other passages. Briefly, she had a panicked thought that perhaps the marks were leading to something deeper into the cave, but she had to believe that it was a way out, or she would simply lie down and die right here.

Lindsay was skeptical of the last choice. The passage looked smaller, but it was marked and she took it. Rocks frequently rolled out from under her, and she almost fell several times, catching herself with her hands. Her hands had never been so sore.

She came to a place where she could go no farther. The way was too small. Lindsay screamed in frustration, clutched a rock, and threw it through the opening. "This isn't fair," she cried. "This isn't fair."

She took her flashlight and examined the opening. It was small. Very small. If she took off her pack, she might be able to fit. How would she get it through? She couldn't leave her pack, and if she put it through first, she might not be able to get it back. She took out the fishing line again and tied it to the backpack. She also took off the belt with the flashlight and belted it to the pack. She wrapped the fishing line around her hand and pushed the pack ahead of her. She crawled after it.

The fit was too tight. She couldn't do it. But she could almost do it. She pulled the pack back to her and examined the wall of the opening again, trying to see if there were any rocks she could move without dislodging everything. There were none. This was the opening. She had to fit through it. She thought of the scene where Mammy was fitting Scarlett into her corset to give her a seventeen-inch waist. That was what she needed to be—just a little thinner. *How do I get thinner?* She took off her shirt and pants and stuffed them in her backpack. The light showed a cavern just beyond the Squeeze. *Damn, just a few inches.* She pushed the backpack through, and it went flying out the other side. She had forgotten to wrap the fishing line around her hand.

Lindsay had to get through or die here. She squeezed into the hole, her arms in front of her. It was still too tight. She curled up her legs and pushed. She was stuck. This was it. This would be how it ended. She could barely breathe because there was no room. Then she exhaled all her breath, pushed with her legs, and clawed with her arms. She inched forward. She was dying for a breath of air. But she was in too tight. She couldn't expand her lungs to take in a breath. She panicked. She pushed with her legs again with all the strength she had left in her body and propelled herself forward. Her chest was past the tight spot. She lay still for a moment, gulping in air, trying to calm herself. She could see the beam from the flashlight. Her head was out of the tunnel.

Lindsay pulled with her arms and tumbled down a short embankment in the dark to the hard cave floor. She shifted to her hands and knees, breathing hard, raspy breaths. She stayed there, on her hands and knees, unable to move, not so much from pain as indecision. She was so tired, so tired. She reached for her pack and the flashlight and got her clothes. As she was putting on her jeans, she noticed that she had no panties. She was too tired to see if she could reach them in the cave. Someone would just have to find them in later years and guess what they were doing there.

Lindsay picked up her things and started walking. Several passages led off the cavern. She looked for one with the markings. It was still there. The way was still marked. She walked on, stopping once to take a drink and eat a nutri-bar. She continued, following the markings through passages, breakdown rooms, and through other small places, though none as tight as the Squeeze. As she reached a large oval passage, her flashlight flickered and went out. She shook it. Nothing. She turned it off and on. Nothing. It was dead. "No!" she cried. "Why is this damn cave so big?" She fumbled in her backpack for the candle and matches. It was then that her dark-adapted eyes saw that the cave was no longer pitch black, but gray. She rubbed her eyes and looked around her. In the distance she saw the sun coming over a rise. She seemed to be standing in a road lined with rocks. Had she finally gone mad? Had she died in the Squeeze? She stood there, shielding her eyes from the light that was getting brighter. Then she heard voices. First muted, then higher pitched.

"Look, over there, who is that?"

Lindsay slumped to the ground. She was too tired to be relieved. She sat in the middle of the road and waited.

"How the heck did you get in here?" said a male voice. "Don't you know this is off-limits except for tours?"

What? What kind of tour? thought Lindsay. *Who would go on a tour like this?*

"Don't you know caves are dangerous?" said the voice. *Yes, I do know that,* she thought.

"Just what are you doing here?"

"She's hurt." This was a female. She heard other voices. Someone shone a light in her eyes. It hurt. She shielded them. "Stop that," said the kind voice. "Can't you see her eyes are photosensitive? She needs help. Can you walk? We saw you standing a moment ago."

For some reason Lindsay was having trouble forming answers. She thought she could walk. She tried to stand. She had run out of adrenaline. She was cold.

"Hell, she ain't but a little bit of a thing. I'll carry her." This was yet another voice. "It ain't that far to the entrance."

Lindsay felt herself lifted and conveyed. She didn't protest. She tried to say thanks, but the words didn't come. Or perhaps they did, for the man said, "You're welcome, little lady."

The sunlight was painful. Someone handed Lindsay a pair of sunglasses. "You're about as scraped up as anybody I've ever seen," said the voice who carried her. She looked toward the sound and saw a giant of a man in khaki shorts, a yellow T-shirt, and a beard. He had two children and a woman gathered around him. Lindsay assumed them to be his family.

"Thank you," she said again. "Can I have a drink?"

"Someone give her some water." An order from someone.

"What you need is Gatorade, little lady. Rachael, give the lady some of your drink."

Rachael dug into a bag as large as she was and came out with a bottle of a green-colored drink and handed it to the man. He unscrewed the cap and handed it to Lindsay. She drank half the bottle before she stopped.

"Now, we need answers to some questions." Lindsay looked up at a thin young man in a T-shirt that said: Cumberland Caverns. "Just how did you get into the Caverns?"

"What time is it? What day?" Lindsay asked.

"Uh, it's 10:00, Tuesday morning."

"Ten A.M. Tuesday," she repeated. The math wasn't hard to do. She had been in the cave about twenty-two hours.

"Now just what are you doing here and how did you get in?"

"I came in through Hell Slide Cave."

"Now, that isn't true. You're mixed up. Cumberland Caverns doesn't connect up to Hell Slide Cave."

"Why is it called Hell Slide Cave?" asked a child.

"Nevertheless. I am here. And that is where I entered."

"Maybe she found a route," said the man who carried her.

"No. The only cave that connects to Cumberland Caverns is Henshaw Cave. None of the other caves connect. You must have slipped through the Henshaw Cave entrance."

"No. I came through Hell Slide."

"Maybe she came through the Grand Serpentine." This was from the kind woman who had helped her in the cave. She handed Lindsay a cold paper towel to wipe her face. "It is close to the caverns, and many people have thought that there is a connection."

Lindsay shook her head.

"Why is it called the Grand Serpentine?" asked the kid, who Lindsay now saw was a boy of about seven.

"Because the passages are all curvy like a snake crawling," his father said, making a serpentine motion with his arm.

"It's not the Grand Serpentine," said Lindsay. "It's *grande serpiente.*" She had just had a flash of insight, of all things, about the name of the cave.

"Is she delirious?" asked a woman whose voice she hadn't heard before. "Shouldn't we get her to a doctor?" It was the wife of the man who had carried her, whose name she thought was Rachael.

"It's Spanish for 'large snake.' The Spanish named it, probably after something the Indians named it, and the name became corrupted."

"How do you know?" asked the first kind woman, who also wore a Cumberland Caverns T-shirt.

"I just know," she answered.

"Look, lady," said the angry young man, "whoever you are. You can't just come into Cumberland Caverns and walk around without a guide. What were you doing in there? You didn't mess anything up, did you?"

Lindsay looked at him for a moment. He was younger than she had first observed, perhaps twenty. He had blond curly hair and blue eyes. Girls probably considered him handsome. Lindsay thought him callow. She wondered if that meant she was getting old.

"My name is Lindsay Chamberlain. Dr. Lindsay Chamberlain. I am a forensic archaeologist, and I did not willingly go into Hell Slide Cave, but was kidnapped and left there to die. I am quite cross about it, as I have just spent the last twenty-two hours trying to get out. I am very tired. I must look like hell, and I want to talk to the police."

FIFTEEN

THE FIRST SHERIFF wasn't much help. Since Lindsay claimed to have been deposited by her abductors in Hell Slide Cave, it came under the jurisdiction of Ellis County, where she was kidnapped. The sheriff of Ellis County wasn't in town, and Lindsay had to make her complaint to a deputy.

"You can't tell us anything about the men?"

"Only what I have told you."

"And you don't think it is this Denny Ferguson or his kin?" asked the deputy. "Now why is that?"

"Because of the way I was treated while kidnapped. It was not vindictive. It was detached, almost professional."

"You think maybe you are just being nice. You know, you may have gotten that Stockholm syndrome that some kidnap victims get."

"Deputy, I was in their hands all of about twenty minutes, and we had little interaction. Stockholm syndrome takes a little longer. I'm attempting to describe to you my observations, and I happen to be particularly good at observations. I'll write up a report, sign it, and give it to you. Do with it what you will, according to how professionally you see your job." She rose and left the office, stopping outside to lean against the building, shaking with anger. She must look like a homeless person, she thought. She had gone straight to the police. The tour guides had given her a Cumberland Caverns T-shirt. That was the only thing clean she had on.

"Are you going to be okay?" asked Laura, the female tour guide who had driven her to the police and waited outside for her.

"Yes. I'm fine. Would you take me to my motel?"

"Sure."

Her Rover was still parked in front of her motel. It was a

welcome sight, a piece of home, familiar. She had no keys, however, to get into her room.

"Do you want me to stay and help?" asked Laura.

Lindsay smiled at her. "That's very kind, but no. I just want to get some sleep."

Lindsay went to the desk. A cheery clerk was on duty, one she hadn't seen before.

"Good Lord, what happened to you?" The girl looked at Lindsay's T-shirt. "Oh, you've been to Cumberland Caverns. You must have been on the wild tour."

"You could say that. I've lost my purse and can't get into my room. My name is Lindsay Chamberlain."

"Oh. You're in luck. Someone turned this in last night." She put Lindsay's purse on the desk.

"Did you see who left it?"

"I wasn't on duty then, but Gary was. He could tell you this evening. He comes on duty at six."

"Thank you. Do you know if I had any calls?"

"Let me see—yes, a guy named Derrick Bellamy. He called three times."

Lindsay smiled. "Thanks."

Derrick—she would call him. After a shower.

Lindsay checked her purse. Everything was there, her motel key, her car keys, her billfold, her money. They hadn't taken a thing, apparently, except her sense of peace. She went back to her motel room with her purse, still dragging her backpack behind her.

She was tired. The first thing she wanted to do was sleep. She went to the bathroom and looked in the mirror. An absolute stranger looked back at her. Her face was swollen, she had two black eyes and a fairly deep scrape on her forehead and cheek. Her hair did not look much different from the five hundred-year-old head of hair she had seen in the cave. It was dusty—the color was lost—and was disheveled beyond belief. She had wanted the sheriff to see how she looked coming out of the cave, so she had not cleaned up. A look in a mirror would have changed her mind. Maybe they would have taken her more seriously if she had cleaned up. Lindsay shook her head. As tired as she was, she was going to take a shower.

Lindsay started peeling off her clothes. Another shock. She had scrapes, scratches, bruises, and dried blood all over her body.

She grabbed a brush and brushed the tangles from her hair and stepped into the warm shower. Her body stung when the water hit the cuts and scrapes. She squeezed shampoo out into her hand and massaged it into her scalp. After her hair was clean, she soaped up her hands and gently washed her body. A washcloth would be entirely too painful.

She didn't look much better cleaned up. The wounds were redder and the bruises more vivid. But she felt a little better. She applied Neosporin to the wounds she could reach, put on a fresh pair of panties, and was headed into the bedroom for a nightgown when someone knocked at the door.

"Lindsay, it's me, Derrick."

"Derrick." She grabbed a towel and rushed to the door.

He stood in the doorway a moment looking at her face, shocked, then came into her room, shutting the door behind him.

"Lindsay." He put his arms around her and hugged her. She flinched in pain.

"I'm sorry. Lindsay, what happened? Your face!" He cupped her face in his hands. "I just came from the sheriff's office. They said you had made a complaint to the sheriff about being kidnapped and in a cave. It didn't make much sense. I got here late last night and have been looking everywhere for you." He hugged her again, more gently this time.

"I'll tell you the whole story when I'm rested. Right now, I need you to put antiseptic on some of the cuts I couldn't reach," she said.

"Cuts?" he followed her into the bathroom.

She took off the towel and Derrick gaped at her cut and bruised body.

"Lindsay! My God." He put some of the antiseptic cream on his fingertips and applied it to the scrapes on her back.

"Lindsay, I had no idea—have you seen a doctor? You need a tetanus shot."

She shook her head. "I'm exhausted. Will you watch over me while I sleep?"

"Yes, but do you expect someone will come back?"

"I don't know."

"Sure, I'll watch over you. When you wake up, I'll take you home."

"I haven't talked to the guy who identified the skeletons yet."

"Lindsay, walk away from this. Look at what you've been through. I've just spent a frantic night wondering what happened to you."

"No." Lindsay's voice came a little too loud even to her own ears. "You don't understand what they did to me, what they took away from me."

She put her hands on his chest. For the first time, he saw the condition of her hands. They were scratched and bruised, and her nails were broken past the quick. They looked as if she had clawed her way out of solid rock to the surface. He took her hands in his own and kissed them.

"You're right, perhaps I don't," he said.

"I almost died a hundred times. I've almost been trapped between rocks, with only a drawn-out death to wait for, I've almost fallen into a pit that I couldn't even see the bottom of, I was almost stuck in a tunnel with no room even to breathe. I've had to do things that I wouldn't have thought possible I could do. I have to find out who did this to me, and I'm going to start where I left off before I disappeared. I want you to help me."

"Will you at least see a doctor first?"

"Yes, I'll do that."

Lindsay put on a nightgown and combed her hair into a ponytail on top of her head and climbed into bed. Derrick tucked her in and kissed her cheek.

"Sleep well. I'll be here when you awaken," he said.

She closed her eyes and went immediately to sleep.

Lindsay awoke with a start, reaching for the flashlight she

had forgotten to turn off. She felt panicked. How long had the light been on that bright?

"It's okay, I'm here."

Derrick. He had come looking for her. She was safe.

Lindsay raised up in a bed. She remembered now. She was safe. "What time is it?" she asked.

"Nine o'clock." Derrick sat on her bed and gathered her up in his arms.

"You mean I've only been asleep five hours?" She rested her cheek against his chest. It felt safe.

"No. Seventeen hours. It's nine in the morning."

"Ten hours more than usual, so I should be well rested." She pushed away from him and swung her legs over the side. Everything about her ached. "I'm so sore," she groaned.

"I found a doctor in town. He said I could just call when you awoke, and he'd fit you in."

"Thanks. I think I'm up-to-date on the tetanus."

"It won't hurt just to let him have a look."

She gripped the edge of the bed and started to rise. Pain shot through her hands. "I need a manicure," she said, looking at them. "They look pretty awful. I'll take a shower and get dressed. You can call your doc."

Lindsay showered and dressed. With her hair clean and brushed, and bandages covering the deeper scrapes on her face, she didn't look quite as bad, but her face was still swollen. She put on a pair of khaki pants and a brown blouse and surveyed herself in the mirror. Not half bad, but she wouldn't want her parents to see her like this. She opened the door and walked out of the bathroom.

"You have a visitor," Derrick said.

"Well, I see Little Rabbit had a time with the old tar-man." John West rose from the chair, holding a gray stuffed animal under his arm.

"Hello, John." She held out her hand. He took it, and looked at it in his hand, much the same way he had before.

"I see you did have a bad time," he said again. "Here, I brought you something. A cute cuddly rabbit didn't seem to fit. I thought Bugs more suitable.'' He handed her a stuffed Bugs Bunny.

''Thanks.'' She caressed the soft coat on the rabbit.

''I'll go and order breakfast,'' interrupted Derrick. ''Come to the restaurant when you are ready. John, why don't you join us?''

''No, I have to get back. But thank you.''

Derrick left and closed the door behind him.

''Your boyfriend is very trusting. I'm not sure I'd leave you alone with another man,'' said John.

''You wouldn't trust me?'' asked Lindsay.

''I wouldn't trust the other man.''

''Derrick is a pretty good judge of character.''

John smiled. ''Other than some scrapes and bruises, you seem to be all right.''

''I am now. But I need to find out who did this.'' Lindsay looked down at her hands, then back at John.

''Why don't you let the authorities find out who did it?''

''You as well as anyone should understand that I can't depend on them to get to the bottom of this,'' she said. ''I appreciate the gift. Does this mean we are friends?''

''No, we are still enemies. The gift is sort of an apology.''

''Apology for what?'' she asked.

''For not believing my father, I suppose. I can't apologize to him, because he doesn't know I didn't believe him.''

''About what?''

''Father goes to bed early and gets up early. Yesterday morning at five o'clock after he arose, we were having coffee, and he said that an ancestor had come to him in a dream that night and told him you were trapped in the earth, that the ancestor heard your cry on the wind and saw your struggle to get out. Father wanted me to get in touch with you or tell someone.'' John paused. ''See, I had told him of your problems and about the dead men in the cave,'' he continued, ''I thought that was where his dream came from, and it may have been. But I should have honored his request. Later, when your friend Derrick called, asking if I mentioned any place you might have gone, that he couldn't find you, I...well, perhaps if I had called him earlier—''

Lindsay shook her head. ''No one could have helped me where I was.''

''Nevertheless, I dishonored my father by not doing what he asked, by assuming that he didn't know where his own dreams came from.''

''I may have seen one of your ancestors in the cave,'' said Lindsay.

John raised his eyebrows, and Lindsay explained what she had stumbled across.

John was silent for a moment, surprise evident in his voice. ''So you were in the cave of the Uktena?'' he said.

''It seems so.''

''Interesting. The cave of the Uktena is a myth, I had always thought.''

''Myths and legends often have some basis in fact.''

''The conquistador held the Ulunsuti in his hands? What did it look like?''

''It was very large, bigger than an ostrich egg, and crystal clear,'' she told him. ''I would have liked to have gotten a better look, but—''

''I understand,'' he said.

Lindsay got up and fished in the backpack.

''Give this to your father. He'll appreciate having a scale of the Uktena.'' She put a crystal in his hand.

John stared at the clear-faceted crystal in the palm of his hand, then at Lindsay. ''Thanks, he will appreciate it.''

''I believe one of your ancestors may have led me out of the cave,'' she said. John raised his eyebrows again, and Lindsay explained about the smoked markings she followed. ''They may have been from someone else, I don't know. But they led me out of the cave.''

''You've had an interesting adventure, Rabbit. I'll tell my father and see what he makes of it. You'd better go eat. Your boyfriend is waiting.''

''Thanks again for coming all this way to give me the rabbit, even if it was for your father.''

"You're welcome." He kissed her cheek, looked into her eyes for just a moment, then backed away.

"I lost the hat you gave me," she said. "It fell off when they kidnapped me."

John went out to his truck and came back with a cap with the West Builders logo. "This is mine," he said. "If you don't mind wearing my cap, you can have this one."

When Lindsay went to the restaurant where Derrick had ordered her eggs, bacon, pancakes, and orange juice, she wore John West's hat.

"YOU DON'T SEEM to have any serious injuries," the doctor told her. "If you have any intestinal or gastric distress for any length of time, we might need to check for any parasites you may have picked up. But I imagine water that deep underground is probably cleaner than the water we get here. You may have some scarring on your face."

"A little dermabrasion will fix it," his nurse said quickly. "I had a friend with bad acne scars. She got a little abrasion, and now she has the prettiest skin."

"That's true," said the doctor. "There's nothing wrong that can't be fixed. And there's a chance you will have so little scarring you won't need anything done to it."

Lindsay thanked them for seeing her on short notice and for their kindness. Derrick was in the waiting room of the small clinic. "Fit as a fiddle," she told him. "I just need aspirin, plenty of water, and rest."

"Good. Can I take you home?"

"No. I also need peace of mind, and I'm going to get that before I leave town. I'm going to see this Dr. Olin Ballinger, the orthopedist who thinks he can identify bones." Lindsay saw Derrick's jaw tighten. "I have to do this," she said.

"Yeah," he answered.

Dr. Ballinger's office was in a new medical complex. The recently planted trees and shrubs hadn't had time to take hold yet. They looked frail. The entranceway smelled like new paint. Lindsay found the office number on the directory at the front entrance. It said Olin Ballinger, M.D., Sports Medicine and Orthopedic Surgery.

"Great," she said. "He treats jock injuries and does forensic anthropology in his spare time."

Derrick cast Lindsay a sideways glance. They took the elevator to Ballinger's second-floor office.

"You're a little tense, aren't you?" Derrick said.

"Why shouldn't I be? You don't see me doing knee surgery in my spare time, do you?"

They entered Ballinger's office. The waiting room was plush, done in light blues and salmon pinks—soothing colors, Lindsay supposed. The receptionist was behind a sliding window.

"Just sign your name," she said, looking sympathetically at Lindsay.

"I don't have an appointment today." Lindsay said.

"Dear, I don't think we have—"

"I did have an appointment late Monday afternoon." The woman's friendly smile was fading. Lindsay could tell she put a high value on promptness. "However, I was delayed by my kidnapping and attempted murder." A look of surprised horror came over the woman's face. "I'm Dr. Lindsay Chamberlain, and I was hoping you could fit me in. I don't want to get in front of these people who've been waiting. I'll be glad to wait until Dr. Ballinger has a few minutes."

"Oh, yes, I remember, Dr. Chamberlain. It's about those, uh... We wondered what happened to you. We called Dr. Prescott—he said—well—"

"Dr. Prescott? Is he using that title?"

The woman looked surprised. "I just assumed—I mean, he is the coroner."

"I see. Regardless of what Mr. Prescott may have told you, I'd like to talk to Dr. Ballinger."

"Please take a seat. I'll go see if he's free."

Lindsay and Derrick took a seat directly in front of the receptionist's glass room.

"A little hard on the woman, weren't you?" said Derrick.

"Was I?"

"Are you sure you're up to doing this now?"

"I'm fine." She hadn't meant to sound so sharp. She reached for his hand. He squeezed it reassuringly.

Lindsay and Derrick waited an hour. Lindsay flipped through magazines without much interest, always fighting the feeling that she had to be constantly on the move, or—or what? Die? She sighed.

Finally, the nurse called them into the office. Dr. Ballinger was a large man, relatively slim, with dark receding hair, an expensive suit, Rolex watch, and gold-rimmed glasses.

"I'm not sure what I can do for you. This business," he waved his hand as if the business were there somewhere in the office, "is an official matter."

Lindsay ignored his claim to official secrecy. "How did you identify the bones found in Hell Slide Cave?"

"I did surgery on Mr. Hillard. I know my work. I had dental x-rays for Mr. Darnell. The other, I forget his name, was identified by his driver's license, found with the body, I believe. The coroner was satisfied. The circumstances were very clear."

"Did you examine the bones for any other cause of death?" asked Lindsay.

"They were caught in a rock slide."

"Do you have the x-rays?" she asked.

"I'm not sure you have the authority to view them," he answered.

"Do you know that you commingled the bones?"

"I what?"

"Commingled the bones. You do know what that means, don't you?"

"Yes, I know what commingling is." His tone was decidedly unfriendly now. "However, I dispute that allegation."

Lindsay took out the photographs of Blaine Hillard's remains and laid them out on the table, pointing to Hillard's two left ninth ribs. Dr. Ballinger refused to look.

"Dr. Ballinger, why are you afraid to examine these photographs?" asked Lindsay.

"I don't need to. I remember working with the bones. No commingling took place."

"Dr. Ballinger. Every competent bone expert in the world would identify both of these bones as left ninth ribs. Unless you contend that Blaine Hillard wore one of his ribs upside down. This petulance you are showing is childish and unprofessional." Derrick quietly reached for Lindsay's arm and gently squeezed it.

"Dr. Chamberlain, I've given you enough of my time—"

"Did you know that Blaine Hillard may have been hit with a tire iron before he was covered with rock?"

"I didn't find—"

"You didn't know how to look."

"I assure you, I'm competent to deal with bones."

"Then you can't have failed to notice that the rates of decomposition among the skeletons are not the same. Why didn't you report that to the authorities?"

Lindsay had caught him totally off guard. He stared at her. "What?"

"I could see that in these photographs. It would have been very evident in the bones. I can't understand why you kept this from the sheriff."

"I didn't—" He struggled to recover himself. "I think you had better go. I'll not sit here while you impugn my integrity."

Lindsay rose. "Dr. Ballinger, I just spent the last day buried in a cave fighting for my life. I believe that wouldn't have happened to me if you'd been more competent in dealing with these bones. I can show you on the skull where I think the tire iron fracture is, and I can point out the inconsistencies in decomposition, but I am unable to persuade you to look at the photographs. However, you can be assured, with reasonable people I can be very persuasive." She gathered up the photographs, turned, and walked out, leaving Olin Ballinger staring angrily at her.

Derrick escorted her to the car. He said nothing until they were outside.

"That's the last time I loan you my copy of *How to Win*

Friends and Influence People. You were a little hostile in there, weren't you?''

Lindsay leaned against the car. ''I am so angry.''

''I see you are. That's why you need to let the authorities take care of this.''

''I will, but I have to show them the way first. When a death has been officially closed, it's hard to get it reopened. Look,'' she said when she saw the hard set of Derrick's face, ''I need your support.''

''I've always given you my support. But I'm having a hard time dealing with this desire for detective work you've suddenly acquired. It's like you've become addicted to danger.''

Lindsay stared at him openmouthed. ''You act like you are blaming me for getting thrown in the cave. None of this is my fault.''

''I'm only blaming you for agreeing to look for a murderer. Murderers will tend to act like murderers if you get in their way. Give me the keys and I'll drive.'' Lindsay threw him her keys and got in the passenger side. When Derrick got in, he looked over at her. ''I didn't mean to come down so hard, at least not right now.''

Lindsay looked at him, into his eyes. He looked troubled and she felt guilty, and felt angry for feeling guilty. ''I know I behaved very unprofessionally in Ballinger's office,'' she said.

''He'll get over it. I'm concerned about you. You're a walking time bomb.''

''It's the anger. It's a thing, like the darkness was a thing that swallowed me in the cave when the light was off. I never knew dark could be so dark. There's no place in your house you could go in the middle of the night, turn out the light, and have it be as dark as it was in that cave, and it was pervasive. My anger is that pervasive, aimed at no one and everyone. I feel like the only way to get rid of it is to find the people who did this to me. If it has to do with Ferguson, then nothing I've done so far had anything to do with what happened to me. As for Ken Darnell and his death, I've only asked a few questions here and there. I've hardly done any investigating at all."

"You think it is someone connected to the cave murders—were they murdered?"

"It's possible that the skull fracture was caused by something other than falling rocks, but I'd have to look at the bones. And yes, I think what happened to me is connected to what happened in the cave to Grace Lambert's brother. I don't really think it is the Ferguson family who did this to me. It just seems too relentless for them to follow me all the way up here—and what about Gil Harris? His death is not related to the Fergusons, but he did know Grace's brother."

"Okay. Where do you want to go now?"

At that moment, Dr. Ballinger came hurrying out of his office and started down the street. Lindsay and Derrick watched him. He was heading toward the coroner's office.

SIXTEEN

"I WONDER WHAT they are going to talk about?" mused Lindsay.

"Did you get any sense that Ballinger or Prescott could have been among the men who kidnapped you?" Derrick asked.

"I couldn't tell. But why would they?" she asked.

"To save their reputations?" asked Derrick.

"No. They've got bureaucracies to do that for them. But something's up. I don't suppose we could listen in?"

"No," said Derrick, starting the Rover. "We can't." He drove back to the motel.

They pulled into the parking space near the stairs that led to Lindsay's room. She turned to Derrick before they got out. "Thanks for staying with me."

Derrick leaned over and kissed her gently. "We'll get through this. If you want to talk about being in the cave, I'll listen."

Lindsay said nothing until they were in the room with the door closed and locked. "Maybe it would help to face it," she said. "I don't ever remember being so constantly terrified. It's like being lost in some other dimension where there's no time and every step's a trap."

Lindsay sat down at the small table in the corner of the room, and Derrick sat opposite her. As she told him the story he reached for her hands and held them, listening quietly.

"We'll find out who did this," he whispered when she had finished.

Lindsay shook her head. "I don't know how. I still can't think clearly. I'm not sure what to do next."

"Since the bones of that Hillard fellow are commingled, and his wife seems to be so cooperative, you could get an exhumation order. Like the guy said, at least the body doesn't have to be dug up. If you see the bones themselves—"

"That's a good idea. If I can just examine those bones, I can get a lot of answers, I—"

Derrick's gaze fell upon the backpack Lindsay had in the cave. It was leaning against the nightstand, the yellow flashlight still dangling from it by her belt. "Why don't you send that to the FBI crime lab? There may be fingerprints on something in there."

"Of course. I should've thought of that. I'll call Agent McKinley, the FBI agent in charge of the Gil Harris case. Maybe when I tell him what's been happening, he'll share some information with me."

Derrick went to his truck to get one of the boxes used for packing artifacts, while Lindsay called Agent McKinley.

"Dr. Chamberlain. How are you?"

"Recovering," Lindsay replied.

"I've done a little caving before. I can't imagine anything more frightening."

"Neither can I," she said.

"You think all these events are connected?" He spoke her thoughts.

"They might be. From the photographic evidence I've seen, I think there's a definite possibility that Ken Darnell and the other cavers were murdered. I'm going to try to get a look at the bones. Is there anything you can tell me about the crime scene at the Rock Shelter Site?"

There was a moment of silence on the phone, and Lindsay thought he was hesitating, then she heard paper shuffling in the background.

"Not much. We interviewed some hikers passing through the area just before dark, hurrying to find a camping spot. They remembered the cars in the parking area used by the site crew. We did discover there was an extra white van parked there at that time. We almost missed that. According to the description, it wasn't unlike the university vans. The hikers were sure there were two of them. There should've been only one. But so far we haven't been able to trace it. None of them got a look at the license plate."

Lindsay was quiet a moment. "My kidnappers used a van."

"Hmmm. Can you send me a description of everything you remember?"

"Yes. I'll do that immediately. Give me your fax number." Lindsay found some stationery supplied by the motel on her nightstand and wrote down the number. "Anything else?" she asked.

"The top of the cliff was rocky. The only things we found were some beer bottle caps and a piece of chewed gum that the lab says was fresh. The chewer was a nonsecretor, so not much there. There was one thing interesting, though I'm not sure it'll help. The lab guys said there was a good impression of a molar that had an extra cusp."

Lindsay was silent for a long moment.

"Lindsay, does that mean something?"

"I don't know...something in the back of my mind. Anyway, there's some things I noticed in the photographs." She told McKinley about the possible fracture with a tire iron and the different rates of decay she believed she saw in the photographs.

"I can call the authorities in Ellis County and encourage that the case be reopened," he said. "That's all I can do, encourage them. Do you think you might find anything else on the bones if you had them to examine directly?"

"I can't promise. But we'll never know unless we try."

Lindsay asked him where she could send her backpack, and he dictated the information to put on the label and where to send it.

"The lab'll be able to come up with something in a backpack full of stuff. Don't worry. I think we'll find who dumped you in that cave."

Derrick had packed and taped the box when Lindsay got off the phone. "From this end it sounded like a productive conversation," he told her.

"McKinley's going to try to reopen the Darnell case."

"That'll be good. With the authorities working on it, no

one will have a reason to want you out of the way.'' He grabbed her around the waist and kissed her neck, nuzzling her ear. ''In the meantime,'' he whispered, gently easing her toward the bed, ''we can take our vacation together here.'' A loud knocking interrupted their intentions, and they both glared at the door.

''What now?'' Lindsay said as Derrick released her and answered the knock.

A slim man dressed in khaki-brown entered, held out his hand, and introduced himself as Sheriff Struen Prescott of Ellis County.

''Are you related to...?'' began Lindsay.

''Yes, the son of a bitch is my cousin and a pain in my ass. If you can show me where he has been derelict in his duty as coroner, I'll see he gets his butt kicked in the next election.'' Both Lindsay and Derrick were speechless. The sheriff smiled. ''I like to be direct. Now, I got an interesting call from an FBI agent. He suggested that if I reopened the case, there might be a big arrest and publicity in it for me, not to mention getting some criminals off the street. I told him I kind of like that idea. Tell me about this caving accident you think might be murder.''

Lindsay invited him into her motel room and showed him the pictures. ''It's suggestive, but I can't know for sure unless I see the bones.''

''I'm working on it right now. Already called the Hillards. Talked to a fella named Clay Boshay. You'd of thought Christmas and Halloween fell on the same day. Getting a court order for the other two shouldn't be any problem.''

''Sheriff, I have to say, you are about the quickest official I have ever seen.''

''Yes, I am. Do what needs to be done and don't fiddle-fart around, that's my motto. I got a clean county to prove my methods. Would be cleaner if Tucker weren't screwing up so much. Don't know exactly how many homicides he's messed up. He's both stupid and slippery at the same time—bad combination. Knows how to shift blame. Always did, even as a kid. I got more whippings for things that bastard did. But it sounds like you can give me what I want."

"Where can I look at the bones?"

"My office be all right?" he asked.

"Sure."

Lindsay could not see the bones until the next day. The sheriff, true to his nature, got the exhumation orders in a hurry and had them executed before anyone was the wiser. The bones of Ken Darnell were at his office before Jennifer Darnell's lawyer arrived to protest.

Clay Boshay and Lorinda Hillard came to the sheriff's office to await the findings. They were dressed as if coming to a funeral: Clay in a suit, Lorinda in her Sunday best, a dark lavender cotton dress with lace trim. They rose to greet Lindsay when she came in.

"Look, we really appreciate what you did," said Clay. "This means a lot to Lorinda here. I'm sorry about all that's happened to you." He grimaced as his eyes darted over Lindsay's bruised and bandaged face.

"I don't know what I'll find," Lindsay told them.

"At least we can rest easy knowing that somebody who knew what they were doing looked at the bones." Lorinda looked past Lindsay. Lindsay turned and saw Olin Ballinger and Tucker Prescott come into the office.

"Boy," said Clay, "if looks could kill, you'd be a dead woman."

Not for the first time, she wondered if they might have been the ones who kidnapped her. Lindsay left them and went into the next room, where Derrick was laying out the bones. She had asked for his help because she wanted it done quickly. The bones were lying on sheets on three tables—three skeletons. She went to Blaine Hillard first and to the misplaced rib. Derrick had already found it and set it aside.

Olin Ballinger and Tucker Prescott, the coroner, followed her in and didn't look happy about it. There was another man there also. He had a pad of paper and a pencil. "Dr. Ballinger wanted to observe," said the sheriff. "And, of course, we always have the coroner in when we deal with dead bodies."

If he had any sarcasm in his voice, Lindsay didn't notice. "This here is Darrell Mannville. He owns the newspaper here in town. We believe in freedom of the press here, don't we, Darrell?"

"Yes, sir, sheriff."

Lindsay decided she didn't want to ever be on the wrong side of Sheriff Struen Prescott.

She put on latex gloves and picked up the switched rib and examined it closely. She walked to the other skeletons and picked up a rib from the remains identified as Roy Pitt. "This is the rib that goes to Blaine Hillard." She gave Ballinger a brief glance. He stood with his mouth turned down in a sour expression.

She asked Derrick to start looking at the bones of Roy Pitt for any cuts or anomalies. She picked up Blaine Hillard's cracked skull and examined the injuries. Looking at the skull close up, it was obvious that he was murdered.

"Sheriff," she said. He came over to look at the skull. "These fractures here and here were probably made by the falling rocks. See how the depressions are rounder and the cracks radiate around each. Now look at this wound. See how it is slightly L-shaped. The bottom of the depression is overlapped by this fracture." She looked up at him.

"Go on," he said. "I'm following."

"When anything like glass or bone is hit, fracture lines radiate out. A fracture line will terminate at another fracture line."

"Yes. That's how we determine the sequence order of bullet holes through glass and such. Go on."

"This L-shaped injury has fractures that radiate out until they just run their course. However, the fracture lines for this injury over here—" she pointed to a depression on the upper occipital, "the ones we think were done by rocks—terminate at the fracture lines for the L-shaped cut."

"The L-shaped wound was first; the others happened later," Sheriff Prescott said. "Hell, I should have done the bones myself, and we wouldn't be here now."

Lindsay smiled. Ballinger and Tucker Prescott looked ill at ease.

"Yes," she said. "That's right. Look at the L-shaped injury. It was probably made with a tire iron or—"

"Crowbar," said the sheriff. "Seen that kind of wound before."

"Yes," said Lindsay. "That's a possibility."

"I've found something here," said Derrick.

Lindsay came over to the table where Derrick was looking at the bones of Roy Pitt. She knew he didn't particularly relish the work. Derrick was not a "bone person," but she knew he could competently lay them out and look them over for signs of trauma. He hated looking at bones that had anything left of the flesh, and the two skeletons of Roy Pitt and Blaine Hillard, though basically skeletonized, were still articulated to a great degree and had quite a bit of gristle on them.

He showed her a rib and pointed to a cut. Lindsay made a motion with her hand as if stabbing someone underhanded with a knife. Derrick nodded.

"It looks like we have some stab cuts here," she said. "The knife hit the rib and the vertebrae. It looks like someone came up behind him and stuck the knife in his kidney, nicking the eighth rib."

The sheriff came over to look. "Yes. See that, too. It looks like we've had a murderer running around with two years of undeserved freedom after committing a crime in my county. I don't like that."

"Interesting that you have two types of murder weapons," said Lindsay.

"Yes. It is," said the sheriff. "I'm going to have to ponder over that one."

Lindsay moved to the skeleton of Ken Darnell and picked up the skull. Most of the bones were disarticulated with only a few telltale ligaments here and there. She held the base of the skull in her hand and looked at the face. Just then Jennifer Darnell's lawyer burst into the room to protest. He had a piece of paper in his hand, shaking it.

"I don't know how you did this, Struen Prescott, but you've gone too far. He wasn't even from your county—"

"Didn't have to be from this county. Just had to be killed here."

"Jennifer Darnell protests most strenuously, and I have a court—"

"You can tell Jennifer Darnell she can relax," said Lindsay, interrupting the lawyer. "These aren't the bones of her husband." Everyone in the room looked at her in amazement. For the first time, the sheriff didn't see how she arrived at her conclusion. Nor did Derrick, who knew her methods well. The reporter furiously scribbled on his pad.

Lindsay had seen these teeth before. She was looking at the defleshed skull of Denny Ferguson.

SEVENTEEN

THE REPORTER WROTE furiously on his pad, taking down the rush of ensuing accusations that Lindsay's announcement provoked. When Sheriff Prescott decided that the ruckus had had its effect, he cleared the room so Lindsay could analyze the skeletons in relative peace, though she could hear the ranting outside the door—threats of lawsuits by Clay and Lorinda, angry excuses from Dr. Ballinger, insults hurled at her. The noise didn't last long. The sheriff let the reporter get his fill and sent everyone home.

It was late when Lindsay finished. She found no more points of trauma on the bones that she could distinguish from damage caused by the rocks. She did find evidence that rodents had gnawed Roy Pitt's and Blaine Hillard's remains extensively. She found none on Denny Ferguson's remains. She examined the x-rays that were labeled Ken Darnell but really belonged to Denny Ferguson and noted the name of the dentist: Terence Wilson, D.D.S. She made a mental note to contact him, though perhaps she should leave that to the police.

As she was about to lay the x-ray down, she saw another anomaly. In the upper left corner, along the edge, was a fingerprint. Nothing unusual about that—this x-ray had been handled by a half-dozen people. What was unusual about this print was that it was part of the x-ray image. It had been left on the film at the time the x-ray was made by whoever developed it. Unusual for a dentist's office, Lindsay thought, but interesting. She placed the x-ray back in its envelope and attached a note to the sheriff to have it delivered to Agent McKinley to be matched.

The last thing she and Derrick did was to take samples of detritus from the auditory meatus, the eye orbits, the skull vault, and the pelvis, and bag and label them. An examination of the detritus would probably reveal soil differences and insect casings that would verify the differences in decomposition rates and places. But, of course, with the skeleton identified as Denny Ferguson, it was a given that his body decayed at a different time. He was alive when the others were reported missing and already dead.

"That was a circus," said Derrick, driving back to the motel.

"Wasn't it though? Denny Ferguson..." Lindsay frowned.

"I'm not sure I understand this," Derrick said half to himself as he pulled into the motel parking lot.

Lindsay was quiet. She got out of the car and walked to her room and leaned against the wall as Derrick opened the door, a frown still creasing her forehead. She slipped off her shoes and sat down cross-legged on the bed.

"That's why all this happened to me. I had the feeling all along—the attacks on my reputation, the calls and trespassers at my house—that someone was trying to get me to go home. Trying to kill me in the cave was the last desperate act," said Lindsay.

"What do you mean?"

"I mean that when they found out I was coming up here to investigate the death of Ken Darnell, they knew that if I ever saw x-rays, photographs, or the skull itself, I, above all people, would recognize Denny Ferguson," she said.

"I can buy that. But who are they?" asked Derrick.

"Kelley. Kelley Banks. Ken Darnell is her uncle. She knew I was coming here, and it angered her. She pretended to be concerned for her aunt. Ken Darnell went to her for a body, and she supplied him Denny Ferguson."

"But that would mean Ken Darnell isn't dead," Derrick said.

"Exactly."

Derrick sat on the bed facing her. "I still don't understand the timing. The dead cavers were reported missing when? February two years ago. Denny escaped this past April. The bodies were discovered this May."

Lindsay nodded. "Yes."

"What do you think happened? Do you think Ken is still alive?"

"Yes, and I think we can get the FBI to look for him."

"Why?"

"Because I can link him to Gil Harris."

"Just because Harris met Ken once—"

Lindsay shook her head. "The chewing gum they found on the cliff. It has an extra cusp—possibly Carabelli's cusp."

"Okay," said Derrick. "Let me get this straight. The person chewing the gum on the cliff where Gil Harris was killed had Carabelli's cusp?"

"Yes, an extra cusp anyway. I'd be willing to bet it was an upper molar," she said.

"What does that have to do with Ken Darnell?" Derrick asked.

"You know that it's a hereditary trait and relatively rare. Joshua Lambert, nephew to Ken Darnell, has it. Ken Darnell could also have it; certainly someone on the cliff the night Gil died had it. Gil Harris was a caver and knew Ken Darnell. A tenuous connection, but a connection nonetheless. What if Ken was following me and Gil recognized him? It makes sense."

"It's a good enough connection to interest McKinley," Derrick said and pulled Lindsay to him.

She put her arms around his neck then abruptly pulled away, looking past him at herself in the mirror at her skinned-up face and touching her forehead and cheek lightly with her fingers.

"You'll look fine," said Derrick, grinning broadly. "You look great to me right now."

She looked back at Derrick's face as if he were suddenly turning into a unicorn before her eyes. "What?" he asked.

"My face and your smile."

"What about them? Are my teeth falling out?"

"I just had an idea." She hopped off the bed and paced the floor, stopped, and stared at Derrick, but all her attention was turned inward. "Do you have your camera with you?" she said at last.

"Yeah."

"There's a picture I want you to take." She went to the phone and called Agent McKinley, explained her idea and what she wanted him to do.

"That's a long shot," he said at last. But she could tell by the tone of his voice that he'd bought into it.

"You'll do it, then?"

"Oh, yes. It's a very interesting long shot. And this Carabelli's cusp thing—well, that's interesting, too."

"Good. These are the measurements I want your people to take. These specific ones are very important." Lindsay gave him directions on what she wanted done.

"Sure thing," he said.

"I'll be damned," said Derrick when Lindsay had hung up the phone.

"What do you think?" she asked.

"Interesting idea, and it might even be true," he said.

"Can you get the picture?" she asked.

"You show me, and I'll get it." He kissed her. "Your lips aren't sore, are they?"

"They're about the only parts of me that aren't."

"Good." He kissed her again.

Derrick and Lindsay changed and drove to McMinnville. They stopped at a Wal-Mart so that Lindsay could get a pair of sunglasses and a large hat, and they both bought Cumberland Cavern T-shirts.

"Don't we look like tourists?" she said, wearing her new T-shirt and sunglasses, her long hair tucked under her large hat. Derrick had put on his shirt and tied his long hair into a low ponytail. His camera hung by a strap around his neck.

"We look like we got lost on the way to the beach."

Lindsay smiled. "Yeah. But I don't want them to recognize me. How do I look in a hat?"

"You were born to wear them."

They drove to Everything Sporting in Derrick's jeep and parked a couple of blocks away. It was their good luck that there was a small cafe across the street with a clear view of the large picture window of the store. It was rather bad luck that Jennifer and her boyfriend, Craig, were in the cafe. They were sitting in the back, drinking coffee and chatting with the waitress. Derrick and Lindsay sat in a small booth by the front window.

"Where you folks from?" They looked up to see a smiling waitress putting menus in front of them. Lindsay had the urge to bolt from the coffee shop. She felt as if her hat and glasses looked like a Halloween costume.

"Oak Ridge," said Derrick.

"Oh. I see you've visited Cumberland Caverns. Did you like it?"

"Unforgettable," said Lindsay, smiling.

"I don't like caves myself. I'll be back when you've had a chance to look at the menu."

"Do you think I should leave?" Lindsay asked when the waitress was out of earshot.

"You can. Now that I know who they are, I can take it from here."

Lindsay started to stand, but so did Jennifer and Craig. Lindsay sat back down as Jennifer walked in her direction, leaving Craig to pay the bill. Lindsay averted her face and looked down into her purse as Jennifer passed. Jennifer turned to look at Derrick, as many women do. She smiled, and he gave her a dazzling one in return. She left and crossed the street back to her store. Craig followed shortly, not giving them a glance.

"That was close," said Lindsay.

"Why don't you go mail your backpack to the FBI," Derrick said, "and I'll get the photograph. You can meet me down the block."

"All right. Derrick, be careful."

"I'm just going to take a picture. I'll be fine."

Lindsay left him, with some misgivings, and mailed the package off to the FBI by next-day service. She faxed a description of everything that happened to her to Agent McKinley. With those tasks done, she drove to the place where she was to meet Derrick. He wasn't there, so she pulled into a parking space and waited, constantly glancing down the street looking for him. After about twenty minutes, she was beginning to feel uneasy and wondered if she should go look for him. She had opened the door to get out of the Rover when she saw him leave the cafe, holding a bag of something and walking up the street toward her.

He grinned when he got to the car, reaching into the sack and pulling out a Styrofoam cup and a spoon, which he handed to her through the window. "I got you some ice cream," he said.

"It took me a while to get the picture," he added. "Both of them went to an office in the back of the store and stayed a while. I was kind of worried. They had a couple of clerks waiting on people, so there wasn't any reason for either of them to come out."

"What did you do?"

"I did a little looking around. They have some pretty good stuff."

"Did they see you?"

"Sure, but they don't know me from Adam. They came out and told the clerks they were leaving. Seems as though they're going to a party tonight. Jennifer gave me another smile and asked me if I found anything I liked."

"Indeed?" said Lindsay, taking a bit of ice cream.

"I said yes, I found some things I liked very much," he said, and Lindsay rolled her eyes. "Anyway, they went out the back, and I reckoned that they had a private parking lot behind the store. I left as quickly as possible without causing suspicion, though I don't suppose that would have mattered. I was in luck. Around back was a place I could hide behind the Dumpsters. I got a good shot by the car with the telephoto lens."

"Perfect."

"I think so. We'll get it developed and send it off."

They drove to a one-hour photo store and waited for the print to be developed, and Lindsay sent it by same-day service to Agent McKinley with instructions.

"Expensive," commented Derrick. "I hope they spring for it."

"Right now I don't care," said Lindsay. "I want this over with as quickly as possible."

Derrick reached for her hand and held it. "Are you feeling better?"

"I'll be all right. I may have to sleep with a night-light on for the rest of my life, but I'm all right. Where to now?" she asked.

"Dinner and dancing. We are going to relax the next couple of days before I have to go back to Cold River."

Derrick had found a small restaurant that had dancing. There weren't many people there, the band was lousy, and the lighting was too bright, but it was a welcome change from the past few days and for a few hours Lindsay forgot about Ken Darnell, Denny Ferguson, and caves. She laid her head on Derrick's shoulder on the way back to the motel and fell asleep. She jerked abruptly awake when they passed a car with its lights on bright.

"You okay?" asked Derrick.

"Fine. Are we about there?"

"Almost."

They slept late in the morning and ate a late breakfast in the motel restaurant. Lindsay kept looking at her watch as she ate, wondering how Agent McKinley was faring, wondering if he got the photographs. He'd said he would take care of it himself. Had he? The Lambert farm was not that far.

"You can't let it go, can you?" said Derrick.

Lindsay didn't realize she'd been gazing off in the distance and that Derrick had been trying to tell her about Cold River.

"I'm sorry. No I can't. Not until I know who did this to me."

"You still think Kelley Banks was involved?"

"Yes, she's the one who knew Denny Ferguson. His body type is not unlike Ken Darnell's."

"What about Ferguson's escape? How did she arrange that?" asked Derrick over his coffee. "It's not an easy thing to do, I imagine. I'm not saying you're wrong about her. It's just that breaking someone out of jail's a tricky process."

"I don't know. Maybe Ferguson did it himself and she took

advantage of it. I haven't figured that out yet,'' Lindsay admitted.

''Okay. How did they do the dental x-rays?'' asked Derrick.

''I don't know that either. Maybe Kelley had Ferguson see her dentist and somehow changed the name on the charts. Maybe the fingerprint will provide a clue.''

''I don't know, Lindsay. All this sounds too complicated to me. I think you need a simpler hypothesis. I just can't see her coming up with the plans and follow-through necessary to break him out of jail and alter the records in a dentist's office,'' said Derrick.

''If she had the help of her uncle Ken and his wife, Jennifer, she must have been in on it—and with their money, she could have pulled it off,'' answered Lindsay.

''Still...'' Derrick was unconvinced. ''What motive would Kelley have that would be worth the risk?''

''Money,'' answered Lindsay. ''The combined insurance policies were worth over a million and a half dollars. Perhaps more. Kelley's just three years out of law school in a struggling practice. She probably had lots of school loans to pay back. I imagine her uncle and Jennifer didn't have too hard a time tempting her.''

''Maybe,'' said Derrick.

''Look,'' said Lindsay. ''Let's go to a lake, rent a boat, and relax all day. I promise I won't even think about any of this. It will just be the two of us having a good time, and you can tell me all about Cold River.''

Derrick smiled and picked up the check the waitress left on the table. ''Sounds good to me.''

It was dark when they arrived at the motel. Lindsay felt relaxed and pleasantly tired. ''I saw that *Tremors* is on TV late tonight,'' she said.

''Haven't you seen that a dozen times?'' asked Derrick.

''Yes, but it always cracks me up.''

They changed clothes and curled up on the bed with their backs against the headboard, supported by pillows, and settled in to watch the movie. Lindsay laughed herself silly. Derrick, merely amused, shook his head at her and smiled. During a commercial, he went to the vending machine and brought them back cold drinks.

"All right," he said, opening a can and handing it to her. "You've been good all day. I know you want to talk about it."

"What?" she said, smiling and sipping the cold drink.

Derrick ignored her. "Pitt and Hillard died first, and probably in the same place, probably the cave, probably at the time they were reported missing."

"It looks like you've been wanting to talk about it, too," Lindsay said.

"I do," he said.

Just then the phone rang. It was Agent McKinley. "Hello, Lindsay. You put the place in quite a buzz up there."

"Yep. Did that."

"I've got some news for you. You were right on the money. I got the picture of Ken Darnell from Grace Lambert like you said, and our people made estimates of size from the car he was standing by, blew up the face to actual size, and did the same with Craig Gillett. My guy said that you can't change some measurements, just as you said, like pupil to pupil. They are virtually certain it's the same guy. I saw the images superimposed. He's had a nose job, implants in his chin and jaws, changed his hair color, and taken up weight lifting. God, those people are thorough. How did you get on to it?"

"Several things came together. Grace Lambert has Indian ancestry, and it shows up in her bone structure and teeth. When Craig smiled, I noted that he has edge-to-edge occlusion. That's more common among Asians and Native American. It just clicked the other day after we discussed Carabelli's cusp. And when the nurse I saw after the cave experience suggested that a little sandpaper would erase any scarring on my face, that got me to thinking about Ken's so-called skiing accident in Colorado just before he disappeared two years ago. His sister, Grace, talked about how banged up he was. I realized that he could have been recovering from plastic surgery and just pretending to have gone to Colorado and had an accident. The broken leg during their visit could have been an act.''

''You sure do draw a lot of conclusions from one look inside people's mouths, don't you?'' Agent McKinley said. Lindsay thought she detected a hint of incredulity in his voice.

''Yeah, occupational hazard, I guess. What are you going to do now?''

''I've called the police in McMinnville. They'll arrest Ken and Jennifer Darnell and hold them for the FBI. The Darnells are implicated in four murders now. I've alerted the insurance companies. They are happy, as you can imagine.''

''The Darnells have probably already left town,'' Lindsay said. ''People who plan as meticulously as they do would already have an escape plan laid out.''

''I don't doubt it,'' he agreed, ''but they'll be found.''

''I suggest that you might look for a way to check Kelley Banks's financial records,'' said Lindsay. ''I'll bet she paid off her student loans and had money to invest. She's Denny Ferguson's attorney and Ken Darnell's niece. She has to be in on it.''

''Poor Grace,'' said Lindsay, when she had hung up the phone. ''This isn't what she expected. I've no doubt she'll regret the day she ever asked me to look into this for her.''

''Look at it this way,'' said Derrick, putting an arm around her. ''Her brother is alive. You found that out.''

''Yes, but this business is going to upset the whole family,'' she said.

''Are you thinking about the little girl?'' asked Derrick.

''Marilee. Yes. She's so cute and so smart. But she's not my little girl.'' Lindsay sounded wistful.

''You know, Lindsay—'' he began.

''What?'' she asked, sensing where he was headed.

''Now is not the time,'' he said, and Lindsay didn't pursue it.

They were quiet for a while, content to watch television.

''What was the purpose in waiting so long to have the bodies discovered?'' Derrick asked after a while.

''I suppose to completely divert suspicion. Jennifer was already well off. They could afford to wait for such high stakes,'' said Lindsay. ''Maybe, too, they didn't have another body. They're not that easy to come by, you know, ones that won't be missed or be identified as someone other than who you want it to be. They have to be the right sex, the right size, the right age, the right ethnic group. I guess they thought a convicted escaped killer who fit the description would be ideal. Kelley sure had me fooled. She seemed to really care about her client.''

''Are you so sure about her involvement?''

''She has to be in it. The Denny Ferguson connection can't be a coincidence.''

''Anyway,'' said Derrick. ''It's over for you.''

''Yes,'' said Lindsay. ''It's over for me.''

EIGHTEEN

ROBERTO LACAYO KNEW they were getting close to the place where he had to make a decision: go to Santa Elena or go with Piaquay. He was beginning to appreciate the beauty of this land. Perhaps he had appreciated it for longer than he had been willing to admit. Why had he not escaped long ago, headed to the far south, looking for a Spanish fort? Because traveling alone in this land is dangerous, *he said to himself, but that wasn't all of it.*

Piaquay stopped to make camp. It was earlier than he usually stopped for the day, but Roberto quit trying to guess how he made decisions. He watched the Indians in their usual practice of building rock pedestals on which to put their possessions, dragging up a log to sit on. They never altered their habits in some things. In others, such as building a fire to cook their food, they sometimes did and sometimes did not. Roberto never understood why, and they would not tell him. It came as a surprise to him how much he wanted them to like him.

He found a log he liked and could drag, and he placed it near them. They sat and ate while Nayahti told stories of the things he saw while he was traveling. Roberto could understand a little of what he said, enough to know he exaggerated, but he also knew that Indians were born storytellers, constructing long, wonderful narratives about places and animals, war and hunting parties. Later, Kinua played his pipes. Roberto looked up at the green canopy above him. It was like a cathedral. He closed his eyes and listened to the high-pitched melody drift around him. It was unlike the music of his homeland. It reminded him of the deep forest, green ferns, and flowing rivers of this land. He wondered if that was what they thought about when they composed their music.

The music stopped, and Roberto opened his eyes. It had

grown dark, and his companions were making ready for sleep. Roberto felt lazy. He also felt he had to answer a call of nature. He rose from his log and walked into the woods.

He had just finished his task when he suddenly found himself flat on the ground, a knife poised above him. His attacker was a mere shadowy figure, but he heard the French curses. Roberto tried to talk to him in the little French he knew.

"Are you lost, as I? I can help you!"

Surely the man was mad to attack in the dark. They fought, but he was strong, very strong, and Roberto was tired from the day's travel. Then, just as suddenly as the man appeared, he was gone. Roberto sat up, blinking back the blood running into his eyes from a cut on his forehead. He wiped his eyes with his sleeve and saw that Piaquay had pulled the man off and slit his throat.

Roberto was breathing hard, gasping for air. Piaquay hauled him to his feet and dragged him back to camp.

"Sleep," he said.

"What if there are more?" said Roberto, feeling his ears, realizing both of his lobes were torn and one of his earspools gone. He winced as he thought he would have to cut the dangling tissue in order to look normal.

"There are no more. Sleep." Roberto then saw Quanche and Minque silently slipping back into camp.

In the morning, when the sunlight filtered through the green canopy, Roberto and the others examined the dead man. There was a fog in the woods, and the air was cool. Roberto shivered as he looked into the face of his attacker. He had fair skin and hair and a wispy beard. The man was half naked and thin. A madman, *thought Roberto,* probably lost or held prisoner, perhaps tortured by the Indians or the Spanish. *It could be either. He was French. Roberto had felt the man's fear the night before. He felt sorry for him now. He understood how this strange land could drive you mad with fear and loneliness, until you learned how to live in it.*

"I will bury him," said Roberto.

"Why not let the coyotes have him?" asked Piaquay.

"He was lost and afraid. I will bury him."

To Roberto's surprise, his companions helped him dig the ole. They first softened the ground with sharp sticks, then ound wide thin stones to dig out the dirt. With all of them orking, it did not take long.

Roberto laid the Frenchman out in the grave, bowed his ead, and muttered a Latin prayer over him. He knelt and put e rosary in the dead man's hand.

"This will help you, my lost friend," he whispered.

They covered him with dirt, and Roberto piled as many ocks as he could find over the grave.

"Your beads," said Piaquay. "They were sacred to you."

"I made the first rosary. I can make another, and it will be acred, too. I thought he needed it on his journey."

Piaquay nodded. Roberto thought he seemed to understand.

"It is time for you to make a choice, my friend," Piaquay old Roberto. "Which path will you take?"

LINDSAY WAS RIGHT. Jennifer and Ken had disappeared. She gave them a pretty good chance of not being found. Those wo knew how to plan and be patient. The next morning she drove home. Derrick wanted to drive with her, but she knew he needed to get back to his site, and she told him she would be fine.

"And, Derrick," she said as she started to get into her Rover, "perhaps we can talk after you get back."

"Perhaps we can," he said and kissed her. He watched her drive away. In the rearview mirror she saw him get in his Jeep and start off in the other direction.

Her trip home was uneventful. She was thankful for that. Susan had returned to Lindsay's house with Mandrake.

"The calls stopped, so I decided it would be all right to come back," Susan said. "Mandrake's fine."

"You went above and beyond in taking care of my place. Thanks."

"That's all right. That was a strange end for Denny Ferguson."

"Yes. If it weren't for Mr. Kim and his family, I could almost feel sorry for him."

Lindsay wrote Susan a check and paid her extra for her time and effort. Susan tried to decline, but Lindsay insisted. "It meant a lot to me to have you take care of things."

It was good to be home. Everything in the house was as she had left it. It was familiar. Susan had left her kitchen stocked, and Lindsay made herself a taco salad for dinner, watched some TV, and went to bed early. She took the phone book before she turned in and looked at the listings for plastic surgeons. She was not vain, but she didn't want to look in the mirror every day and think about the cave. Or maybe she was vain, she thought to herself; there's nothing wrong with looking good.

In the morning she called and made an appointment with a plastic surgeon she had heard about from another faculty member. She was lucky. There had been a cancellation, and they would fit her in the next week.

LINDSAY PARKED at the medical building and followed the directions given to her over the phone. She still had misgivings about coming. Her scrapes might not warrant such dramatic treatment, she thought as she walked down the long hall, passing the doors of other medical professionals. Timothy Scott, M.D., P.C., Pediatric Medicine, one said. Where had she heard that name? Oh yes, Kelley Banks's boyfriend. Kelley Banks, thought Lindsay, was having a time explaining to the authorities how her client ended up being misidentified as her uncle.

Terence Wilson, D.D.S., P.C., Dentist, the door past Timothy Scott's said. Lindsay passed it, stopped, and looked again. Side by side. What a coincidence. The dentist whose name was on Denny Ferguson's x-rays had an office next to Kelley Banks's boyfriend. She walked on down to the end of the hall to her appointment. While she waited, she tried out different scenarios in her mind.

Kelley went to visit Denny in jail about his appeal, told him that it wasn't going well, reminding him what an injustice had been done to him, how he deserved to be free—that she had a plan that would free him.

Drink this. It will give you bad stomach pains and they will have to take you to the hospital. You can escape from there. After we have you out of jail, I'll have a dentist look at your teeth. That was how you got caught the first time. Crooked teeth.

Kelley's boyfriend, Timothy Scott, was probably friends with the dentist next to him—the dentist may have been in on it. Anyway, it would have been easy for Scott to pop in and out of his friend's office. Perhaps he purloined a key. He could make a file, change the label on the x-rays. Ken may have gone to this dentist before. Maybe made a point of it so that he would have a file there. It would have been much easier for Scott to have altered the records than for Kelley to have done so. The unidentified print on the false x-ray, whose was it? Sloppy for a dentist. How about a pediatrician not used to developing dental x-rays?

Lindsay guessed that Kelley's tuition had been expensive and she had massive loans. Agent McKinley hadn't verified it with her, but he wouldn't. She wasn't really in on the investigation anymore. Lindsay wondered if Timothy Scott was Kelley's boyfriend before or after the scheme was concocted. She imagined he had some pretty hefty expenses himself, opening up a practice. Lindsay was so lost in thought the nurse had to call her name twice before she heard it.

The plastic surgeon, Dr. Lacey, told Lindsay that she thought there was a good chance her facial injuries would heal without much scarring, but it would be a simple outpatient procedure if she needed anything done. Dr. Lacey was a competent woman, and Lindsay liked her. She and her nurse were riveted by Lindsay's explanation of how she came by the wounds.

"Have they caught the guys who did that to you?" asked her nurse, a young black woman who looked to Lindsay as if she was sixteen. *I am definitely getting old,* she thought.

"No. There are leads, but so far they haven't found anyone," she told them. They shook their heads at man's inhumanity to man.

She left, still deep into her thoughts as she walked back to her Rover. *It could be a coincidence,* she thought. After all it was a coincidence that she picked this plastic surgeon to consult. She wondered who had done Ken Darnell's plastic surgery. She couldn't imagine the nice Dr. Lacey being involved in this, but then, the surgeon didn't have to know Darnell's intentions. *But this is too close to home,* she thought. *Colorado.* It popped into her head. *Of course, he would have it done out of town; he probably really did go visit Colorado.* She must have said it aloud, for she heard a voice say it back to her.

"Colorado? Hello, Lindsay."

Lindsay looked up and was startled by Dr. Timothy Scott. Apparently, his car was parked next to hers. He was getting out of it.

"Oh, hi," she said. "How are you?" Fear ran down her spine. She dropped her keys on the ground and hurriedly picked them up.

"Visiting me?" he asked.

"No. Dr. Lacey, the plastic surgeon. I may have some scarring on my face."

"Yes. I heard what happened to you. But it doesn't look too bad from here."

For some reason that made Lindsay angry. She smiled tightly at him, got in her Rover, and drove off. She was right. *It was him,* she thought. There was something about the careful way he talked to her, the measured calmness in his voice, that convinced her. *It was him.* She drove to her office.

There was no one in the lab. Students were still off on their summer vacations. She unlocked her office and went in. It was as she had left it. Familiar, comfortable, like her house. There was a package lying on her desk. She sat down at her desk and opened it. It was the knife from the Lamberts' field, the one Joshua traded his tooth to Marilee for. The note said that it was French, not Spanish, the kind used by French soldiers who were battling the Spanish conquistadores for a foothold in the Americas. They wrote a long report on it. Lindsay laid the pages on the table and examined the knife. It looked as though it had once had a handle, but only a thin metal hilt mained. The blade had been relatively thick. The restorer ad done a good job with it. It was gray and heavily pitted ut had a slight sheen. She thought Joshua Lambert would be leased with it.

She looked up when her door opened. Timothy Scott was tanding in the doorway. She gripped the knife and put her ands in her lap. He came in, closed the door, and locked it.

"You know, don't you?" he said.

"Know what?" she asked.

"Let's not play games. I doubt if either of us has the mental trength for it. All this is a strain, isn't it?"

"Why did you do it?" asked Lindsay.

"Money." He was very calm. "Look, Denny Ferguson was waste to society. He won't be missed by anyone but his nother and a few odd relatives."

"What about Blaine Hillard? What had he done?"

"He was just a poor guy worth more dead than alive. Besides, I didn't kill him. Roy Pitt did. I didn't even know about ll this then."

"Who was Roy Pitt?" Lindsay asked.

Scott shrugged. "Some loner friend of Ken's. The two of hem came up with the idea together."

"But Ken stuck a knife in his back instead," said Lindsay. *Two methods of murder, two murderers,* she thought. Scott nodded his head. "Then I guess the problem was to find a body to substitute for Ken." She wondered if she could make t past him or if she could grab the phone and punch in a number. No, he would have her before she could do that. *Keep him talking,* she thought, while she made a plan. "And along came Denny Ferguson. What did you do—have Kelley give him a drug to simulate appendicitis, help him escape, then take him to the dentist whose office is next to yours?"

"I knew that's why you were there, checking up on your theories."

"No. I was really there to see Dr. Lacey."

"Oh." That seemed to disconcert him. "But you saw the names on the offices, and you figured it out, didn't you?"

"Yes."

"You're too smart for your own good."

He's starting to get hostile. Ready to do—what? she wondered. *Keep him talking.*

"Did Kelley know?"

"About Ken's fraud? Yeah, she knew. She was desperate for money, too. And crazy about her uncle. He generated loyalty like that, in women anyway."

"What about killing Denny? I have a hard time seeing her go through with that."

"I told her that the dentist had to put Ferguson to sleep to pull a bad tooth. I said he died and that, rather than turn the body over to the authorities, we should just put it to good use. She bought it. Ken had already approached me about finding a body to substitute for him. Denny was perfect."

"You killed him?" she said.

"Yes. I told him I had dental training. I got into Dr. Wilson's office at night. Denny—stupid bastard—thought it was neat to sneak in and use the equipment to make the x-rays. Thought he was going to get a dental makeover. It fit into his criminal sensibilities. It was pretty easy. Dr. Wilson and I have adjoining doors. I took the x-rays, labeled them, and put them in Ken's file. Wilson was Ken's dentist. Neat, huh?"

"Yes. Neat. How did you kill him? Lethal injection of some kind?"

"Yes, very fitting, don't you think?"

"You killed him at the Lamberts', didn't you? Told him he could hide out there while they were on vacation. When he was dead, you decomposed the body in their shed. You even killed the neighbor's calf and pretended it caught its head in a broken wall of the shed so you could mask the odor. Everyone would think any telltale odor was the decomposing calf." Lindsay watched the surprise on his face as she talked.

"You are very clever. How did you work that out?" he asked.

Lindsay shrugged. "I'm an archaeologist. We have to be very clever and look for all the clues to be able to generalize behavior from the skewed data we dig up."

He smiled slightly with one side of his mouth. "You're

ght, of course. And you know how easy it is to decompose corpse in the summer if you have the proper place and can t the right bugs. Inside that shed at the Lamberts' place it ts up to 120 degrees every day when it's closed up. There as nothing much left but bones inside of two weeks."

"Too bad about the neighbor's calf."

"Yes. Another sacrifice for the cause. But they would have st killed it and eaten it anyway."

"It must have been hard to put clothes on a skeleton."

He laughed. "That's true. I had to stuff the bones in the ants, hoping they weren't in too much disarray. It was not asy. I was afraid the crime scene would look too staged. See, e read a lot about what we were doing and knew that some ime scene professionals could detect things like that. Staging nd posing and all that." He laughed again. "But after all, is was just small-town stuff; we really didn't expect to deal ith an expert crime unit. Jennifer was a big help. You've et detail-oriented people? That's Jennifer. She doesn't miss thing. You'd have thought she was decorating her living oom. She arranged for Dr. Ballinger to identify the bodies, o. She knew he operated on Blaine, and dropped the sug-estion to the coroner, who jumped on it. He got Ballinger to D the others, too. Ballinger himself sent off for Ken's x-rays om Dr. Wilson, so it all seemed on the up-and-up. No one ad a clue until you turned up on the scene. That was a real care. We knew if you ever saw that mouth—"

"You and Ken put me in the cave?"

"You would have had an easy death, like Denny. We veren't sadistic. It was your idea to lose yourself in the cave."

He took a hypodermic needle from his coat pocket. This vas it, Lindsay thought. She held tightly to the knife in her ap. He approached.

"Don't move," he said. "This won't hurt."

Lindsay stood. The desk was between them, but he was etween her and the door. He was in somewhat of a bind imself, she thought. He couldn't come around or she would un and flee out the door. And it was hard for him to reach across the desk. He pulled a small gun from his pocket. N such a bind after all.

"Just stay still and give me your arm." Lindsay did sta still, but she didn't hold out her arm to him. "You aren going to cooperate, are you?" he said. "Well, I don't suppos I can blame you. Move away from the desk, back against th wall."

"Look, it's useless to kill me. Your fingerprint develope into Denny Ferguson's dental x-ray."

He looked alarmed, then smiled. "Good, good. You almos had me. Clever. I'd lie, too, about now."

"It's true," she said.

"I don't believe you. Now, do as I asked." He gesture with the gun.

"Will you answer one more question?" she asked.

"Why not?"

Good, he wanted to put off killing her. "Why did you ki Gil Harris? That has completely stumped me."

"Well, what do you know. Something you couldn't figur out. Well, I can't blame you there. It was completely out o the blue. Not that it will matter to you, one way or another but I didn't kill him. Ken did. We were following you, Ke and I, trying to get you to call off your investigation and g home. Why didn't you just go home? All of this could have been avoided."

He seemed to be getting frustrated. She had to calm hin down. "It didn't occur to me to go home."

He shook his head as if he found that amusing. "We triec everything we could think of to make you go home," he continued. "We even shot your tire, but you knew that, didn' you?"

"Yes. What about Gil Harris?"

"I'm getting to that; be patient. Ken got the idea of disabling your Rover. We figured if you didn't have transportation, you would just give it up after everything else that happened to you. See, we tried every way in the world not to kill you. We only killed when it was completely necessary. Ken even laughed at our efforts—started calling us Wile E. Coyote and you the Road Runner. We aren't bad people."

No, thought Lindsay wryly. *You just do bad things.*

"Gil Harris saw us," he continued. "That wouldn't have been so bad, but he recognized Ken. Can you believe it? After all that plastic surgery. I didn't recognize him. Jennifer didn't. Nobody else did."

"It was dark," said Lindsay. "It muted the differences, probably. And I imagine he heard Ken's voice. We had just been talking about Ken, and Ken was already on his mind."

"That makes sense." Scott seemed to appreciate the explanation.

Lindsay had been moving slowly around the desk as they talked. Now they were both in front of it.

"Back up, I said." He was nervous. It must have been easier with Denny, who hadn't known what was coming. Lindsay imagined it was harder for Scott when his intended victim knew what was going to happen. He was not a natural-born killer, but he was still a killer.

"So Ken killed him," she said.

"Yeah. We marched him up to the cliff with a gun on him. Ken said he had a proposition he wanted Gil just to listen to, that he didn't want to hurt him. He hit him with a tire iron when his back was turned. Just stunned the damn fool. He got up and tried to fight. I tried to calm him down, tell him it was just an accident, but he knocked me to the ground. Ken hit him again and killed him." Scott sounded as if he regretted it. Probably that was the one that made him feel like a killer. He could rationalize the other, but not Gil.

"That must've been nerve-racking," Lindsay said.

"It was. We waited on the cliff trying to decide what to do. We hadn't planned on anything like that. It rattled us both. We went back to the van and left. Then Ken got the idea we could use it to our advantage. It would be more dramatic to throw him off the cliff. I didn't want to go back, but Ken said that what we wanted was for you to go home. He said if a dead body didn't do it, nothing would. You've got to be the most relentless person I've ever met."

"You actually went back?" Lindsay was surprised.

"Yeah," answered Scott. "Ken loves to live on the edge. I think he enjoyed the risk of it"

Lindsay moved suddenly, picking up the telephone receiver, hitting his gun hand and stabbing him in the neck with the knife in one motion. She had decided on the plan when she first saw the gun and had mentally practiced it while he talked. She knew she could do it. If she could climb the wall of that shaft in the cave and hang over a bottomless pit, she could do this.

She bolted, unlocked the door, and nearly flew up to the main office. Dr. Kerwin, the acting head was there, so was his secretary, Edwina. They stood and blinked at her when she tried to tell them to call the campus police. Finally, she reached for the phone and called them herself.

NINETEEN

AGENT MCKINLEY CALLED. Lindsay was in her office working on an article. "Just wanted to catch you up on the latest. We have a tight case against the lot of them. Even if confessions weren't pouring out of Kelley Banks and Timothy Scott, we would have enough evidence. That was his thumbprint on the x-ray. He was very surprised. By the way, Scott's wound in the neck was superficial, and he's recovered nicely. So if you're the kind who worries about that kind of thing, don't. When we find Ken and Jennifer Darnell, we've got them, too. Seems little Miss Meticulous Jennifer missed a couple of things. First, we got a partial fingerprint of hers off the burned-out bulb from the flashlight."

"You're kidding. You mean mine didn't smudge it?"

"You didn't have any fingerprints to speak of. By that time you had worn yours off in the cave, and your skin was very dry from being dehydrated. Luckily, you didn't happen to rub hers off when you removed the bulb. Luckily, too, you kept the bulb."

"Harley told me to never leave anything in a cave except footprints." Her mind flashed to her panties and she smiled.

"Harley?"

"An old boyfriend."

"Good advice. Apparently Jennifer didn't know that the West Builders cap in the back of their van belonged to you. She just thought it was left over from construction workers. It had a couple of your hairs in it, along with some root tissue. So, if you'll give us a sample of your DNA, we'll match it up and place you in the van."

"That's really good news. I can't tell you how relieved I am," she said. "I meant to ask Scott, while I had him here holding a gun on me, why they put a magnifying glass in the backpack. Everything else was regular caving supplies."

Agent McKinley laughed. "I know the answer to that one. Jennifer thought you would have one, because you were supposed to be going to the cave to do detective work."

"Oh." Lindsay shook her head and smiled.

She hung up, feeling better. She was having fewer nightmares now, fewer incidents of waking up in a panic. Oddly enough, she found she slept better without a night-light. It was the light that seemed to trigger her attacks—fear that she had left her flashlight on, that its batteries would run down and she would be in the darkness forever. She looked up from her thoughts to see Grace and her family standing in the doorway.

"Hi," said Marilee, smiling and waving her tiny hand at her.

"Hi, yourself," said Lindsay. "Come in."

"I came to apologize," said Grace. "I know I wasn't very gracious when you came out to the place to bring Joshua his knife. I know—I knew then—that none of this is your fault. Ken did terrible, terrible things. It's just that it hurt, and right or wrong just doesn't seem to make any difference in the hurt."

"I know," said Lindsay. "He's still your brother."

"Yes. He always will be. And I am glad he's alive. But it just doesn't seem like the same person I knew and grew up with did all those things. I'd like to blame it all on Jennifer, but I know that's not fair."

"I'm very sorry about Kelley," said Lindsay. "I know she wasn't involved in any of the really bad things." Lindsay selected her words carefully in front of Marilee and Joshua, though she had imagined they had heard the worst.

"No. She may be disbarred, but they don't think she'll have to go to jail."

"We really want to say we're sorry for what Ken tried to do to you," said Miles. "That must have been just a terrible ordeal."

"It was. I can't deny that, but I'm better. How did you like the knife, Joshua?" she asked.

"Neat. Did it belong to the guy you found in our field?"

"Maybe. Can't say for sure. I can say he is definitely European."

"How did he die?" asked Joshua.

"Don't know," said Lindsay. That wasn't true exactly. From a nick on the front of his cervical vertebrae, she suspected his throat was cut, but she didn't want to say that. "He's still being analyzed. My students are having a good time with him. They are putting his skull measurements in a computer model. We can probably come up with what section of Europe he came from."

Grace and Miles merely nodded.

"What's his name?" asked Marilee.

"The students call him Pierre. We don't know his real name. We do know he was between sixteen and twenty years old. He had no diseases that we could see on his bones, but he didn't get enough to eat to keep him healthy. Let's see." She wrinkled her brow trying to remember. "He was left-handed, and probably a soldier. He limped with his right leg, because he had a healed wound to his right calf that had been made with a sword. That makes us believe he was fighting with other Europeans, since the Indians didn't have swords."

"Maybe they thought he was an Indian," said Joshua, "because of the ear whatchamaccallits."

"Could be," said Lindsay. "At that time the French and Spanish were fighting over the New World; your knife was French. It's an interesting puzzle. But we're learning things about him. As I said, my students are having a great time."

Marilee tugged on her mother and whispered in her ear. "Go ahead," her mother said.

Marilee took something from her mother's purse and gave it to Lindsay. "She made that for you," said Miles.

It was a plaster cast of Marilee's hand in a paper plate, spray-painted silver and decorated around the edge with a red crayon in a zigzag that looked liked an Indian. Lindsay fought back tears as she hugged Marilee.

"I really like this," she told her. "Thank you."

They left, and Lindsay sighed and thought about Derrick. She was reaching for the phone to give him a call when Dr.

Kerwin walked into her office. "We have a prospective student," he said. "At least that's what she says she is."

"You have doubts?" asked Lindsay, raising her eyebrows at him.

"She may be, well, a spy," he said in a low voice.

"A spy?" asked Lindsay. "To spy on what, for whom?"

"You'd better talk to her." He walked out, leaving Lindsay bewildered.

She was enlightened when a young Native American woman walked through the door and sat down in a chair. "That guy's weird," she said.

Lindsay grinned at her. "He thinks you may be a spy. We don't get many Native Americans wanting to be archaeologists."

The woman, who looked about nineteen, grinned back, showing a beautiful even-edged occlusion. "I don't suppose you do. Some of my relatives think I'm nuts."

"What can I do for you?"

"I want to be an archaeologist."

"Tell me about it," said Lindsay.

"I'm a Lumbee Indian. You know what that means, don't you? We are the original lost tribe."

Lindsay did know. The Lumbees are the largest Native American population in the southeast and have utterly and completely lost their original Indian culture. When they were first reported and written about in the 1800s, they spoke only English, lived like whites, and bore no trace of the culture from which they came.

"Many people," said the young woman, "including other Indian tribes, don't think we are really Indians, but we are. Look at us. Where else did my black hair and shovel tooth incisors come from?" The woman's dark eyes shone with earnestness.

"I agree," said Lindsay.

"I want to find my history and the history of my people, and I figure this is the career to do it with. With the new stuff they're doing with DNA and everything, I think there is a good chance I can."

"You're right," agreed Lindsay.

"I have this idea that maybe some of our culture did survive, it's just hidden."

"Where?" asked Lindsay.

"In family stories handed down generation after generation. I want to collect them and compare them with known Indian myths and legends, and with historical accounts. I know there is something there. Things just don't completely disappear."

"That's a very good idea," said Lindsay.

The young woman smiled again. "And I think there is something I can find out in the family names as well. You know, don't you, that even though a lot of people don't think our ancestors were the Indians who absorbed the Roanoke colonists into our tribe when they mysteriously disappeared, we have more than two dozen surnames from people in the Roanoke Colony among our people. I think that says a lot. I think that maybe that's what happened to our culture. We absorbed so many Europeans into it, their culture began to dominate." She raised her chin as if expecting Lindsay to disagree.

She did not. "I have often speculated about that," Lindsay said, "and believe that the whole question of where the Lumbees came from can be solved by looking at those things you mentioned, including the designs on their art and belongings passed down through the generations."

"Art. I didn't think of that one," she said. "That's a good idea, too." She pulled a small pad and paper from her purse and began to write. "I write down all the ideas where I can get clues," she said. "This is something I really want to do. I know our history is out there somewhere just waiting to be dug up in some fashion. Do you think I can come to school here and work on it?"

"I think that is a very valid direction for research. And assuming your grades are fine, I'm sure you can come here. By the way, my name is Lindsay Chamberlain. I guess Dr. Kerwin told you. What's your name?"

"Bobbie. It's really Roberta—one of those family things you get stuck with." She wrinkled her nose. "Roberta Lacayo."

Author's Note

JUAN PARDO'S SECOND expedition took place from September 1567 to march 1568. For purposes of this story, I had his expedition take place in the summer. Unlike de Soto's expedition, Pardo had no horses.

Residents of Tennessee may notice that I took some liberties with their geography. The caves of Grand Serpentine and Hell Slide do not exist, nor does Ellis County.

The stories of Piaquay and his people, though based on what is known both historically and archaeologically about the Indians of the southeast, are fictional, as are the archaeological sites Lindsay visits.

Estaban Calderón is fictional, but there is historical and archaeological evidence that his portrayal is consistent with events surrounding expeditions of Spanish conquistadores of the period through what is now the southeastern United States. The character Roberto Lacayo is also fictional, but explorers did become lost and lived among the Indians, where they learned native languages. When found by subsequent expeditions, many became interpreters between the Spanish and native people.

Bones don't lie.

But forensic anthropologist Lindsay Chamberlain had not bargained for *this* kind of trouble when she signed on with the archaeological dig at the Jasper Creek Site. Who is the mysterious woman unearthed in burial twenty-three? Since she's only been in the ground fifty years or so, she certainly isn't party of the ancient Indian village they have been excavating. The trouble is, she's not the only unexpected find. Body after body has surfaced in the town of Merry Claymore, and some of the graves are very fresh.

When the local sheriff asks for her help in identifying the victims, Lindsay can't say no. As she and her crew are drawn into the maelstrom of suspicion, accusation, and terror raging between those who want the truth unearthed and those who want it to remain buried, Lindsay's special expertise with bones could be the death of her.

A Rumor of Bones is the first volume in the Lindsay Chamberlain mysteries, which feature solutions to crimes that did *not* happen just yesterday.